Sign up for our newsletter to hear about
new releases, read interviews with
authors, enter giveaways, and more.

http://www.ylva-publishing.com

EMMA WEIMANN

Acknowledgments

Little did I know that the project that started years ago as a short story would evolve into two short stories only to end up as a novel. Those two ladies sure have come a long way and taken a special place in my heart.

I couldn't have finished Sam and Gillian's story without the help of some great women. First of all I want to thank Cheri for her time and constructive criticism. She encouraged me when I needed it and kicked my butt when I deserved it. Thanks!

Thank you, Henrietta, Erin, and Blu, for taking time out of your busy schedules and test-reading my story.

And—last but not least—a big thank-you goes to my wife, Daniela, who not only shared her experience as an animal keeper but decided to share her life with me as well.

CHAPTER 1

"BUT YOU'RE A WOMAN."

This guy really was one of the most obnoxious building managers Sam had ever encountered in her life. She lifted the gray shirt away from her body and stared down at her bra. "Yes, I am. All woman." She looked up again and ignored the way Mr. Hayes clenched his jaw. "I'm here to paint the Wallace's apartment."

The guy stared at his calendar. "But I was told a Sam Freedman had been given the job."

Sam fought the urge to knock him over with the dusty loudspeakers on his desk. "Sam is short for Samantha. And that would be me. We've already been through this twice. Why don't you simply call the Wallace's and ask them?" She pushed down on her urge to groan out loud. How could a guy like this get a job in one of these expensive apartment complexes?

He browsed through the diary on his desk. "I can't. They're on vacation." With a frown he gazed at the paint, the brushes, and the ladder she had brought with her. "All right. I'll show you to the apartment. But I'll check up on you from time to time. Just so you know." With those words he left the room.

Sure. Asshole. Did he think she would steal thin air out of an empty apartment? Shaking her head, Sam picked as much of her stuff up as she was able to carry. The handles of the buckets cut into her fingers. She would need to come back for the ladder.

Mr. Hayes stood in the hall, arms akimbo and with a frown that would make children cry. "The service elevator isn't working. We need to use the other one. Try to behave as low-key as possible."

Following him through the high-ceilinged foyer, Sam tried her best to be quiet. This building emanated the atmosphere of a church, built to impress and show off to visitors. It certainly worked on her.

They passed a gurgling fountain with slate-stone water steps. Sam didn't even want to guess what that thing had cost. She miraculously managed to get all of her stuff into the glazed elevator, the buckets firmly planted between her and Mr. Hayes, who glared at her with narrowed eyes.

Seconds felt like hours. Finally the elevator dinged.

"Here we are." With a sneer on his face he watched her struggle to carry the equipment out of the elevator.

Sam set the buckets down on the floor. The hall was empty. "So which number is it?"

"Apartment seven," Mr. Hayes spit out behind her. "Down the hall, last door on the right."

Before Sam had a chance to respond, the door to her left opened. A woman with long dark hair, dressed in a bright red pantsuit appeared in the doorway. "Gillian, honey," she called back into the apartment. "Hurry up." She turned toward Mr. Hayes. "Hold the elevator, will you?"

"Sure, ma'am." He nearly fell over himself to make sure that he pressed the elevator button in time.

Sam barely stopped herself from rolling her eyes. The same man who hadn't thought twice about letting her do all the heavy lifting was now nearly killing himself to make sure that the elevator's doors stayed open for the femme fatale. It was always the same. When a woman had boobs the size of watermelons, a waist like a wasp, and the brain of a dodo, men went crazy. Sam grinned. Well, on the other hand...she cast a glance at pantsuit woman. *She really has nice breasts.*

A second woman stepped out of the apartment and closed the door behind her. "All right. I'm ready." She glanced at Sam before gazing down and walking past her toward the elevator.

5

Yeah, that's how insects must feel when being gazed at by a mantis with green eyes.

"Wow, those two were hot." Mr. Hayes was almost drooling all over his shirt.

This guy really is a living cliché. Sam crossed her arms over her chest. "Do you have the keys for the apartment?"

"Yeah, yeah. Come on." He walked away, again leaving her to carry everything.

What an asshole. She hoped he would leave her alone as soon as she was settled with her stuff. But first, he would probably tell her exactly how she was supposed to do her job.

Sam sat on the floor and leaned her protesting back against the wall behind her. A long, hot shower was in order tonight. And a cold beer. And a pizza.

Satisfied, she looked at the fresh white walls. As much as her back hurt after eight hours of painting, she'd done well today. The two smallest rooms were finished. The big room was left, which meant one more day of manageable and well-paid work. The apartment owners had been so happy about her willingness to start right away that they didn't even try to argue about her hourly rate. Which had been a nice surprise. Rich people were often the most annoying clients.

It was her luck that the apartment owners were relatives of one of her oldest and nicest customers. Old lady Henderson had probably not only put in a good word for her but also taken care of the payment negotiations. Which was just fine with Sam.

She opened her water bottle and took a sip. Working in a building like this was unusual for her. Often they were occupied by high-earning professionals with jobs that demanded they stay overnight in the city while their shiny, happy families lived their shiny, happy lives in not-so-little houses in the suburbs. Her take on this was: boring jobs, boring neighborhood, boring lives, and more money than anyone needed. She sighed. A life that could well have been hers.

The ringing of her cell phone brought Sam out of her musings. "Yeah?"

"Hi, Sam, this is Linda. How are you doing, good-looking?"

Ugh. A call from her friend and co-worker usually meant more work or a shopping spree for something that was on sale somewhere. "I'm doing all right. What's up?"

"I'm just on my way to Mr. Zimmer's for the electric installation. Say, are you coming tonight?"

Shit. "To the party?"

"What other event do you think I'm talking about?"

Sam raked a hand through her hair. She had totally forgotten about the invitation. "I don't know. I only have two days to paint a whole apartment."

"Aw, come on, Sam. You owe me."

Yeah, and you remind me of that every single time you want something. "All right. But I can't promise that I'll stay for long."

"Great. See you tonight, love machine."

Sam let her head fall back against the wall. *Shit. So much for a nice, relaxing evening at home.*

CHAPTER 2

SAM SIGHED AS ANOTHER ONE of these sterile, electronic songs started to play. The music sure fit this place. Both were boring and superficial. With a sigh she shifted on her barstool.

"Here you go." The bartender set down a glass of something that looked a lot like liquid clay in front of Sam.

"What's this?"

"The beer you ordered."

"Ah, shit." She couldn't believe this. What was wrong with a normal beer? "Come on. I ordered a beer not some chemical experiment."

The bartender wiggled his fingers goodbye and turned his attention toward another customer.

With disgust Sam stared at the microbrewery crap in the glass before her. Who drank beer out of a glass anyhow? This party was even worse than she had feared. She cast a glance at the group in the corner. Linda was hanging all over the latest object of her lust. *I bet she won't be going home alone tonight. Maybe I should just leave and head over to The Labrys.* Her favorite lesbian bar was like a second living room where she spent time with friends who shared her view and lifestyle whereas this crowd was clad in Brooks Brothers, Vineyard Vines, Hilfiger, and other expensive brands. The Pulse was the kind of LGBT club that attracted the rich, the beautiful, and the androgynous. Or at least those who wanted to be like that. So not her kind of place.

Sam glanced at the huge clock on the wall behind the bar. Nearly nine. The Labrys was already open. Linda wouldn't miss her here. On the other hand...Sam sighed. Her friend would hunt her down tomorrow if she just disappeared. Not that sitting alone at the bar, several feet away from where the party was actually happening, was so much better.

Sam gripped the glass. At least the crap was cold. She took a gulp. A fruity taste spread over her tongue. *Yuck.* How could people drink stuff like that? Disgusted, she set the glass down.

A leg brushed against Sam's as someone climbed on the stool beside her. Expecting Linda's wrath, she turned her head and was mesmerized by a pair of intense green eyes. A pretty blonde with skin as pale as porcelain held her gaze. *Where have I seen her before?* Sam couldn't remember and somehow it really didn't matter at all. This woman was a beauty. *Pale and perfect.* So perfect that one didn't dare to touch because running hands over skin like that could easily become an addiction. Sam's mouth was dry. She licked her lips. Some addictions were dangerous...but worth the risk. *And that black dress*...oh boy, if that wasn't the epitome of tailored understatement. This woman was beyond classy, probably in her late thirties and way out of Sam's league. The stranger looked very much like the Chanel No. 5 type with a white picket fence around her house. Sam cast a glance at the other woman's hands. No ring. Flirting couldn't hurt much. *Right?*

"Hi there." Sam put on her best pick-up smile, a mixture of confidence and interest that she hadn't used in a while. She held her breath. Either the other woman would get up and leave or...

Green eyes narrowed, assessing her. "Hi."

Yes. Now the next step. "My name is Sam." She held out her hand.

"Hello, I'm Gillian." The stranger took the offered hand.

A shiver ran down Sam's spine. Gillian's hand was soft and warm. If the rest of her body had the same quality...

Gillian leaned over, giving Sam a throat-clenching view down the front of her dress.

Oh, yeah. Great tits. Sam admired firm breasts, cupped by a lacy bra. *I think I'll skip The Labrys. This could be real fun.* "Would you like something to drink?"

"Wine would be great. White, please."

Sam hadn't missed the slight hesitation. Still, being allowed to order something to drink was definitely the next step on the way to a hopefully promising night. "White it shall be. Is Chardonnay okay?"

"Yes." This time the smile reached those incredible green eyes.

Gillian obviously wasn't a talker but she was beautiful. Conversation wasn't what Sam had in mind for later anyhow. Two women could have fun without speaking. There were other things one could use a mouth for and she was very much looking forward to exploring those kinds of possibilities...if Gillian was up for it.

It didn't take long for the barkeeper to set down the glass of Chardonnay in front of Gillian and from her expression the wine's quality was satisfactory.

Good. Sam decided to up the game a bit. She rubbed her knee against Gillian's. When the other woman didn't shy away from the contact, Sam moved her hand to Gillian's leg and leaned closer. "So, what brings you here tonight?"

"I was looking for company." She put her hand over Sam's.

Sam's stomach did a slow roll. *Wow. Score.* "Really?"

"Yes, really." Gillian's voice shook a little. She took a piece of paper out of her handbag and pushed it toward Sam. "But not here. I own an apartment nearby. Here is the address and my name."

Holy cow. This woman really did know what she wanted. "Sounds good to me."

Gillian beamed. "Great."

Sam glanced at the piece of paper. "How far from here is your little love nest?"

"It's a ten minute walk to the apartment. I'm going to leave now but I'd appreciate if you could wait a bit before following me." She scraped a hand through her hair. "What is your last name?"

Sam raised one eyebrow. "Why?"

"I need to give the doorman a name."

No way I'm going to give her my real name. Sam looked at the beer label. "Sam Cellar."

"Sam Cellar?" Gillian furrowed her brow.

"Yeah, something the matter?"

"No. That's fine. Sorry." Gillian shook her head and got up from her stool. "See you in a few minutes." She slowly withdrew her hand, tickling Sam's wrist before letting go.

Heat shot through Sam. "You will." With a grin she turned her attention back to her beer and took another sip of the awful brew. Now, this was going to be a hell of an interesting night.

CHAPTER 3

"GOOD EVENING, MRS. JENNINGS."

Gillian smiled at the elderly doorman. "Good evening, Thomas. There will be a visitor arriving within the next ten to fifteen minutes. A friend. Her name is Sam Cellar."

Thomas' face showed his standard expression of polite indifference. "Yes, Mrs. Jennings."

"Thank you, Thomas." Gillian's high heels echoed loudly on the marble floor. She stepped into the elevator and punched the button for her floor.

Excitement tingled through her when she thought about the night that lay ahead. Part of it was the thrill of having sex with a stranger—a female stranger—in her deceased husband's apartment. The other part was the thrill of danger. Sex with strangers was never totally safe—something she was well aware of. So far luck had been on her side. Meeting women at the city apartment was as safe as encounters of this sort could get. Most of them had been at least pleasant. *Let's hope the new conquest will be as hot as she looks.*

The elevator dinged, and the doors opened. There was no one to be seen in the short hallway as Gillian fumbled with the key for the apartment. Finally, the door opened, she stepped inside and slipped out of her coat. Her new conquest would be here soon—if she hadn't chickened out. For a short moment back in the bar, Gillian had been sure that Sam wouldn't agree to her offer. Hooking up with the butch looking woman had been a spur of the moment decision. Gillian's other "dates" had been chosen more carefully and been more...sophisticated. *I just hope this one doesn't bite me in the ass.* She grinned. *Well, at least not more than I want her to.* Sam's cocky smile had done funny things to Gillian. And that body certainly had looked hot. *Really hot.*

Gillian kicked off her shoes and for a moment reveled in the quiet surrounding her. No outside sound invaded the apartment. It was the perfect refuge, a sanctuary of peace amidst an avalanche of noise in the busy city of Springfield. However, she very much doubted that this had been the main reason why Derrick had chosen this place. He had probably gone for the anonymity and luxury it provided. Which suited her just fine.

She went over to the sideboard, opened a drawer, and took out a silver-framed photo, staring into the eyes of the man she had married a long time ago. A man who had betrayed her.

Cheated on her. "Well, here you go, Derrick. Hot date number seven. It's a shame you can't be here to witness it." She took a deep breath. "Rot in hell."

Straightening her shoulders, she pushed the photo back into the drawer. Time to freshen up. She wanted to be as sexy and desirable as possible when Sam arrived.

Sam looked up at the apartment complex in front of her. More and more of those glass and steel things had appeared over the past years. Springfield nowadays was a rather busy town. And people living in places like this certainly had enough money to spend their nights in clubs like The Pulse. Probably every night. Sam wrinkled her nose. *Let's hope she's worth my time...*

A uniformed doorman appeared from inside the building.

Sam strolled over, nodding her head in greeting. "Hi, I'm here for Mrs. Jennings."

The doorman squinted. "Are you Mrs. Cellar?"

"Yes, that would be me, and a good evening to you." *Snobby little man.*

His gaze intensified. "Samantha?"

Sam's heart stopped beating for a moment. *Shit! Thomas.*

"Girl, is that really you? I nearly didn't recognize you with that short hair and," he looked her over, "those clothes."

For a moment, she considered turning around and leaving. Surely no sex, no matter how good, was worth this kind of trouble. Sam forced herself to calm down. Thomas had always been kind to her. It would be rude to leave without a few words. "Thomas, right?" She held out her hand. "How are you?"

"Good, good. Getting older every day." He gripped her hand. "How are you?"

It was true. He was a lot older than the last time she had seen him around...*wow, twenty years or so. I must have been around seventeen back then.* Now gray dominated his hair, and he sure didn't stand as straight as he had back then. The wrinkles on his face looked as deep as the Grand Canyon, but the kindness in his eyes was the same. Sam returned his smile and winked at him. "I'm all right. Thanks. But I'm getting older as well."

"Oh, come on." He took a step back and looked her up and down. "Look at you. Healthy as a horse and as beautiful as a blazing sunset."

Sam chuckled. "Thanks. I've never been compared to a sunset before."

"How is your family doing?"

Sam pushed her hands into the pockets of her trousers. *What am I supposed to say? Haven't seen the bastards for ages?* She simply didn't want to talk about it...about them. Not with Thomas. Not with anyone. "Maybe we can chat another time? I have an, ugh, appointment." Gosh, that sounded so lame. She wondered whether he had any idea why she was here.

He laughed. "Sure, no problem. I'm off in half an hour. So I'm probably not going to see you again tonight."

Relief flowed through her. As nice as Thomas was, she just wasn't ready to be drawn into memories of their shared past. "Maybe another time. It was nice seeing you."

"Likewise. Give my regards to your parents."

"I will." *When hell freezes over.* Sam crossed the hall, feeling his gaze following her. Shit, that had been weird. Weirder than weird. She couldn't even remember when she had last met someone she knew back in what she called nowadays the "dark ages". *Well, you knew it would happen one day. Just be glad it was Thomas instead of your father or brother.*

The elevator dinged its arrival.

Sam stepped inside. She leaned her forehead against one wall, letting the cold of the stainless steel reach through her brain. Her mood for sex had been pulverized. However, the prospect of spending the night alone in her flat, haunted by memories of the past, wasn't appealing either. She had about two minutes to make her mind up. Go home? Drive to The Labrys and get drunk... and most likely end up in a stranger's bed? The stranger and sex part was something she could have here and now as well. Without getting drunk first. Sam raked a hand through her hair. She would stay, try to get in the mood again, enjoy a night of hedonism and be out of here in the morning. Determined, Sam stepped out of the elevator and walked down the hall. Apartment 241. Taking a deep breath, she knocked.

"There you are," Gillian said with a smile when she opened the door.

For the second time tonight, Sam felt herself drawn into those unbelievably green eyes. They reminded her of the emerald earrings her grandmother used to wear for special occasions. As green as Ireland's hills, the old lady had always said. Sam swallowed. "Hi, yes. Here I am."

"Please, do come in."

Wide-eyed, Sam stepped inside. Dark brown and black leather furniture dominated the room. *This is her place?* Everything was practically screaming "testosterone". Sam could envision a stuffy lawyer or a banker hit by his midlife crises choosing this interior. But certainly not a woman like Gillian. Sam crossed her arms over her chest.

"Do you...would you like something to drink?"

"Yes, please, a beer would be great." Sam followed Gillian into the stainless steel kitchen. Speechless she looked around. All the latest gadgets were assembled in this room. Not a single speck of dust seemed brave enough to hang around. This is *a showroom. Beautiful but sterile. Oh please...don't let her be like that kitchen.* Sam needed to let off steam tonight. She wanted to forget and to get lost. If this kitchen reflected its owner's attitude...then this evening was destined to be a disaster.

Gillian removed a bottle of beer from the Subzero refrigerator. After twisting off the cap, she handed the opened bottle over.

Sam mentally gave her a point—the beer was a pricy brand but acceptable. Not the same kind of shit as in the club. Raising the bottle with a thankful smile, she drank deeply, enjoying how the smooth, cold drink went down, before focusing her attention again on Gillian, who had poured herself a glass of white wine. Sam cleared her throat. "Live here long?"

"No." Gillian frowned. "I don't live here. It's just a place I use from time to time if I want to stay in the city."

"So, you don't own it?"

"Oh, yes. I do." Gillian must have found something very interesting at the bottom of her glass because she continued to stare into it.

There was certainly an interesting story lurking behind those words. *Come on. She asked you here for a hot night. For sex. Either leave now or get on with it and find out if this is going to be fun or not.* "Well, here we are." Sam took another gulp of beer before setting the bottle aside and stepping closer to Gillian. "Let's not waste more time." Sam lowered her voice. "I can't wait to taste you, Gillian."

EMMA WEIMANN

Gillian's eyes were round as she looked up, away, then with a quick brush of her eyes, back at Sam.

Like a spooked animal. Sam bent her head and brushed her lips over Gillian's. Once, twice, enjoying their softness before breaking the contact again.

Gillian blinked, a slow smile spreading over her face.

Sam smiled. *All right. That is a good sign.* "I love the way you feel," she said, touching Gillian's face and brushing a stray lock of blonde hair out of the woman's eyes.

"I love the way you kiss," Gillian replied after a moment's hesitation. She nuzzled Sam's palm and pressed a tingling kiss to the center.

Yes. This is going to be fun. "Oh, the rest of the night will be more than nice, I promise you." She kissed Gillian again, this time no gentle brush of lips but a bit more roughly, more demanding. Missionary style or cuddling wasn't what she had in mind for tonight. Either Gillian would play along or not. Better to find out now.

To Sam's delight Gillian opened her mouth, her tongue touching Sam's. The sensation was wet and soft, sending shivers down Sam's spine, urging on the desire that all but vanished downstairs.

Sam sucked on Gillian's tongue until she let out a muffled moan, her body flexing and arching.

Gillian grabbed Sam's hand and brought it to her breast.

Sam cupped the heavy weight of Gillian's breast and let her thumbnail scratch at the nipple that was prominent through the light fabric. Gillian's jerk and sharp intake of breath encouraged her to take the sensitive nipple between her thumb and forefinger, rolling it gently while she bit down on the lush perfection of Gillian's lower lip.

It was maddening, how playing with Gillian's breasts increased Sam's own need and desire. She whispered in Gillian's ear, "You're going to be a good fuck, aren't you?"

Gillian gulped and stared, not speaking even when Sam took hold of her nipple and gave it a twist that had Gillian squeaking, but not pulling away.

"Want to play with me, Gillian?" Sam asked, releasing the abused nipple. "I wanna play a bit rough. Wanna play with me?"

Gillian flushed. She was obviously fighting inner turmoil as she regarded Sam with a mixture of curiosity and caution.

To Sam's satisfaction, there was not a shred of regret or fear in her expression. It seemed that so far, she had done and said the right things. Encouraged, she moved closer to Gillian until their bodies were touching in all the right places. "Tell me, Gillian," she said pitching her voice low. "How do you want to come tonight?"

"Excuse me?"

"I want you to tell me how you want to come," Sam repeated. "What do you like? Do you want me to take my time, or would you like to come hard and fast? Would you like my mouth on you, or do you want me to watch while you take care of yourself? Do you like anal stimulation? Are there toys you want me to use? Tell me. I want us to make the best use of our time."

Gillian's eyes were dark pools of desire.

Sam tried to ignore her own rising hunger while Gillian nibbled on her bottom lip, clearly unsure about how to continue. But Sam remained silent until Gillian finally asked, almost shyly, "You really want to know what I like?"

Sam nodded and put some distance between them. "Yes. I want us both to have a good time, Gillian. Talking can be foreplay, too." She tilted her head to show that she was listening closely to whatever Gillian chose to say. At the same time, Sam began to massage the crotch of her jeans, where the seam rubbed against her pussy, stimulating herself with a hint of pain, and a whole lot of arousal. "Like I said," she went on, her voice getting rough, "I absolutely think it's hot to hear you, to watch you telling me how you want to be pleased."

Gillian's gaze flickered down to Sam's busy hand and remained there. Her breath hitched as the color rose in her cheeks.

Sam spread her legs wider, thrusting her hips a bit, really getting into it.

Gillian's pupils dilated, her blush deepened. "I want you to take me right here." She glanced up at Sam.

Sam groaned. The expression in those green eyes took her breath away. There was hunger and raw lust, mixed with shyness and vulnerability—the most endearing emotional mix. Thinking about getting Gillian off right here and now was a definite turn on. If she was only half as wet as Sam had become just by thinking about it...well, she would find out soon enough. Sam stopped stroking her denim-clad crotch and pulled off her jacket, holding eye contact as she draped the garment over the back of a chair. She slowly rolled up her shirt sleeves, showing off her muscular forearms. Keeping herself in shape was important to Sam and physical labor had given her a sturdy musculature that she knew most femmes found attractive. Gillian wasn't any different, if Sam read her admiring gaze correctly. She reached out to unbutton Gillian's dress. "Really thoughtful of you to wear a dress with buttons in the front. That way I don't have to rip it off."

Gillian's eyes followed the path of Sam's fingers. Delightfully pale flesh was exposed as Sam slowly flicked the buttons open one by one until she was able to slide Gillian's dress from her shoulders and let it fall to the floor in a puddle of black satin, leaving her in a black lacy bra and matching panties.

Holy... Sam let her gaze travel over Gillian's body—the full breasts almost spilling from the bra's lace cups, the small waist and flat belly, the curve of hips that flowed into sculpted thighs. It was clear that Gillian worked out, probably with a private trainer or in one of those fancy studios. But wherever and however, the woman's body was perfect, and Sam had a hard time not drooling.

Gillian blushed brightly under Sam's scrutiny but remained where she was.

Sam whispered, "You are gorgeous, Gillian. Absolutely stunning."

Her statement brought a pleased smile to Gillian's face. She breathed a short, "thank you."

"I'm going to touch you now and I won't stop until you've come at least once," Sam said. She waited a moment to let her words sink in and to gauge Gillian's reaction before closing the space between them in a single step. Sam cupped Gillian's sex. Those panties were already as soaked as a wet sponge.

Gillian whimpered.

Sam increased the pressure slightly and purred. "I promise to make you come right now if you promise I can take my time with you later. Deal?"

Gillian nodded. The muscles in her thighs trembled.

"Take off your bra."

Gillian hesitated, but she undid her bra with shaking hands and let it fall next to her dress on the floor.

Sam licked her lips. Gillian's breasts were firm and round, the nipples pert and just begging to be touched.

"Good girl," Sam said. "Now your panties. Get them off." She took her hands away.

This time Gillian complied without hesitation.

Sam took a step back to admire the view.

Gillian stood naked, shivering in the cool air while Sam's gaze lingered on the short, damp curls between her legs.

Definitely a natural blonde. A memory of another blonde, equally beautiful, arose. Cheri. Sam's first love. And the chaos that had erupted after Sam's mother had found them in bed together. She shook her head, desperate to cling to the reality of this moment.

"Are you okay?" Gillian's soft voice cut through the darkness of Sam's memories.

"Yes, I was a bit lightheaded there for a moment." Sam plastered a grin on her face. "No wonder. Looking at you. You're exquisite, Gillian."

A shy, yet pleased smile crossed Gillian's face. "Thank you." She swallowed. "I think you are too. And very hot."

An ache of hunger settled in Sam's belly, replacing the knot of anger that had spread from her memories. *She's real. You're real. You're going to enjoy this night and forget about the ugly stuff.* "So, two beautiful women. One naked. The other horny. What should we do about it?"

Gillian's lips trembled. "Fuck me."

Sam held her breath. Those words from the naïve-looking woman in front of her wiped every other thought and memory from her mind. "I will. The whole night." She took a step toward Gillian and touched those wonderful breasts, slowly stroking the nipples.

Gillian moaned and pushed against Sam's hands.

Fire surged through Sam. This was it. *Life. Joy. Fun.* Desire flared strongly inside her. She crossed the remaining distance between them and pushed a knee between Gillian's legs.

Gillian grasped at Sam's wrists to keep her balance.

Moisture seeped through Sam's jeans where the hot pussy was pressed against her thigh. Sam's arousal heightened. It was an itch that she was more than ready to scratch. She stifled a moan, not wanting Gillian to know how much she was affecting her. "Put your hands on the wall behind you and leave them there."

Gillian had to release Sam's wrists, but Sam took hold of her hips, steadying her until Gillian complied. Her body formed a graceful curve; skin and muscle tightened beautifully. Gillian's eyes drifted shut.

"Look into my eyes, Gillian. Look at me. I want to see your gorgeous green eyes when I fuck you."

Gillian's eyes opened.

Sam put more pressure on Gillian's pussy, knowing the denim fabric would feel harsh to the ultra-sensitized flesh. "Spread your legs wider for me."

Gillian shifted, making it easy for Sam to replace her thigh with her hand.

That was what she had been waiting for. Sam eagerly slipped her fingers through the slick folds. "You're so wet. I like that."

"Please," Gillian hissed, pressing harder against Sam's hand.

Sam didn't need more encouragement. Her blood pounded in her ears as her excitement surged. She rubbed her thumb around Gillian's clitoris, spreading slippery moisture, and leaned forward to take Gillian's mouth in a kiss. Her other hand found Gillian's breast. The nipple hardened instantly in her palm. She rubbed the wet clit more firmly.

Gillian's moan sounded more like a growl.

Riding the power wave that dominance gave her, Sam broke the kiss. "Want me to make you scream when you come?"

This time Gillian whimpered in reply.

Sam took that as a yes. She pushed a finger into the hot wet channel of Gillian's pussy and after a few thrusts, added a second. This felt so damn good.

Gillian cried out sharply, closing her eyes. Her head slammed back against the wall when Sam added a third finger.

The muscles in Sam's forearm began to burn as she pumped her fingers in and out, finding a rhythm that had Gillian's hips rising to meet her.

Sam had a hard time concentrating. The smoothness of the inner walls that gripped her fingers drove her own arousal constantly higher and higher. She thrust harder; increasing the pace until Gillian mindlessly ground her pussy against Sam's hand. The aroma of feminine arousal was heady, mingling with the fragrance of Gillian's perfume producing a scent that Sam found absolutely intoxicating. Withdrawing her fingers and ignoring Gillian's wordless cry of protest, Sam went down on her knees and scooted forward until she was positioned between Gillian's spread thighs. "You make me so hot, Gillian. I'm going to make you come now." She had to crane her neck as the position was awkward, but this was how Sam wanted to have Gillian. She pulled one leg over her shoulder. *Better.* Slowly, she licked and teased around Gillian's clit, enjoying the taste of Gillian's desire.

Gillian's moans intensified.

Settling her mouth over the nub of flesh, Sam flicked her tongue—first slow, then faster. When she heard the first moans she shoved her fingers into Gillian's heat; pushing them in as far as they would go before drawing them out again, until her fingertips were poised at the opening.

Gillian's muscles fluttered, like a greedy little mouth trying to suck Sam's fingers inside.

Sam stopped licking and pushed her fingers into Gillian several times, the movements smooth and powerful. "That's me fucking you," she said somewhat breathlessly. A sense of triumph was growing, fuelled by Gillian's groans and the slickness that oozed from the wet opening. Sam fastened her mouth over Gillian's pussy and lapped at her clit.

Gillian's hands fell on the back of Sam's head, clutching her short hair, holding her in place. Gillian was trembling all over. "That feels so good."

Sam curled her fingers, seeking that special spot inside all women. She knew she found it when Gillian bucked wildly, almost spraining Sam's wrist.

Sam increased her tongue's pressure against Gillian's clit and was soon rewarded. Inner muscles spasmed hard around her fingers and she tasted a gush of slightly bitter fluid—sure signs that Gillian had climaxed. But Sam was far from finished. She gentled her licking at first, to soothe the heated flesh, and then smoothed the flat of her tongue over Gillian's clit.

Gillian stiffened and shuddered through a second orgasm, her hands still fisted in Sam's hair.

Breathless, Sam carefully removed her fingers before she pressed a light kiss against Gillian's pubic curls.

Gillian buckled.

Sam caught her and allowed her to slide down the wall. Cradling Gillian in her arms, she placed a kiss on her slightly parted lips, surprised at the feeling of protectiveness that bubbled up inside her. She sat with Gillian in her arms for some minutes, the quietness of the apartment only interrupted by the sound of their breathing.

Cradled in Sam's arms, stars danced before Gillian's eyes. Her whole body tingled. "Wow," was all she was able to mutter.

"Wow?" Sam chuckled. "Good wow?"

"Unbelievable wow." Gillian turned her head and nuzzled Sam's throat, planting a gentle kiss on the soft skin. She felt safe. And relaxed. And simply very, very good. "You are a wet dream come true."

"It is going to be a rather cold dream for you if we stay like this much longer."

"So?" Gillian smiled. "What do you suggest?" She hoped that Sam wanted to stay and go another round or two or three.

Sam cupped Gillian's breast and caressed the nipple under her finger. "I'm sure that somewhere in this apartment is a perfectly fine bed."

Gillian moaned. Sam's touch was driving her crazy. *I'm not going to survive this night.*

Sam kissed Gillian tenderly. "You're a very responsive woman, very sensual, very arousing. I love that. And I'd love to spend the whole night with you."

Yes. Yes. Gillian tried to gather herself to form a coherent sentence. "Thank you for asking me what I wanted. I...I really liked that, as you can tell."

"So, want to show me your bed?" Sam's grin was positively devilish.

"Hell, yes."

Sam laughed and took her hand away.

Gillian groaned in protest.

"Come on. We have to get up so we can lie down again."

It took a moment for them to untangle their limbs. Gillian took Sam's hand and drew her toward the bedroom.

Sam stopped. "Hang on a second. Would it be okay if I took a quick shower?"

Gillian nodded. "Sure." She pointed toward the door leading to the bathroom. "That's the bathroom. Help yourself. Towels are in the cupboard. And there's another door that leads directly to the bedroom, where I'll be waiting for you. Naked." She smiled. "Unless you don't want to shower alone?"

A smile spread over Sam's face. "Not this time. But hold that thought for later tonight. Now, off you go, warm the bed and wait for me. Won't take long, all right?"

Gillian nodded and watched Sam close the bathroom door behind her. The room felt empty and Gillian shuddered.

She walked into the bedroom and stared at the king-sized bed in front of her. Rubbing her hands over her face, she remembered the very first time she had set foot in this room. How surprised she had been back then about the huge bed, wondering why Derrick needed something like that in an apartment he used for only the odd night he had to work so late that he didn't want to disturb them at home. *How naïve and stupid I've been.*

A lot of her questions had been answered as soon as she had opened drawers and found sex toys she hadn't even known existed. And DVDs that had blown her mind. She had watched him with his sluts—and she had thrown up.

Running a shaking hand through her hair, Gillian sat down on the bed. What a stupid fool she had been. Setting aside her life for Derrick, supporting his career. "Your little housewife has changed, you bastard." Her voice sounded as raw as she felt. "And I'm going to be happy."

Sam couldn't believe her eyes when she entered the bathroom. A lot of money had been sunk into this place. A free-standing, oval bathtub stood in the center of the room. It was light grey on the outside and white on the inside, matching the cool, understated, and good taste evident everywhere in the apartment. It could easily accommodate two people, and Sam smirked as possibilities came to mind. Well, a bathroom could become an amazing playground with a little imagination. And Gillian sure did seem open to possibilities. *Maybe later.*

Giving in to her curiosity Sam opened the glass and steel bathroom cabinet. Body Lotion, a toothbrush, aftershave... *aftershave?* Did Gillian invite men as well? Sam scowled and closed the cabinet. Time to shower. She shed her clothes and stepped into the luxurious separate shower enclosure. The teak beneath her feet was smooth and cool, and she noticed with delight that the high-tech showerhead was adaptable. *Come to Mama.* Within seconds, Sam was enjoying the hot water cascading down her body, imagining that it washed away all memories of a past that had left more than enough scars.

It was time for good memories. With a grin on her face Sam recalled Gillian's expression when she had let herself go, the feel of that soft skin beneath Sam's hands. She imagined flicking her tongue over Gillian's clit. A rush of arousal hit out of nowhere. *Yeah, that's it.* Slowly adjusting the water temperature, Sam guided the pulsating jets over her body, circling her breasts. She growled. The powerful spray caused the most delightful sensations, and Sam would have liked to build up her arousal and savor the moment, but she knew she had to hurry because Gillian was waiting for her. Wasting no more time, she positioned the showerhead between her legs. The pulses hit her and caused a pleasure close to pain. "Yes. God, yes!"

She closed her eyes and imagined Gillian kneeling on the shower floor, licking her pussy, tongue-fucking her while Sam rode that beautiful face. A low groan escaped her. The orgasm built quickly, and it wasn't long before a climax ripped through her.

Opening her eyes, Sam stared at her arm. Teeth marks indented her skin where she had bitten into her hastily raised forearm to stifle the noise. She touched the marks with trembling fingers. Fortunately, they were superficial. That had been one hell of an orgasm. She leaned against the tiled wall, breathing heavily through her nose, and let the hot water run down her neck. She needed a moment to come down from such a high. *Wow.*

With genuine regret, she got out of the shower. She dried herself with one of the fluffiest towels she had held in her hand in a long time and Sam found herself imagining drying Gillian with one of those later. Man, had she misjudged the potential of this date. She would have to thank Linda for dragging her to the party, although the notion of showing gratitude had Sam grinding her teeth.

There were nicer things to think about. She laid the towel over the rack in the corner and walked to the door that led into the bedroom. There was no need to get dressed. *I hope she hasn't gone to sleep.*

Sam opened the door and stopped dead in her tracks.

Gillian lay naked on the bed, the fingers of her right hand placed over her pussy; the other hand busy playing with one of those tempting nipples. "I thought you would never come back. So I started on my own." Her voice was husky, with a slight tremor to it.

Heat shot through Sam. "Don't you dare." She crossed the distance to the bed. "Away with those hands. Now."

Gillian giggled. "Or?"

"Or else." Sam jumped on the bed and replaced Gillian's hands with her own. This was going to be a fun night.

CHAPTER 4

WAKING UP IN HER OWN bed was good but the sound clawing its way into her bedroom wasn't. Gillian clenched her teeth against the deafening noise of grinding beans. She hated the digital super-automatic espresso machine that Derrick had insisted on buying. A simple coffee machine would have done the job as well. And at this very moment Gillian also hated Tilde, her Swedish au pair, who had insisted on keeping the machine.

A glance at the clock revealed that it was already three p.m. The kids would be back in around two hours. Gillian sighed and stretched lazily, grinning when her sore muscles protested against the movement. *Gosh, it's going to take another day or two before I'm able to move again without thinking of last night.* Of Sam. Butch as butch can be. And yet...never before had anyone been so attentive to Gillian's needs. She brought her fingers close to her nose and inhaled deeply. Even though she had showered before leaving the apartment, a whiff of her own scent still clung to her fingers. A smile spread over Gillian's face. She clutched the sheet to her chest and closed her eyes. Her body tingled all over as she remembered those hands on her body, in her body.

Somewhere inside the house a door slammed.

Gillian cursed and rolled out of bed. *I can't go through the day constantly thinking of sex. And Sam. Stunning Sam.* Gillian hadn't gotten enough of those hard muscles under soft skin. The only drawback had been Sam's obvious dislike of being touched intimately. Gillian sighed. *I need a cold shower. A very, very cold shower. Again.*

Fifteen minutes later, Gillian stood at the kitchen window and watched Mrs. Storm, one of the biggest gossips in the neighborhood, inspecting their neighbor's garden over the picket fence. Mrs. Storm was like the Spanish inquisition. An inquisition Gillian had banned from her house after Derrick's death. Which had made Mrs. Storm very suspicious of all things going on inside the Jennings' home.

Gillian picked up her freshly brewed cup of coffee and entered the four-season room. She opened the sliding doors to the garden and let the scent of flowers and earth wash over her. A huge lavender bush towered beside the doors. Butterflies and bumblebees swarmed around it as if the plant was some kind of insect drive-through. Smiling, she settled down in her favorite armchair and took a sip of the dark brew. The children would soon be back from their grandparents. *Enough time to think and drive yourself crazy. Hooray.* She let her head fall back and closed her eyes. *What am I going to do?* As nice as these nights in the city were, reality hit hard the next day. She was still no closer to finding out what she wanted to do with her life. Without a husband, she had a lot of options. But there were the kids to consider. And the neighbors. And the parents-in-law. *You know that you're a lesbian. You know that some day you'd like to be in a relationship with a woman. And that the kids will be part of the package. But how? And where am I going to meet Ms. Right?*

Gillian sighed. Maybe moving away would be a good first step. But the children would miss their familiar surroundings, wouldn't they? These kinds of questions had been driving her crazy for months. *I guess I just have to do it, to take a first step.* If only she had an idea of what the correct first step was.

"Did you have a nice night?"

Gillian groaned, opened her eyes, and found Tilde standing in the doorway. "Thanks, yes. Nice night. Not much sleep. Feel like crap now."

"Sounds like a lot of fun."

Gillian grinned. "Yes, it was fun. Sit down."

"I'll get myself a coffee. Be back in a moment."

With her long black hair and brown eyes, Tilde didn't look like an au pair from Sweden but she really had been one of the nicest surprises in the past year. She was loyal and funny, and the children loved her. Having another grownup in the house was a wonderful thing. Even more so because Tilde was the most nonjudgmental person Gillian had ever met.

Seconds later, she was back with a cup of coffee.

"So, you're ready for the invasion?" Gillian stuck out her tongue.

"No. Are you?"

Gillian shook her head. "No. But with a bit of luck Margret will have a migraine, and the chauffeur will bring the children."

"Wouldn't that be nice?"

They smiled at each other. They shared a distaste for Gillian's mother-in-law, a snobbish matriarch, whose world was simply black and white. One mistake Gillian would never repeat again was to fall in love with someone without getting to know her future parents-in-law. "I'm thinking about selling the house and moving." Gillian held her breath. It was the first time she had voiced her thoughts. This was only Tilde, but still...

Tilde leaned back in her chair. "Where to?"

And wasn't that the question? She couldn't imagine living in the city, without a garden. Would moving to another suburb change anything? Wouldn't there be the same kind of snoopy people and uptight neighbors? "I'm not sure. But I'll start making appointments with real estate agents. I need to start somewhere."

Tilde grinned. "All right. But Mrs. Storm will be devastated."

"Ain't that the truth." Gillian couldn't help laughing. "I'm sure she will camp outside the house to make certain that nothing escapes her eagle eyes."

The ringing of the phone cut through their laughter.

"Want me to get it?" Tilde set her coffee aside.

"No, that's fine." Gillian got up. "Let's order pizza tonight and watch a movie with the kids, shall we?"

"Great idea."

Gillian picked up the phone in the kitchen. "Hello?"

"Gillian. You have to come over." Margret's voice screeched through the receiver like a hot water kettle about to explode.

"Why? What happened?"

"You won't believe what your daughter did! I expect you to pick up the children. Now!" The busy signal replaced Margret's voice.

"Oh shit." Gillian rolled her eyes, walking back to the winter garden. "Tilde, order a bottle of schnapps with the pizza. We will need it."

CHAPTER 5

SAM STARED AT CRUMBLED PIECE of paper in her hand. By now she knew Gillian's mobile number by heart—even though she hadn't dialed it once. But she had thought about calling Gillian around a hundred times...at least.

The memory of Gillian's warm, soft skin beneath her fingers had not vanished one bit since Sam had left the apartment. The way Gillian's face had flushed during orgasm made Sam's heart beat faster every time she thought about it and the little sounds Gillian had made when Sam's tongue had danced over her clit... they were like an earworm, playing again and again in her head.

Sam rubbed her eyes. *Shit, it's as if she bewitched me.* Sitting down on a lone paint bucket in front of her van she fumbled with her mobile phone. *Should I call her?* They had agreed that calling for a new "date" would be all right if either of them felt up to it. That had been four days ago. Sam grimaced. *Is it too late to call again after four days? Or too early?* She would really like to see Gillian. The sex had been great. And the mystery around her had captured Sam's interest. Was she a housewife? A player? A professional? Had she bought the expensive apartment herself? Questions over questions were running through Sam's head.

"Sam?" Linda's voice echoed from their small office.

Sam sighed and turned around. "Yes?"

"Why is the coffee empty?"

"Because you drank the last cup?"

"Very funny." Linda stepped out of the building, holding a coffee can—bottom up—in her hand. "There's no more coffee. The can is empty. And you're responsible for shopping this month."

"Oh shit." *I'm really losing it.* Sam got up. "I'm sorry. I forgot."

Linda narrowed her eyes. "Yesterday you forgot an appointment with a potential new customer and on Monday you left your tools behind." She laid a hand on Sam's arm. "What's up with you?"

Sam put the piece of paper with Gillian's phone number into her pocket. "Nothing." She took a step back and picked up the paint bucket. "I need to go but I'll buy some coffee later today. Sorry."

"I don't care about the coffee." Linda grinned. "Well, that's not true. But I do care more about you."

"I don't want to talk about it." Sam heaved the paint bucket into her van. With a satisfied thump the bucket settled between one broken hammer that Sam had wanted to throw away for days, a cable spool, a torque spanner, several screwdrivers and two toolboxes. *Gosh, I really need to clean up here or I'll be able to open my own DIY store in the van.*

"You never want to talk about 'it'," Linda growled. "You mope around for days and days until either your sister or I threaten you with bodily harm. And even that doesn't always work."

Sam sighed. Linda wouldn't give up. "I just need to think things through before talking about it."

"That's fine. But most of the time you think so damn much that your brain is about to fry before you give." Linda crossed the distance between them. "Too much thinking is like a short circuit fault about to happen."

Sam couldn't help but grin. "A short circuit fault?"

"Well, yeah." Linda shrugged. "Too much thinking and 'boom'." She threw her hands in the air.

"Boom." Sam laughed. "Back to watching too many cartoons again?"

"No. And you're deflecting. Once again."

"I just...I don't know what to say." How was she supposed to talk about something if she hadn't figured out herself what exactly bothered her? She had a hot night out. Great sex. And yeah...maybe she wanted to do it again. With Gillian. So why was this driving her so crazy and making her think so much? And feel so much?

Linda sucked on her lower lip. "All right. Can I ask some questions?"

Sam nodded. There was no way of stopping Linda anyway. "Yeah, go ahead."

"Who was the woman that you talked to at the birthday party?"

"You're nosy." *And she knows me too damn well.* "And?"

"She's...she was a...we had a fun time that night." Sam stuffed her hands into the pockets of her jeans.

"Right. And you've not been yourself ever since why?"

"I..." Sam groaned. "All right...I would like to see her again. Satisfied?"

"Well, you must have been very satisfied if you want to see her again." A smirk lit up Linda's face.

"It's not—" *like that.* Sam just stopped herself from dragging her thoughts out in the open. "She was hot. I'm just not sure if seeing her again would be a good thing."

"Why not?"

'Cause I felt too much and I'm too interested and there's someone in that building hanging around who knows my family. "I don't know. And I really have to hurry or I'll be late. I'll bring back some coffee tonight."

"All right. I won't pester you anymore. For now. And I'll stop at Coffee Beans later and buy some coffee myself."

"Thanks." Sam was dizzy from relief that the interrogation was over. She had no doubt that Linda would have another go. She was like a Terrier on a hunt once she got scent of something interesting. Sam sat down in the driver seat and started the car. The drive to her new job wasn't a long one; the job itself would be rather boring. Which was usually fine with her. She didn't need another broken water pipe. Yesterday evening she had been sure that small webs had grown between her fingers. However, a boring job meant that she would have more than enough time to think about Gillian all day long.

What am I going to do? Sam drummed her fingers on the steering wheel. *Maybe I'm overcomplicating things. Maybe I should just call and see her again. Get her out of my system. But what about Thomas? What if he's working again? What if he wants to talk about the good old times?* A bitter taste spread in Sam's mouth. She couldn't hide forever. *You knew that one day something like this would happen. Be happy it's only Thomas you met.*

Twenty minutes later Sam parked her car in front of her customer's house, took out her mobile phone and dialed Gillian's number. *It's now or never.*

The neighbors' sprinklers all started to shut down one after the other, leaving behind wet grass and a flock of happy birds hunting for insects.

Gillian stopped at her front garden, breathing heavily. Sweat trickled down her face and coated her whole body. It was around eight o'clock and already way too warm to continue with her run. Which is why she had cut it short today.

"Hello." A voice like fingernails on a chalkboard clawed across the quiet lawns.

Shit. Gillian was tempted to ignore the earsplitting call and rush into the relative safety of her home. Maybe she could pretend that she just hadn't heard Mrs. Storm. She turned and hurried toward the entrance.

"Hello, Gillian. Wait. I haven't talked to you in ages."

Gillian sighed, stopped and turned around.

Mrs. Storm made her way across with the determination of a Mississippi River steamboat.

Gillian plastered her best fake smile on her face. "Good morning, Mrs. Storm."

"Well, it would be a good morning if it wasn't so unbelievably hot."

"Yes, it seems to be another one of those days."

Mrs. Storm looked at her watch and then back at Gillian with a bright smile on her face. "I'd love a cup of coffee, dear. I have around half an hour before I have to be home again and I would simply love to chat a little. It has been way too long..."

Oh. No. You don't invite yourself in our home. "I'd love to Mrs. Storm. Really. But I have to shower." Gillian pointed at her sweaty clothes. "And afterwards I have to make some urgent phone calls that I simply cannot delay." Gillian put on the fake politician smile that she had learned from Derrick. All she wanted was to escape her nosy neighbor and get out of the sun that was already starting to burn down on her like a mega-spotlight.

Mrs. Storm shook her head. "I really wonder what au pairs are all about. Even though you have one you never seem to have time to sit down and chat with one of your oldest neighbors."

Nosiest neighbors is more like it. "Well, there's simply so much to do every day. And without a husband..."

"I'm happy to help if you'll let me know how I can support you." Mrs. Storm took a step closer, an eager expression on her face.

Shit. "Well, Mrs. Storm—"

Gillian's mobile phone blasted the opening theme of "Desperate Housewives" into the air.

Thank God. She squinted at the display. *Whose number is that?* "Yes, hello?"

Mrs. Storm took another step closer.

Gillian turned away, the phone pressed to her ear.

"Hello, is this Gillian?"

"Yes?"

"It's Sam."

"Oh." Heat shot through Gillian's body, followed by several very vivid memories that would make Mrs. Storm keel over. "Hang on a second, please." She turned to her neighbor and nearly bumped into the damn woman by doing so. "Another time, all right? This is one of those phone calls I was talking about earlier."

Mrs. Storm's face lived up to her name.

Gillian hurried toward the house. *Sam. Wow.* She had thought so often about their night together but hadn't found the courage to call. She shut the door behind her and walked into the living room. "Hello. How are you?"

"Fine. How are you?"

"Very well, thank you." Gillian sat down.

For a moment only Sam's breathing was proof that the connection was still working.

"So..."

"I'd like to see you again. That's why I called. To see if you want to see me, too."

Gillian got up, unable to sit still when thinking about the implications of what Sam had just said. "That would be nice. I'd love to see you again." *And feel you. Taste you.* Her head was spinning.

"Yeah?" Sam cleared her throat. "Great. Sounds great. Would you...should we meet at the apartment again?"

"Absolutely. Yes. When?" Gillian groaned inwardly. *One word sentences. Very, very sophisticated.*

"What about Friday at eight p.m?"

"Yes." Gillian hurried into the kitchen and looked at the calendar. Angela had a sleepover at a friend's. Michael would be fine with Tilde. They adored each other and wouldn't miss her for one second. "Friday works for me."

"Wonderful. I look forward to it. And Gillian?"

"Yes?"

"I'd like to have you all night."

Gillian's brain nearly fried when she thought about the promise behind those words. She cleared her throat. "Likewise."

"See you Friday."

"Yes. Goodbye." Gillian stared at the phone in her hand. Sam wanted to see her...to touch her again. The whole night.

CHAPTER 6

GILLIAN BLINKED, WAKING UP FROM a dream filled with pleasure and heat and fun. She snuggled deeper into the covers, trying to hold on to the wonderful feelings the dream had left behind.

The sound of running water invaded her mind. She slowly opened her eyes. White wardrobes. *This is no dream.* She was in the downtown apartment, she wasn't alone...and she had fallen asleep on her lover. *Damn.* She closed her eyes again and drew the cover over her head. *How embarrassing.* She had fallen asleep on Sam. Gillian peeked out from under her shelter. Two a.m. And Sam was still here. Which had to be a good sign. *Right?*

With a sigh Gillian stretched muscles that whined about being overly used. *What a night.* She was quite sure that there wasn't a millimeter on her body that Sam hadn't touched or licked in some way. And yet, imagining that it was Sam showering in the next room...a prickling sensation rose over Gillian's whole body. The sex had once again been great, wonderful, and fulfilling. And tonight Sam had even been open to being touched. Not too intimately. But she had been different compared to their first time together. There was no doubt that Sam was an amazing lover. *I wonder how she acts outside the bedroom?* Gillian sighed and burrowed deeper into the pillow. *Let's be honest. You'd like to see her again. But how do I ask her?*

Sam looked into the mirror. "What do I do?"

Her reflection didn't answer.

Why did this happen to her? Why be interested in someone who was supposedly only into one-night-stands? Well, technically a two-night-stand...Truth was that she would love to meet Gillian outside the bedroom, to get to know her a bit...to chat about normal things, to hear about Gillian's life. *Maybe I won't even like her once we've spoken more than five sentences that don't evolve around sex. She's out of my league. And I don't know anything about her. Maybe she's even married. Has a husband who loves to hear about her hot little adventures.* The thought made Sam sick. But she had to know. If Gillian was married and just used her as a distraction or whatever...then Sam wouldn't see her again and that would be it. She wouldn't invest more

HEART'S SURRENDER

time into "this"—whatever "this" was. If Gillian was interested and if there was a chance to get to know her a bit more...Sam grimaced at her mirror image. *I'll take it one step at a time.* She knew that she was a good fuck buddy and Gillian was a great lover. But after the bad experiences Sam had had with relationships in the past, she wasn't sure if she was up for more. Relationships scared the shit out of her. On the other hand... Gillian was intriguing and fun. *What to do?* Sam turned around, took a deep breath and entered the bedroom.

Gillian lay naked on top of the covers, her eyes closed, her face relaxed and soft.

She's beautiful. Sam remained standing in the doorway, arms crossed over her chest, and enjoyed the sight before her. Her gaze wandered to Gillian's hands. Those fingers had touched her and brought her amazingly close to losing control; something she hadn't done in a long time.

As if sensing she was being watched, Gillian opened her eyes, her gaze seeking Sam's.

Once again, Sam found herself the focus of an intense green-eyed stare that seemed to go straight through her. For a long moment, she held Gillian's unblinking gaze, then went over to the bed.

"Hi, stranger," Gillian finally said in a voice so low that chills went down Sam's spine.

"Hi there yourself," Sam purred, crossing the distance between them. She crawled unto the mattress and reached out a hand, slowly caressing Gillian's cheek. Sam took her time stroking Gillian's brows, her eyelids, the lines of her lips and her nose before asking, "How are you doing?"

Gillian chuckled. "My throat is a bit hoarse but beside that... I think I never felt more alive." She touched Sam's thigh, her touch as soft and gentle as a butterfly's. "Thank you."

Sam grinned. "You're a truly attractive woman, Gillian. I can't get enough of you." She traced the line of Gillian's jaw with the backs of her fingers. And it was true. The longing to touch Gillian was greater than the longing to guard herself. *For the moment at least.* "I think you've put a spell on me."

"I did?" Gillian's laughter curled around Sam's heart. "Well, I think it was the other way around."

Sam steeled herself against the rejection she was sure would follow. "I know it's early and all that. But would you like to meet again? Next Friday or so?"

Gillian grimaced. "I can't."

Two words with the power to shred a heart. Sam looked away. What had she thought? That Gillian really did want to spend more time with her? "It's all right. I really enjoyed tonight." Sam kissed Gillian's forehead and got up from bed. With a swift move she collected her underwear from the floor.

"Wait." Gillian stared wide-eyed at Sam. "What's happening here?"

Sam avoided Gillian's gaze. She felt a lot like her fifteen-year old self when her dad had asked what she was doing out late with his chauffeur's daughter.

"I'd love to see you again. It's just that I can't next Friday."

"Oh." Sam froze.

Gillian's brows furrowed. "Did you think I didn't want to come? To see you again? Ever?"

All Sam wanted was to slip into her clothes and run. That was exactly what she had thought.

"Sam? Look at me, please?"

Sam forced herself to meet Gillian's eyes and was caught by the vulnerability she glimpsed there.

"I don't have time next weekend. But I could meet you for dinner during the week...if you wanted to?"

Sam turned around and slowly put her underwear on the black leather chair that stood in the corner. *Dinner. She wants to have dinner?* Sam turned around and stepped closer to the bed. "You'd like to have dinner with me?"

Gillian nodded and patted the place to her left. "Yes, dinner with you. Only food and talk. I can't stay away from home for a whole night on a weekday. Though I have no idea how I'll survive not touching you. Or being touched." She grinned. "Come here."

As if remote-controlled, Sam crossed the distance to the bed and crawled back next to Gillian. *She wants to have dinner. And talk.*

"You look like a deer caught in headlights."

Sam swallowed around a throat that was still alarmingly dry. "I feel a bit like it."

"Why?"

"I..." Sam sighed. "I would like to spend some time outside of bed with you. Like to talk and get to know each other a bit. But I...I believe that we don't run in the same circles."

Gillian shrugged. "That's probably true. But it's also true that I don't like my kind of 'circles' very much."

"You don't?"

"No. I don't."

"Oh."

Gillian snuggled closer, her naked body touching Sam. "You're cold." Gillian drew Sam closer. "Come here."

And Sam complied. She snuggled as close as she could, one hand on Gillian's hip, the other on Gillian's side. "And you're nice and warm." She let her hand travel from Gillian's hip to her breast.

"You do have wandering hands."

"Yes, do you mind?"

Gillian smiled and shook her head. "No, I don't. But before we forget everything else...So, are you free on Wednesday evening? For dinner?"

"Yes." And even if she wasn't she would cancel everything else for this date.

Gillian swallowed. "And would you mind just having dinner with me? Just talking?"

"That's a toughie. Only talking?" Sam still hadn't processed that Gillian was possibly interested in more than just sex.

"Yes."

"I'd love to." She caressed Gillian's breast. "I'd love to learn more about you." Her caress became more intense until Gillian's nipple was as hard as a rock. "But I'd also love to touch you some more tonight."

"Please," Gillian breathed. "Yes."

"So, all talked out now?"

"Kiss me, you goof."

Sam rolled on top of Gillian. "Your wish is my command." Sam rubbed her breasts against Gillian's, skin sliding on skin. "You're bossy." She planted a kiss on Gillian's lips. "I like that."

Gillian returned the kiss with a ferocity that scorched Sam from the inside out. Heat centered in her pussy. *She drives me crazy.* Sam took Gillian's mouth in another kiss, nipping the bottom lip and drawing a whimper from her lover. Desperately needing to feel more of Gillian, Sam began to massage Gillian's breasts, finally bending her head to suck first one nipple, then the other into her mouth, alternating between the two.

Gillian moaned, shifting her legs wider apart.

After releasing a rosy nipple with a wet pop, Sam found herself fascinated by the goosebumps that followed every touch on the flawless skin under her. "You like that, don't you?"

"I love it. I love your touch."

Sam smiled before she slid down Gillian's body, pausing to kiss the firm, smooth belly. A faded scar from a C-section caught her eye. She hadn't noticed it until now but had seen those before on sexual partners. *So she has kids.* For a moment Sam froze. Kids did fit into the white picket fence picture she had of Gillian's life outside the bedroom. *She wants to see you and talk to you on Wednesday.* Sam would concentrate on this. Storing away the information she had gotten from the scar, she blew a raspberry on Gillian's belly, making her giggle in reply. Tonight was about touch and feel and lust and fun. Sam pressed more kisses on Gillian's hips and the tops of her thighs.

Soon whimpers and groans rose from Gillian's throat.

These were the sounds that Sam had longed to hear. She continued her slow torture, dipping her fingers into Gillian's wetness and swirling them around the moist folds.

Gillian was staring down the length of her body at Sam, her eyes glazed with lust, her lips parted.

Sam slowly brought her fingers to her mouth and licked them clean of Gillian's juices.

Gillian stopped breathing and licked her lips as if she could taste herself.

Sam's nipples tightened and she whispered, "Turn over, beautiful."

Gillian gazed at her as if stunned. At last, she managed, "Don't you want me to," she cleared her throat, "go down on you for a change?"

"Maybe later," Sam laughed, sitting back on her heels. "Right now, I want you to turn over for me."

Without hesitation, Gillian flipped over onto her stomach.

Sam's mouth went from wet to dry immediately. Gillian's ass was magnificent. Every nerve ending in Sam's body sizzled at the sight of those round, firm, creamy buttocks. Her cunt twitched.

Gillian shifted.

"Relax, Gillian," Sam said, pitching her voice low. "I just want to take my time with you and get to know every inch of your body again. I won't hurt you or do anything you don't want. As soon as you say 'no' I stop whatever I am doing. Trust me."

"All right." Gillian's voice was hoarse.

Sam laid her hands on Gillian's back, gently kneading the tense muscles she discovered. "I want to make you feel good. That's the only thing on my mind." After a few minutes Sam began to move lower to Gillian's thighs, continuing the careful massage until the knots under Gillian's skin were worked out. "You doing okay?"

Gillian groaned with pleasure.

Schooling herself to patience, Sam slowly moved her hands until she reached Gillian's ass, gliding her palms over the plump buttocks until she felt Gillian push back into the caresses, clearly seeking more stimulation.

Sam's own excitement grew by the second. Gillian was like a natural aphrodisiac, and Sam was gushing wet. "You love it when I play with that sweet ass of yours, don't you?"

"Yes," Gillian moaned. "Touch me. Do what you want...anything...just touch me."

Sam laughed softly, slipping a finger against Gillian's asshole, a teasing touch that made Gillian's breath stutter. Sam did not penetrate her. Gillian's eager response so far to anal play made that a distinct possibility that Sam would love to explore—another time. Not today. She stuck the fingers of her other hand in her mouth to wet them, then rubbed the moisture round and round Gillian's tight little hole. Sam kissed Gillian's buttocks and the small of her back, mouthing endearments and obscenities against Gillian's skin.

It didn't take long before Sam was as covered in sweat and breathing as heavily as Gillian. Sam crawled forward until the full length of her body was draped over Gillian's back. She pressed a series of kisses against the nape of Gillian's neck. Her distinct smell, musky and sweet, increased Sam's desire even more.

Gillian turned her head, gazing at Sam over her shoulder.

Those green eyes were unguarded, allowing Sam to see that Gillian was willing to give her everything, to yield herself up completely to Sam's whim. There were no walls between them anymore. As dangerous as this was—she wanted it. She wanted Gillian. Sam took her time peppering Gillian's spine with kisses before she licked and sucked on one of Gillian's earlobes, using teeth and tongue, all the time grinding her pelvis against the naked flesh beneath her. Gillian had to be feeling the damp rasp of Sam's pubic hair on her buttocks, and that thought brought another level of excitement to Sam. This was not a simple act of sex anymore, it was pure adoration from her side. She breathed into Gillian's ear. "I am so hot for you. I have to hear you come again, and this time I want you to bring yourself off. Imagine me touching myself, playing with my pussy while you play with yours."

"Oh, God," Gillian moaned, clearly on the edge.

Sam felt the motions as Gillian began to fuck herself. Sam moved between Gillian's thighs, hauling her up on her knees so that Sam had access to those wonderful buttocks. Wetting her finger once again, she began playing with Gillian's asshole. It was a deeply intimate act that Sam didn't perform often. Trust was needed. And trust was given tonight.

Gillian all but shrieked when Sam dipped the tip of her finger inside the tight hole. There was momentary resistance, then the muscle relaxed, and Sam's finger slid inside past the knuckle. "You all right, there?"

"Yeah. It just...it's weird."

"Do you want me to stop?" *Please don't.*

"No, don't...don't stop."

Soon Gillian was making noises that drove Sam absolutely nuts. This time, she did not deny the groan that escaped her own throat. There was no point concealing how much she was aroused, how much her own body throbbed and begged for relief. The sight, the smell, the sound of Gillian was edged into Sam's mind. She could not control the passion that shook her to the core, nor did she want to. Sam touched her own clit, rubbing it hard, while finger-fucking Gillian's ass. Coordination was not easy, but she had the greatest incentive in the world. "Come on, baby," she whispered. "I want to come with you. Let me hear you. Come with me."

Gillian climaxed, crying Sam's name out loud.

Sam sobbed, driven over the edge right after Gillian. Light burst in Sam's vision as pleasure hummed through her. Spent, she managed to withdraw her finger from Gillian's ass before crashing down on the bed, at the last moment shifting so she did not land atop her lover but beside her.

Gillian immediately rolled into Sam's embrace, her face slack with pleasure.

Sam wrapped her arm around Gillian, careful to not touch her with her other hand. Skin against skin, sweat cooling on both their bodies...as far as she was concerned, intimacy had never felt so good. "You know," Sam remarked, still basking in the afterglow of a powerful orgasm, "that was mind-blowing."

Gillian chuckled, slowly tracing patterns on Sam's arm with her fingernails, scratching lightly. "It was. When I saw you in the bar, the first time...I thought that you would be one of those typical butches. Just doing your thing with me."

Startled, Sam stared. "Doing my thing?"

"Yeah." Gillian blushed. "Doing your thing."

Sam had no idea where this was going.

Gillian brushed her lips over Sam's mouth before continuing, "You're not my first one-night stand, I've had a few these past months but...I made wrong assumptions about you. You're so attuned to what I want, what I need, and I feel so cherished, safe with you. Thank you."

Sam kept quiet. She did not always care about what her bed partners thought, or whether they left her satisfied, but Gillian was different in a way she could not define. Sam didn't know how to reply. The fact that Gillian had kids and maybe was even married and had other one-night stands...*What have I been thinking?* Sam's stomach sank. Her old instinct to flee when things were too much raised its ugly head once more. She pushed it down. *No. You'll talk this through on Wednesday. Calm down. Just a few more days.*

Oblivious to Sam's struggle Gillian rolled on top of her, touching their foreheads together. Her hair hung like a curtain around them, blocking out the view of the bedroom, creating a private space that encompassed just the two of them. "Hey, would you like to shower together?" Gillian asked shyly. "We've gotten dirty...now I guess we'd better get clean."

Sam swallowed hard. The world had gone crazy, she was crazy. "Yes," Sam said, rolling them both over until she was able to tumble out of bed, leaving Gillian flat on her back and breathless. "Race you to the bathroom and that obscenely big tub. First one there chooses position," she continued.

Off she went, a giggling Gillian following close on her heels.

CHAPTER 7

"ANGELA, IF YOU'RE NOT OUT of here in thirty seconds..." Gillian let the threat hang loosely in the air. This was a game she and her daughter played several times a week. Angela was a bit of a slob—with her room as well as when it came to time management. A fact that had driven Derrick mad. He, the perfect lawyer, had always been on time for appointments and had been neat, bordering on anal. Which had driven Gillian as crazy as Angela's behavior did.

"Bye, Mom." Angela waved her goodbye as she hurried down the driveway, lunch pack in one hand and smart phone in the other.

Gillian ran a hand through her hair. "One of these days I'm going to throttle her." She was not a morning person herself. Having children hadn't changed that. But au pair or not—she wanted to be the one to send the children off in the morning.

"I have to run as well." Tilde rushed by Gillian. "I'll be back in two hours."

"Do you have the shopping list?"

"Yeah," Tilde held a sheet of paper in the air. "All under control. And I'll even bring us back lunch."

"It's like standing in the middle of a mad highway rush," Gillian mumbled, before turning back into the house and closing the door. With Angela, Michael, and Tilde out of the house the only sound that reached her ears was the ticking of the kitchen clock. Gillian rolled up the sleeves on her sweater and made her way to the stereo in the living room. Music was what she used as a crutch to find peace when she was alone and solitude threatened to turn into pain.

Moments later Melody Gardot's voice drifted through the air like a sweet-smelling perfume.

Gillian sighed. *Better.* Her gaze went to the sideboard and the portraits, standing there like little beacons of her former life. The picture in the center portrayed Derrick and her, standing together with his parents. Everything looked so...artificial and...happy...and obscenely Disneyesque. She hated that picture as much as her life back then. Gillian put the picture facedown.

There was another one that was as horrible as a toothache. The kids in their best clothes like little soldiers with no smiles on their faces. Gillian rubbed her hands over her face. Derrick had used the same picture for his little happy family shrine at work. One time she had joked half-heartedly that lawyers tended to show off pictures of their families like some kind of trophy they had won. Derrick hadn't gotten the joke which was never meant to be one in the first place. Gillian put the picture facedown with a satisfying thump.

Her eyes wandered to the portrait of Derrick and the Governor, shaking hands in a glossy black and white shot. Important people who helped to speed up slimy business deals. She sneered and put that picture down as well.

The next picture to catch her eye was the wedding picture, taken at a time when she was so sure she was in love with Derrick. Gillian's fingers touched the glass. Had that been really her? A smile as dazzling as Derrick's. Back then she had thought that Prince Charming had stumbled into her life. A law firm partner marrying his secretary...the stuff fairytales were made of. But not every fairytale had a happy ending. She willed her face not to crumple. This had been one huge mistake—on both sides.

She ran her finger over a picture of the kids hugging her. That had been a wonderful summer day out on the boat with Derrick's parents. A smile found its way onto Gillian's face. The kids really were the only good thing that had come out of that damn marriage.

Gosh, she'd love to have a drink. A strong one. Her gaze wandered to the antique oak framed Tantalus that her father-in-law had given Derrick for Christmas several years ago. The sparkly crystal decanters the Tantalus held were beckoning her. Gillian turned away. Alcohol was one of the temptations she had sworn to stay away from. A glass of wine now and then in the evening was all she allowed herself. But never before six. And sure as hell never more than one. Gillian raised a slightly shaking hand to her forehead and closed her eyes for a moment. No alcohol. Coffee it was.

A while later she stood at the kitchen window, coffee cup in her hand. The view outside was peaceful. The neighborhood was a good one. At least that was what Derrick had said. Back then. And part of it was true. It was a safe place with lots of well-trimmed lawns and quiet neighbors. She had even made some superficial friendships. As peaceful as it was—this was not the place she wanted to continue living. Gillian took a sip of her coffee, enjoying the slightly bitter brew. She had never wished for Derrick to die. But it hadn't taken long before she realized that his death had freed her and that his absence from her life was a chance to escape what she had come to despise. Not to go back to her old life. She grimaced. No, that hadn't been all red roses either.

The only problem was that escaping from something was not enough. She still hadn't figured out where to escape to. The only thing she knew with absolute certainty was that she wanted, no, needed to find a life that would give her and the children equal happiness. No more, nor less. If there was one thing she had learned over those past unhappy years it was that she wouldn't be a good mother to her children if she wasn't happy herself.

She took another sip of her coffee and enjoyed how the strong brew tickled her taste buds awake. There was one thing...one person that had brought a tiny piece of happiness into her life. *Sam.* Being with Sam had been different to her former one night-stands...two night-stands... Sam stirred a hunger in Gillian. It wasn't only the sex they had. Gillian grinned. Though the sex was really, really good.

Gillian turned away from the window. She didn't really know what to do with Sam. And what did Sam want from her? Gillian had found her thoughts straying to the other woman more and more often, wondering what she was doing at the moment...and if Sam was also thinking of her. Which was stupid. They had met twice and had spent most of that time in bed, not talking. *But we'll talk tomorrow on our date.*

Date. Gillian chewed on her lower lip. The word sounded strange in her head. She had a date with a stranger who knew her body intimately. But could someone like Sam ever be more than an occasional lover? Besides...would Sam even want to explore the possibility of more? Or would she run screaming into the night as soon as she realized that Gillian came with a package? Well, two packages; one about to hit puberty and the other being a dreamy boy.

She set the coffee cup down. One thing was sure. Neither Sam nor anyone else would ever again be the sole person she'd build her happiness on. As tempting as the thought of finding someone...the special someone was. Nope. No way. Not anymore. Her life, her goals, and her happiness. That was something she would be happy to share with the right person. But she sure as hell would never give it up again. Not for someone else. "All right. Stop this. Time to do something." Gillian picked up the phone and dialed her real estate agent's number. "Hello Caroline. I'm ready for some house-hunting."

CHAPTER 8

GILLIAN ARRIVED A FEW MINUTES late to La Trattoria, the Italian restaurant Sam had chosen for their "first" date. Romance however was not on Gillian's mind. Traffic on the streets had been mad, as had the phone call from her mother-in-law, just when Gillian had been about to leave the house. Thinking back to the call made Gillian grind her teeth. The woman was driving her crazy and brought the term "evil mother in law" to a whole new level. The name Tilde had given her fit—dragon lady.

Thankfully parking spaces were reserved for guests of the restaurant Sam had chosen. Gillian sighed in relief. Maybe the day would get better. It simply had to. Appearing late for the date as if she didn't care wasn't the kind of impression she wanted to give Sam. Due to the stupid phone call there hadn't even been time to obsess about a special outfit for tonight.

Gillian killed the engine, took a deep breath and got out of the car. *Romantic dinner. How do I get in the mood for this?* She closed her eyes and pictured Sam. Beautiful and strong Sam. The woman who had taught Gillian more about her own body and about sex in two nights than any other person had before. She shivered. It would be so much easier if tonight was just another of those hot, sweaty dates they already shared. But this was not about sex and Gillian's nerves were fried. She clenched and unclenched her hands to get rid of the tingling caused by the nervous energy coursing through her body. What if this, tonight, didn't work out? What if they found out that they had nothing to talk about, nothing in common? What if Sam was as much of a bore as Gillian felt most days? Think positive! She looked up at the sky. Dusk was settling on the city. *Maybe we'll like talking as much as we like fucking each other senseless.*

A couple entered the restaurant hand in hand, laughing and happy. In love. The light shining through the restaurant's windows was inviting. La Trattoria looked like a family owned place. Visions of handmade pasta and crunchy garlic bread swirled around Gillian's head. She chuckled to herself. *Bad girl. No garlic breath.* No sex didn't mean no kissing and she was determined to steal at least one kiss tonight. Gillian ran a finger over her lips. Sam was a great kisser.

The aroma of tomatoes, garlic, and fresh bread tickled Gillian's nose when she entered the restaurant. Her mouth watered. *Nice.* She let her gaze wander around. Small niches in the back of the room and a softly dimmed light created a warm atmosphere. Most tables were occupied, but the noise level was low enough to hear the soft Italian music that played in the background. La Trattoria seemed a perfect choice for a romantic dinner on neutral territory.

Some guests glanced her way. With relief, she noticed that she didn't recognize anyone. She realized something else as well—the one face she came to see tonight wasn't here. Sam.

A young woman who was the embodiment of an Italian beauty advanced toward Gillian. She had dark curly hair, a very stylish red dress and legs that went on and on and on. *"Buona sera,* welcome to La Trattoria. How can I help you?"

"Good evening." Gillian took another look around the restaurant, still coming up empty. "I'm supposed to meet Sam here tonight. I believe she made reservations."

The woman slowly looked her up and down. *"Si, si.* Sam is waiting for you. Please follow me." The hostess turned around and went to the back of the room.

They are on a first name basis? Frowning, Gillian followed through a door that was partly hidden behind a huge plant. They walked along a semi-dark corridor until the hostess stopped.

"Sam reserved a private room for tonight. Enjoy your meal." The hostess winked at Gillian, and opened the door to her left.

Gillian fought against the non-romantic urge to whistle. A bouquet of red roses dominated the wooden table in the middle of the room. Burning candles framed a Champagne bottle cooler that held a bottle of Dom Pérignon. And on a chair sat Sam. *Oh my.* Dressed in a dark blue button-down shirt and black slacks, she looked sexy as hell. Knowing what lay under those clothes woke Gillian's desire with lightning speed. She smoothed the fabric of her blouse with shaking fingers, unsure what to do, how to behave on the unfamiliar territory of a real date...with a woman. *With Sam.*

The smile on Sam's face when she got up from her chair and crossed the distance between them was as bright as a spotlight. "Hi there. You look absolutely lovely." Sam picked a rose out of the bouquet and held it out to Gillian. "No thorns."

Gillian took the rose, her throat tightening. She brought it to her nose and inhaled. The sweet scent reminded her of springtime and new beginnings. "Thank you." Not even when they had started to date had Derrick had he ever done something equally romantic. In fact...no-one had ever done something like this for her. She smiled at Sam. "This is...just wow."

Sam let her fingers trail down the side of Gillian's arm before she gently kissed her cheek. "You take my breath away. Thank you for spending the evening with me."

The slight huskiness in Sam's voice sent a shiver down Gillian's spine. Her eyes traced the gentle arch of Sam's lips. Lips she had tasted. Lips that had feasted on her. *Shit. No sex.* This was going to be an interesting evening.

Sam took a bite of her lamb filet, enjoying the mild aroma of rosemary that caressed her tongue. She had been looking forward to the food. La Trattoria was one of her favorite restaurants, the owner, Luca, and his daughter Diana, old friends. As much as she enjoyed the Italian cuisine, the food took only second place tonight. Gillian was the center. And what a beautiful center she was. With her simple light blue blouse, neatly pressed black slacks, and sleek pointed heels, Gillian had taken Sam's breath away when she had appeared in the door. Nearly ten minutes late. Sam had been a nervous wreck by then, afraid that Gillian wouldn't show up at all.

Oblivious to Sam's thoughts, Gillian hummed, seeming to enjoy her tuna. Which was a good thing. The location obviously was a hit. The food was great. Right. So...the small talk was a bit difficult. But that was why they were here. To talk and get to know each other better outside of the bedroom and the shower and... Sam cleared her throat. "So how was your day?"

"Actually, quite good." Gillian speared a piece of tuna with her fork. "I was house-hunting."

Sam nodded. *House-hunting. Right.* "So, what are you looking for?"

"Something not as big as the one we own now." Gillian frowned while chewing. "And in a different neighborhood. A garden is a must. A swimming pool would be nice. For the children. A large master bedroom with direct access to the garden would be great. For me."

Children. One question answered. *How do I ask her if there's a father around? Shit.* Sam took a sip of her wine before asking, "And did you find something?"

Gillian shook her head. "Today was more a confirmation of what I don't want. But that's all right. The search continues next week." Gillian tilted her head and smiled that special smile that caused Sam's stomach to do a flip-flop every single time it was directed her way.

"So," Sam cleared her throat, "you and your children?"

Gillian hesitated for a moment before saying, "Yes, Angela and Michael and well, there's also Tilde, our au pair."

So, wherever the father was, he was not in the picture for the move. Sam shuffled the potatoes around on her plate. *Is she divorced from the father? Or maybe she is divorced from her wife?* Everything was possible. However, Sam was sure these were questions one didn't ask on a first date. "How old are your children?"

"Angela is eleven and Michael is six." Gillian's voice was soft.

"And is it working out with the au pair? Do the children like her?"

Gillian nodded, her eyes sparkling "They love her. She's very down to earth and has a hilarious sense of humor. I wouldn't know what to do without her." Gillian broke the eye contact and concentrated on her food.

So, is this another line drawn? There were a thousand things Sam wanted to ask. Where was Gillian's significant other? Why did they move? Why had she chosen Sam the first night they had met? *Keep calm. Safe questions. I need a safe question.* "And what about pets. Is there a cat or a dog in the picture?"

Gillian chuckled. "No. Angela would love to have a dog. But Michael is allergic."

"Oh, I bet that goes over well with his sister."

Gillian rolled her eyes. "Very true. It took a while before she stopped blaming him for not being allowed a dog."

"Yeah. My sister and I had the same problem."

"You have a sister?"

Sam nodded. "Do you have siblings?"

"No. Not that I know of."

Sam frowned. That was a strange answer.

"So, you never told me how your day was." Gillian leaned forward.

Sam hated first dates. Two strangers meeting, asking questions while trying not to cross invisible borders. Technically they weren't strangers anymore but talking about orgasms and sex toys might not be the right thing to do for tonight. "Well, I think my day was not as interesting as yours. Work mainly."

"What sort of work do you do?"

"I'm a handyman. Or maybe we better call it handywoman. I paint apartments, repair things, and sometimes even build smaller furniture. Stuff like that."

"Wow. So if something is broken you can repair it?"

"Sometimes. No electrical stuff though." Sam grinned.

"Do you like your job?"

"I do. Most of the time. Some clients suck. But most are nice. And we have some elderly clients and they really appreciate that they can rely on us to help them in their homes." Sam laid her fork down. "And that is the kind of work that is satisfying. Not only to repair something or paint something. But to know that I'm making a difference in someone's life." She bit on her lower lip. Saying it out loud like that sounded lame.

"I think it is amazing to hear that you love that part of your job. I always thought that working should be about more than just money. It does make a difference if you love what you do and see a meaning in your job, right?" Her tone was almost wistful.

Sam nodded. "I agree. It's not easy figuring out what you want to do with the rest of your life when you leave school. But later in life...I think it's important to find out who you are and what you want to do. Life is too short to just try to please others or listen to others."

A shadow fell over Gillian's face. "I agree. Though following that rule is not always easy."

"No, it isn't."

They stared into each other's eyes. Gillian was the one to break the silence. "So, what do you like to do in your spare time?"

"I play the guitar. Nothing fancy. Just for my pleasure. I like to read. And I love to spend time with my niece."

An intense gaze met Sam's. "That sounds pretty down to earth."

Sam ran a finger over the foot of her glass. "Yes, I think my wild days are over."

Gillian wiggled her eyebrows. "Wild days?"

Sam snorted. "No. No way I'm talking about those tonight. So, what do you do for a living Gillian?"

Gillian's brow furrowed. "I don't...well, I take care of the kids and the house and stuff like that. But I don't work. Like in an office or so."

Sam was just about to ask Gillian another question when someone knocked on the door and, without waiting for an invitation, entered. *"Buona sera. Buona sera*, Sam. Good to see you."

Sam groaned inwardly. She loved Luca to bits. He was a great guy and something of a father figure. But she had explicitly asked him to leave them alone tonight.

"I don't want to disturb you. Just say hi and ask if everything is fine?" Luca had a shit-eating grin on his face. Where his daughter was slim and an Italian wet dream, he was tubby and radiated an air of snugness. The mix of those personalities was what made the restaurant so successful.

Sam got up from her chair and went over to her old friend, fighting down the urge to throttle him. "Hi, thank you. Yes, the food is delicious as always."

He looked at Gillian and lifted an eyebrow.

I don't believe this. Curious bastard. "Luca, please meet Gillian. Gillian, this is my old friend, Luca." Sam stepped aside and watched Luca and Gillian shake hands.

"Oh, but I'm not that old. How lovely to meet you, Gillian." He waved his hand in the table's direction. "I hope that you enjoy your food and," his voice dropped while looking in Sam's direction, "your company."

Kill me now.

"Thank you very much. The food is absolutely lovely. The tuna is sheer perfection. My compliments to the chef." She smiled at Sam. "And the company is the best I could wish for."

Sam's ears began to burn.

Luca chuckled. "Great, great. I leave you to your food and the good company then." He picked up Gillian's hand and planted a kiss on it.

Sam rolled her eyes. *Ever the charmer.*

Thankfully enough he said goodbye and disappeared again.

Sam grimaced. "Sorry. I think he is a bit curious."

"About?"

Sam rubbed the side of her nose. "You."

"Oh, right." Gillian offered a smile. "How do you know each other?"

Shit. The PG version of that particular story would be a stretch. She sure as hell didn't want to tell Gillian too much about her relationship with Diana. Sam rubbed her neck. On the other hand, if this, tonight, was about finding out if Gillian and she had a chance at anything...lying wasn't really an option. *Try a neutral approach. Maybe she won't ask more questions.* Sam took a deep breath. "I, um...ran into his daughter...and then I met Luca and we liked each other and the food here is exceptional." She looked up again and met Gillian's gaze.

Gillian blinked. "You ran into his daughter? What does that mean?"

Now would be the perfect time for Luca to come back and interrupt them again. Or for a fire alarm to go off. "In a bar." Sam fought against the urge to drop her head on the table. Why hadn't she made reservations somewhere else?

"I'm sorry." Gillian laid her hand over Sam's. "I don't want to pry."

Sam stared down at their linked hands. Gillian's was soft and warm and so very different from her own rough hand, which this afternoon had been stuck in a toilet. Sam snorted softly. "It's not prying. We...we kind of dated a few years ago and remained friends."

"That's amazing."

Sam frowned. "What is amazing?"

"To be able to remain friends after...you know. Not many people can say that."

Sam pressed Gillian's hand. "It works if both parties really want to make it work."

"Is that so?" Gillian's voice had dropped.

Sam suddenly wasn't sure if they were still talking about her relationship with Diana or about something entirely different.

For a long moment neither said a word. Then Gillian let go of Sam's hand, took her chair and set it down next to Sam's. "Hi."

Sam lifted an eyebrow. "Hi."

"As much as I love to talk to you and ask questions and act like a grown-up...I really hate to sit so far away from you that I can't touch you." Gillian's eyes twinkled while her thumb drew lazy circles on Sam's hand.

"Is that right?"

"Yes. No sex is fine. Well, for tonight. But sitting on opposite ends of the table is really, really not."

Sam couldn't help but chuckle. "Yeah, it sucks."

Gillian leaned her head against Sam's shoulder. "So, where were we?"

Sam dropped a kiss on Gillian's head. The scent of cinnamon tickled her nose. She closed her eyes and inhaled. "I like how your hair smells."

For a moment they were quiet.

"I love to be able to touch you," Gillian murmured, breaking the silence.

"I love to be touched by you and touching you." Sam closed her eyes and enjoyed their connection. This date wasn't half as bad as she feared.

Sam stared at the sleek, black, sporty Mercedes. *I bet those are leather seats.* The woman definitely was classy. And rich. Not that there had ever been any doubt about it.

"Thank you for the wonderful evening." Gillian took the keys out of her pocket and opened the car's door. "Let's do it again."

Sam grasped her hand and gently kissed Gillian's palm. "I'd love that. But the next time you'll choose the location."

"Great. Yes." Gillian scanned their surroundings before she stepped even closer, her body lightly pressing into Sam's. "You know that I can't let you go without a goodbye kiss."

"Yeah?"

"Yes. Let me thank you properly for a lovely evening." There was that seductive purr that made Sam's knees go all jelly.

Gillian cupped her cheek and then soft lips brushed against Sam's. She closed her eyes, losing herself in the kiss and in the feel that was equally soft, sweet, and hot.

A moment later Sam broke the kiss as slowly as it had begun. With a last nip to Gillian's lower lip, she let go. "You make it really hard not to do something inappropriate in a parking lot."

Gillian leaned her forehead against Sam's and whispered, "Being grown-up as well as behaving responsibly is highly overrated."

"Yes, it sucks." Chuckling, Sam stepped away and moved one of her fingers across the tempting lips of her lover. "You want me to take a cold shower tonight, right?"

Gillian sighed. "Why should I be the only one being tortured?"

"See you Wednesday?"

"Yes."

"Nine p.m. at the apartment?"

Gillian slipped into the driver's seat. "Yes. But I have only two hours."

"We can work with that." Sam gently closed the door, her eyes never leaving Gillian's until the light inside the car went out.

Shortly after, Sam watched Gillian drive away. Wednesday couldn't come soon enough for her.

CHAPTER 9

"HEY, CHLOE," SAM SHOUTED DOWN the hall. "I'm ready. Come on." Without waiting for a reply she entered the pink nightmare, otherwise known as her niece's bedroom. Nothing much had changed since Sam last set foot inside this room to assemble the new wardrobe several weeks ago. Setting down the hammer and nails next to a pile of books on the desk, her eyes were drawn to a poster that she hadn't seen before. Justin Bieber's face grinned down at her. Sam shivered. *Oh shit. I hope this is just a very short phase in her life.* Sighing, she sat down on the bed that looked as if a tornado had hit it. The room gave her a headache. How could a niece of hers love so much pink and girly stuff? "Chloe. I need instructions. Hurry up."

Chloe whirled into the room, all smiles and energy, her blonde hair held back in a ponytail. "Cool. I want it there." She pointed at the wall above her dresser.

Two minutes later the framed picture of Chloe's cheerleading group hung exactly where she had wanted it. Sam grinned down at her niece. "All right?"

"Yes. Thanks, Sam." Chloe leaned into her aunt's body. "The frame is beautiful."

Sam forced a smile on her face. Little did Chloe know how Sam had abhorred spraying the gorgeous wooden frame in the pinkish color. "Good. Glad you like it. I hear a mega, extra big slice of double cheese pizza calling my name."

"Yeah, me too." Chloe grabbed Sam's hand. "Come on."

When they entered the kitchen, Victoria held out a plate with a huge piece of steaming pizza on it. "Who's hungry?"

"Gimme." Chloe's hand was faster than lightning and, without so much as pause, she consumed a piece of pizza.

Sam couldn't help but grin. Chloe looked like a chipmunk.

"Excuse me child of mine but 'gimme' is not what we say when we want something." Victoria glared at her daughter.

Chloe's cheeks bulged even more. "I'm hungwy."

"Manners, manners, manners."

Sam grinned at her sister. "You sound just like Mother."

The glare she received in return was an exact copy of the one they both had regularly received as kids. "Stop it. I feel like a ten year old."

"Well, then stop behaving like one and sit down. Both of you."

Sam chuckled, picked up a piece of pizza and put it on a plate before offering it to her sister. "Here. Have at it. You behave like a diva when you're hungry."

Chloe chuckled and sat down.

Victoria growled. "Hey, no ganging up on me."

"But we always do, Ma."

Sam smirked. "Yes, Ma. We always do."

"Oh, shut up you two."

Sam accepted the plate that held a huge piece of steaming pizza. She inhaled the smell of cheese and tomato sauce and fresh basil before she took her first bite. The taste exploded in her mouth. She groaned. "That is so amazing. And I'm so thankful for your vacation in Italy."

"You will be delighted to hear that we're going back next year."

Sam nodded. "That's great. The whole summer?"

"Four weeks in Tuscany." Victoria's eyes twinkled. "I'm counting the days."

"Oh, I'm counting with you and I can't imagine what kind of recipes you'll come back with this time." Out of the corner of her eye, Sam noticed how Chloe stuffed a second piece into her mouth as fast as she could.

Victoria cocked an eyebrow. "What exactly is the hurry, Chloe?"

"Ma, I have to call Laurie in," she glanced at the clock on the wall, "about two minutes."

"And why is that?"

"Her birthday party." The unspoken "duh" rang loud and clear in the air.

"Make it five minutes and eat properly. All right?"

Chloe's sigh was pure drama queen. Sam had a hard time not laughing out loud. Her niece was at times a copy of a much younger Victoria.

The next minutes were filled with laughter and stories from Chloe's school. Sam basked in the feeling of family and belonging that always enveloped her at times like this. She couldn't hide her smile when Chloe finally jumped up and Victoria rolled her eyes at her daughter. This was all so familiar and safe. A warm feeling spread through Sam. This was how family was supposed to be. She swallowed the rest of her pizza and patted her stomach. "That was really good. I love your pizza."

"Really?"

Sam threw her napkin at her sister and hit her square in the chest.

Victoria picked the napkin up between her thumb and her forefinger and threw it in the trash can. "Coffee?"

"No, thanks." Sam took the plates and put them into the dishwasher while Victoria busied herself with her shiny coffee machine.

The sound of grinding beans vibrated through Sam's teeth. "A sledgehammer has nothing against this monster." *She took a closer look. I'm pretty sure that the last time the coffee machine was black and not a silver monster of steel.* "A new one?"

Victoria sighed. "Yes."

"From?"

Victoria peered into her coffee cup before she set it down and pressed a button on the steel giant. Dark liquid poured into the cup. "Daddy dear."

"Oh, so what has he done now?" Sam couldn't hold back the bitterness in her voice.

"He forgot to attend Chloe's theater group premier last month even though he promised to be there and take us out for dinner afterwards."

"Sure he did." Sam rolled her eyes. "And a new coffee machine for you is supposed to do what?"

"A new machine for me and a new iPad for Chloe." Victoria held up her hand. "And yes, we did accept the presents."

"I really don't get how you can let that asshole—"

"Stop." Her sister pinched the bridge of her nose. "We're not discussing this again. He is her grandfather. And I'm not cutting him out of our lives. And as fucked up as it is—presents are his way of saying sorry. You have to accept that."

"More his way of buying himself an 'it's all right we forgive you'—again." Sam balled her hands into fists. They would never agree on their father's behavior and the way he tried to manipulate and buy everyone around him—including his family.

"Sam." Victoria reached out and took hold of Sam's hands. "He is her grandfather. And I really don't want to lose another part of my family. I want my child to have contact with him as long as she's up for it. Once she decides that she doesn't want to see him anymore..." She shrugged. "Well, then it is her decision. But until then, he's going to be part of our lives. A very small part as it is."

Sam shook her head. "I'm sorry. I'll never get it. But it's your decision."

"I know. Come on, let's relax a bit on the sofa."

"Yeah."

They settled on the sofa in the living room, Victoria scooting close enough to rest her head against Sam's shoulder.

Anger was still coursing through Sam. Anger about her father's behavior, Victoria's decision to let him stay in her life and, on top of all of that, an anger burning about the way all of this still affected her. Even after all of these years.

"So, what's up in your life?"

"Why?"

"You haven't stopped fidgeting around like a five year old since you crossed the threshold."

"Have not."

Victoria just hummed quietly.

Sam found it hard to breathe. She had been looking forward to and at the same time feared telling her sister about Gillian. Talking about "it", about Gillian, would make everything real and Sam still wasn't sure if that was what she wanted. But her mind and her emotions had been spinning in circles over these past days and she needed to tell someone. "I met a woman."

"And?"

"She's funny. She's interesting. She's," Sam chewed on her bottom lip, "an amazing lover. Sexy as hell." She sighed. "And she's getting under my skin."

Victoria whistled. "Wow. And?"

Sam grimaced. "She has money. Loads of it. She's rich."

"Oh no. What a shame." Victoria laughed out loud.

"This. Is. Not. Funny."

"Oh yes, it is."

Sam's hands curled into fists. "No, it's not."

"I really believe you're the only person that has a problem with having a rich girlfriend."

Sam bit down on the bitchy response that was lingering on the tip of her tongue. Needing some distance, she got up and went into the kitchen. She took a bottle of beer out of the fridge. "It's not funny at all," she said to herself, before opening the bottle and walking back to the living room. She stopped in the open door. "I don't cope well with...you know...rich people." Though it wasn't mainly the money but the behavior that came with it. The whole "we own the world and you" attitude that she hated like an ugly rash.

"So, you can't cope with us, either?" There was a bite to Victoria's words.

"That is not the same."

Victoria made an irritated sound deep in her throat. "Why not? And since when have you become such a snob?" Her sister's voice was so soft that it nearly took the sting out of those words. "Come here." She patted the empty space next to her on the couch.

"A snob? Me?" Sam pointed at her breast. "I'm a snob?"

"Come here, you goof, before I drag you here." Victoria pointedly stared at the empty space beside her.

"As if..." Sam grumbled but sat down. She placed her beer on the low table.

"Oh yes. You are some kind of snob. You don't judge people by who they are but by how much money they have. And you think you're a better person because you're not rich."

Sam leaned forward, resting her elbows on her knees. She couldn't deny that what Victoria said was true. "Can you blame me?"

"No, I don't and you know that. What they did to you was totally, utterly wrong and shitty as hell. But that doesn't mean that every person with more money in their bank account than you is a monster. And I'm sure that whoever 'she' is didn't give off those kinds of vibes or we wouldn't be sitting here, having this conversation."

Sam knew that Victoria was waiting for a reply. She wouldn't let it go. Being the mother of a nine year old made her some kind of Mistress of Patience. *Might as well give in.* "That's not the point. I can't remember one positive experience with white collar people. Not as a child, not as a teenager, and certainly not as a grown-up. I just don't relate. It's not my world."

"Oh, Sam." Victoria rested a hand on Sam's back. "I bet you still don't know much about her, right?"

"No." Sam sat upright. "We haven't talked that much. Just the one date so far."

"You only met once?"

"Well, no. But we only talked once."

Victoria burst out with laughter. "You're unbelievable."

Sam groaned.

"And you have no idea how she made her money, right?"

"No." Sam let her head roll onto the back of the sofa.

"And you pout like my daughter."

Sam growled. "Not true."

Victoria bumped her shoulder. "Yes, true."

"I hate you."

"No, you don't." Victoria rolled her eyes.

"I'm afraid."

Victoria ruffled Sam's hair the way she would with Chloe. Affection was written all over her face. "I know."

"I haven't been in love since Cheri." Speaking the name still hurt.

"Five years is a very long time."

Sam once again let her head fall back. Why couldn't she just let go of the past? After nearly twenty years of leaving her old life behind, it still hurt. And talking about Cheri was just as painful. Her gaze fell on a glass jar that held lots of small notes. "What is this?"

"Good memories." Victoria got up and walked over to the sideboard. "Every time Chloe is overwhelmed or angry about what happened to," she picked the glass up, "her father, we'll write down some good memories." The shaking in her voice was unmistakable. "I do too."

Sam swallowed hard. Even two years after Martin's accident, talking about him was hard for Victoria. They had been a couple for over ten years. One drunken driver later—all had been over. Martin was gone. And Victoria and Chloe left behind. Alone.

Victoria sat the glass down and joined Sam on the couch. She let her head fall down on Sam's shoulder. "I miss him so much."

Sam pressed a soft kiss on her sister's head. "I know."

"And I want you to find the happiness we had. You have to make some good memories and for that you have to take a risk."

A risk was exactly what Sam didn't want to take. Sure, a happily ever after would be great. But how often did that happen in real life? The chance of being hurt, of having her heart ripped out once again were a lot higher. "I hate being a grown-up person."

"So, what are you going to do?"

Sam shrugged. "Well, since not seeing her anymore isn't an option...I think I'll just see where this leads."

"And if it leads to something serious?"

Contradicting thoughts and emotions swirled through Sam like a tornado. However, she had to admit that her heart felt at least a bit lighter now, after bringing her worries and fears out into the light. "Well, if it becomes more serious, I'll come banging at your door in the middle of the night."

Victoria chuckled. "Great. Except the middle of the night part."

CHAPTER 10

GILLIAN TRIED TO CATCH HER breath and, with a slight shake of her head, get rid of the stars that were dancing before her eyes. Sam's warm hand was sprawled across her abdomen and her head was buried between Gillian's legs. Never had Gillian thought that she would be a participant in an orgasm marathon. One thing she knew for sure—there was no way she could go another round.

Gillian looked down at the dark head and nudged it with the fingers of a slightly shaking hand. "Hey, are you still alive down there?"

Sam lifted her head slightly. "Not sure. I think I'm floating. Or dead. Or whatever. But I feel great."

"Well, the French call an orgasm 'little death' for a reason. Though it should be me being a little dead. Not you."

"Well, I'm certainly sure we did it French just a moment ago."

Gillian chuckled. "Come up here and kiss me."

Sam complied and Gillian could taste herself on those lips, that tongue. "I love kissing you."

"I love tasting you." Sam's smile was slow and lazy.

With a quick move and energy she didn't know she still possessed, Gillian rolled on top of Sam, straddling her hips.

Big brown eyes were looking up at her with a trust that she hadn't seen there before.

Running her thumb gently over Sam's lips, Gillian sighed. She would never get tired of this feeling. Her skin on Sam's warm and sleek body that held steel underneath was heaven. "You. Are. Incorrigible."

"Yes," Sam drawled. "And?"

"I love it."

"Me too."

"Good." Gillian captured Sam's lips in a firm kiss, rubbing her thumb over an already stiffening nipple.

A groan echoed from Sam.

"I want to touch you." Gillian bent down, licked the nipple, and then blew hot breath over it. "And I want to bring you the same joy you bring me."

Sam closed her eyes and took a deep breath.

Shit. Afraid that she had crossed a border and walked into dangerous territory Gillian froze.

Sam opened her eyes and met Gillian's gaze, as if searching for something.

Gillian licked her suddenly dry lips. One thing that was surely written in her eyes was pure lust...and need. But she wanted to bring joy to Sam, not fulfill her own needs. And if Sam didn't want to take this next step and didn't want to be touched intimately...Suddenly feeling ill she took her hand away from Sam's breast and whispered, "Sorry."

"No." Sam's hand gently wrapped around Gillian's wrist. Her eyes crinkled into a smile. "Don't be sorry. Never be sorry for wanting me."

"I constantly want you." Gillian's cheeks were suddenly very warm.

"Then show me." Sam grinned. "Just...don't torture me too long or I'll lose my nerves."

Gillian burst out laughing. Somehow Sam always found the right words to take away her fears. "I'm not going to torture you. Promise." She turned her wrist and whispered a kiss on Sam's hand. "I just want to make you feel good."

"You do, Gillian. You really do." Sam drew Gillian's hand closer and reciprocated the kiss she had just received.

For a moment they just stared into each other's eyes, then Gillian allowed the smile that had blossomed in her heart to break free on her face. "I love how soft your skin is." She ran her hand down Sam's ribcage and shivered in response to Sam's moan.

"You're...God..."

"No. But sometimes I sure wish I had some of the abilities that come with that particular calling." Gillian smiled and closed her mouth around an erect nipple, bathing it with slow, languid strokes of her tongue.

Sam's moan vibrated under Gillian's body.

Drunk on emotions, Gillian just couldn't stop touching Sam. Not after being allowed for the first time to touch her as if there were no more barriers between them.

Sam's calloused hand touched Gillian's back, sending shivers up her spine. Gillian let the nipple go and looked up, into Sam's beautiful brown eyes that had somehow turned into something resembling liquid chocolate. *She's so stunning.* Gillian lowered herself into a kiss.

Without hesitation Sam granted Gillian's tongue entry.

Gillian's skin burned with desire. She moved her hand between their bodies, along smooth skin and past damp curls before she slowly dipped into Sam's wetness, working her fingers in slow, drawn out circles.

"I can't..."

"This is going to be a rather quick little death. Promise." Holding herself up with one arm, Gillian initiated another kiss while continuing the caress over and around Sam's clit. Within seconds Gillian's fingers were soaked with her lover's essence. "You're so wet." With a swift move she entered Sam. Deep. Keeping up steady movements. In and out, ignoring the throb that hummed between her own thighs.

"You're torturing me," Sam's voice was raspy.

"No." Gillian curled her fingers and thrust deeply, keeping up her rhythm. "Trust me. I won't."

Sam's breathing was speeding along with Gillian's thrusts. Head thrown back, with closed eyes, she looked almost ethereal in her beauty. "Come for me."

A languid moan filled the room, seconds before Sam's walls contracted hard around Gillian's fingers.

"You're so beautiful." Gillian couldn't and didn't want to stop the words that filled her mind.

Sam threw her arm across her eyes. "Done. No more. Finished."

With a laugh Gillian rolled beside Sam. "I believe we both are."

The demand for a nap tugged on Sam. *Damn. What a night.* She was exhausted, a bit sore and felt like a champ. Who would have thought that Gillian had her number down like that?

A warm hand settled on Sam's arm. "Something was different tonight." Gillian's voice was soft and hesitant.

Sam turned her head. "What do you mean?"

"You...I..."

"Hey, just tell me. What's wrong?"

"You never allowed me to touch you like that before."

Sam swallowed. "I need some time before I trust another person, before I can let go."

Gillian's eyes widened slightly. "You trust me?"

"Yes, just did. And yes, I do."

Gillian chewed on her lower lip. "When did you know that you were a lesbian?"

That sure as hell was a change of topic. "Fifteen. I was fifteen."

"Wow. How did your family take it?"

Sam stiffened. She wasn't ready to tell Gillian the whole sordid story. Not tonight. *Keep it simple and matter of fact.* "I left home pretty early. I was nearly seventeen."

Gillian's brow furrowed but she kept silent.

"It was hard for a few years. But still better than staying at home. My father wanted to send me to one of those camps where they cure you of your homosexuality...or so they say."

"Shit."

Sam couldn't help but laugh a little. "Yeah, shit. That about covers it."

"How did you survive? So young and on your own?"

For a moment Sam struggled with the memories of a pain that had been her constant companion back then. She shrugged. "With luck. I had a few hairy experiences and I slept more nights hidden in alleys and on park benches than a teenager should. Hell, than any person ever should. That's for sure. But I made it. And I believe that running away and struggling for a few years was still the better option compared to being forced into a camp where they teach you to hate what you are, who you are. Who I am." Emotion scratched in her throat. It was time to change the subject. "So, what about you? Do you have a sordid tale to tell?" Sam held her breath. This was a make or break moment. Would Gillian reveal something about her life? Or would she continue to hide?

The sheet over Gillian's breast was moving with every breath she took.

Sam cleared her throat. "You don't have to—"

"My husband died a while ago." Gillian's voice was sharp as a knife. "He owned the apartment but he wasn't so much using it for sleeping after a long workday as for his long line of affairs. Men and women."

That's where the aftershave in the bath had come from. Sam's heart clenched. *Married to a guy. Who had affairs? Bastard.* Sam shifted closer and tangled her fingers with Gillian's, giving them a short squeeze.

Gillian's voice sounded muffled when she continued, "I didn't know...we were married for a very long time. But," she took a deep breath, "we hadn't had sex for some time. Ever since I realized that not only did I not love him but that I was also attracted to women. I couldn't bear his touch. Not anymore. But I wanted to save our marriage or the beautiful picture of a marriage we had been able to paint for others. The kids. I didn't want them to..." her voice trailed off. "I was stupid. And then he died and I found out about his countless affairs. More like a harem. And it had been going on for years and years. It made me sick. But somehow...I'm guilty as well. I should have left him." A fire was burning in Gillian's eyes. "Damn it! We had two children together and my husband slept with everything that had a pulse. When I learned about it, I just wanted to take revenge. I've known that I'm attracted to women for several years. Though I'd never acted on it. But after I found out about Derrick I...I kind of let loose."

Sam shivered. She pushed herself up on her elbows and frowned. "You took revenge by sleeping with a woman after his death?"

"Women...with other women. It's complicated and it sure sounds stupid saying it out loud like that." Gillian grimaced.

Sam was speechless. She had sensed there was a story behind Gillian's behavior, but this sounded absolutely absurd. "And did it work? I mean, did it make you feel better?"

"No...I mean, at first, yes," Gillian brushed her hand over the blanket. "Like I said...I knew for a long time that I was attracted to women but then...no. I felt like an asshole or an idiot. I made sure that the others always knew that all I wanted was sex. I didn't lead them on." A crease appeared on Gillian's forehead. "But having sex with women didn't help me feel better. Not at all."

"I don't know what to say, Gillian," Sam replied at last.

Gillian's head came up, her gaze searching Sam's. "It was an asshole reaction from me. I know that now." She glanced down at the bed sheet, her fingers playing around the edge of the blanket that was draped over her body. "But it's different with you. It was from the first night on. The first time you touched me. With you... it's not only the best sex I ever had in my whole life—" She paused, and went on after a moment, "There's more between us. And I would like to know what this 'more' is."

Gillian's words hit Sam's heart like a sledgehammer. Should she admit her own insecure feelings, or just get up and leave now while escape was still possible? This thing between them could break Sam. She knew that.

"Please, Sam, I...I'd like to spend more time with you, get to know you a bit. You are...you touched something inside of me," Gillian said. She softly brushed her lips over Sam's as if trying to reaffirm a connection that Sam couldn't deny. "I have no idea where to go from here. I have two children, a broken life, and an unknown future. And to be absolutely honest...I don't know what to make of 'us'. If there is an 'us'."

Sam chuckled. Whom did she want to fool? As much as Gillian had the potential to destroy her—Sam realized as well that this between them could be something very good. Something special. "Yeah. That pretty much sums up my own life. Well, except that I don't have children. And I'm not rich."

"Being rich is not all that much fun."

Sam had to agree. Even though she still struggled in life, it was nothing compared to how she had struggled before she had left home. But that was a story she would tell Gillian another day. Swallowing around a sudden lump in her throat Sam asked, "So, where do we go from here?"

"Well," Gillian moistened her lips with her tongue, "I would like to meet again."

"Meet as in 'meet' or as in..."

"Both. Talk, have sex. Eat. Date. Have fun."

"Sounds good to me." Sam bit her lower lip. An idea popped into her head. "Are you free on Friday? For around three hours?"

"Only three hours?"

"Yes. We'll meet at seven and I'll have you home at ten. What do you say?"

"I was supposed to choose the next date."

Sam sat up in bed and hugged her knees against her chest, arms circled around them. "You can choose the next two dates."

A genuine smile lit up Gillian's face. "All right. Are we having dinner again?"

Sam shook her head. "No, better eat something before we meet. So, where do you want me to pick you up?"

"Oh." Gillian bit her lip. "I...I don't know if that is such a good idea."

Irritation prickled at the back of Sam's neck. "I'm not going to kiss you senseless in front of your house."

"I know. It's just that the neighbors are really nosy and I'd rather come out on my terms and not on theirs."

An uncomfortable silence stretched between them.

Sam swallowed around the lump in her throat. That wasn't how she wanted this night to end. She needed to be patient with Gillian as much as she needed Gillian to be patient with her. With a smile Sam reached out and trailed her hand along Gillian's cheek. "All right. Why don't we meet here?"

"That would be great. I'm sorry. I just—"

"I can be patient. Honestly."

Gillian's lips curved into a tiny smile. "I'll need your patience."

Sam captured Gillian's lips in a firm kiss. "You have it. I promise."

CHAPTER 11

GILLIAN GOT OUT OF THE taxi, her gaze firmly fixed on Sam. Gorgeous Sam, dressed in comfortable looking worn jeans, the ever-present Doc Martens, and a black leather jacket, was the epitome of self-confidence and oozing sexiness. This was going to be a long evening of not touching.

Sam stood next to Thomas, the elderly doorman. She was laughing as she ran her hand through her hair, which was a gesture Gillian now recognized as Sam being nervous or embarrassed.

Gillian slightly shook her head. How was it that just after spending some nights with each other she was able to read Sam's body language? And what a nice body that language belonged to. Gillian snorted softly. *Insatiable perv.*

As if feeling her presence, Sam turned around, a million watt smile spreading over her face.

Something fluttered from Gillian's chest down to her stomach. "Hi."

"Hi there."

Gillian turned to Thomas. "Good evening."

"Good evening, Mrs. Jennings. How are you doing tonight?"

"Thank you. I'm fine." She looked up at Sam, unsure for a moment what to say or how to behave with Thomas around. He knew that Sam had been with Gillian that first night but she had no idea if he had any inkling that Sam and she were more than just friends. *Play it cool.* She took a deep breath to settle her nerves. "Shall we?"

Sam nodded. "Yes, it's time. See you, Thomas."

He touched his hat with two fingers in a move that reminded Gillian of one of those navy sailors in a fifties movie. "It was nice talking to you, Samantha." There was laughter in his voice.

Sam winced. "Likewise." She turned to Gillian. "Come on. I found a parking space just around the corner which was something akin to a miracle."

Gillian was still wrapping her mind around the fact that Thomas had called Sam "Samantha." Had that been an educated guess? Or did they know each other? Gillian drummed her fingers on the side of her pants and waited until they were several steps away before she said, "Finding a parking spot here is sheer luck, Samantha."

"Ugh...don't please. I hate the name." Sam wrinkled her nose.

Gillian couldn't stop herself from asking, "How is it that Thomas knows it?"

Sam ran a hand through her hair again, her body as tense as a coiled spring. "That is a long story."

Gillian sighed. It was painfully obvious that Sam didn't want to talk about it. "Maybe another time?"

Relief spread across Sam's face. "Yes, absolutely." She stopped in front of a shiny black BMW SUV and took a key out of her pocket.

Openmouthed, Gillian stared from Sam to the car. "This is yours?"

Sam stuffed her hands into the pockets of her blue jeans, a half-smile on her face. "No, actually it's my sister's car. Mine isn't as nice. And I wanted to impress my date, not scare her away." She winked at Gillian.

"Your date is certainly impressed." Gillian stared at the beige leather seats then looked up and met Sam's brown eyes. "But I would drive with you in a garbage truck if it meant spending time with you."

"Garbage trucks stink."

Gillian chuckled. "I still would. Because I like the girl who would be the driver."

A faint blush colored Sam's cheeks. "Get in or we'll be late."

Gillian settled into the seat, a soft sigh escaping her lips. She waited until Sam was settled as well. "This is like sitting on my sofa at home." She ran her hand over the side of the seat. "The leather is so soft."

"Yeah, my sister clearly has taste."

"And obviously money."

For a short moment Sam's knuckles stood out white against the black steering wheel. "Seatbelt, please."

Gillian decided to let go whatever it was that Sam didn't want to talk about. She put the seatbelt on. "So, where are we going?"

"Oh no." Sam shook her head. "Not telling. This is a surprise. The only thing I'm going to tell you is that the drive will take about half an hour."

"Fine. So, a surprise you say?"

"Yes." Sam started the car.

"And no telling?"

"Nope." Sam continued to stare straight ahead, focusing on the traffic. A small smile was playing around her lips. "Put some music on if you want to."

"No, that's fine. Unless you want to?" Gillian laid her hand on Sam's thigh, enjoying the feel of the well worn fabric under her hand. The muscles underneath, however, were anything but soft...

Sam shook her head. "I like the quiet. I listened to music the whole day while painting a living room. Music helps keep the rhythm."

"Blue, right?"

"Blue what?" Sam frowned.

"You painted the living room blue."

Sam turned her head to Gillian before she focused on the street again. "How do you know?"

Gillian chuckled. "You missed a bit of paint." She reached out and ran her fingers over a blue spot on Sam's temple.

"Well, at least that verifies my story." She leaned into the touch. "Tell me what you did today."

"Gardening." Gillian let her hand fall down again on Sam's thigh, simply enjoying the physical connection. "I gathered that we need to pimp our garden a bit if we want to get a good price for the house."

Sam raised an eyebrow. "Pimp your garden?"

"Well, those were my son's words."

Sam snorted with laughter. "Nice. I don't think I've ever heard 'pimp' and 'garden' used in the same sentence."

"Well, I guess they wouldn't use those words in a garden show on TV."

Easy laughter filled the car. For the next half hour they swapped stories about whatever had happened in their lives over the past few days. From time to time, Gillian tried to guess where they were going. Sam, however, kept quiet. Gillian still had no idea about their destination. The only thing she knew was that they were travelling through the outskirts of Springfield. She couldn't remember ever being in that particular area. The houses looked nice and well cared for. A woman was hurrying along the pavement, holding one child on each hand. Next they passed a man standing on a corner, with his cell glued to his ear. Gillian looked at her wrist watch. "So, thirty three minutes are gone and I still have no idea what you've planned for tonight."

"Well, actually, we've reached our destination." Sam set the blinker and slipped into a free space at the parking lot in front of a large building.

Impressive stairs led up to the entrance. Gillian craned her neck and tried to read what was written on the façade. "A planetarium?"

"Yes. I promise you an evening full of stars and unknown worlds."

"Oh." Gillian grabbed Sam's hand and squeezed it. "That sounds great but doesn't it have to be dark outside?"

"No, we're not using the telescope tonight. We'll be watching a show. They have a state-of-the-art Zeiss Starmaster projector. It's mind blowing."

"I've never been to a planetarium."

Sam stared at Gillian as if she had two heads. "Really? Not even with the children?"

"No. Never."

"Oh. All right. You're going to love it." Sam squinted at her. "You do like pretty stars and the universe, don't you?"

Gillian bumped Sam's shoulder. "Who doesn't?"

"Well, I certainly do. I'm here about twice a month at least. It's just so relaxing to get a perspective on life. What are my problems compared to the mystery and greatness of the universe?"

Gillian nodded. She could definitely relate to that. "I know what you're talking about. It's like looking into the Grand Canyon and realizing how gloriously insignificant our lives are."

"You really get it." Delightful wonder was written all over her face.

"How being 'insignificant' can be a great thing?"

"Yes. Most people would find it depressing. But I feel like," Sam shrugged, "I don't know...free?"

"Yes, it is." Once again, Gillian placed her hand on Sam's thigh and began to lightly rub back and forth. "It's liberating. And I don't find it depressing at all."

The smile on Sam's face couldn't have been wider. "You're going to love the show. Come on."

It didn't take long for Sam to pay for the tickets as not many people were in line at the counter. *That's weird for a Friday night.* Gillian found herself checking out the few visitors that were hanging around in front of the huge and truly ugly red doors that she guessed to be the entrance to the viewing area. Checking people out had become an automatic thing for her. Gillian bit down on her bottom lip. She really needed to get over her fear of what would happen if people found out that she was...a lesbian. Gillian grimaced. She hated that word. It came along with the feeling of being pigeonholed and bullied for loving someone. And even worse—what would her being an "out" lesbian do to her children? What if they were bullied for having a mother in a relationship with another woman? Gillian rubbed the bridge of her nose. Society sucked. To cheat on a partner was condoned in her circles—if done discretely. Fiscal fraud was some kind of sport. But loving someone of the same gender wasn't as hip as some people proclaimed. The fear of being "out" battled against the guilt she felt about hiding and of not feeling comfortable with who she was. She wrapped her arms tightly around herself. Would there ever be a time when she would be confident enough to even hold hands in public? And was hiding fair to a partner?

"Hey, you okay?" Sam's gentle voice tickled Gillian's ear.

Gillian forced a smile on her face. This was neither the time nor the place to talk about her insecurities. "Yes. So, is this," she pointed at the red doors, "where the show is going to happen tonight?"

Sam tilted her head slightly and observed Gillian's face for a moment before she said, "Yes, and they should open the doors any second now."

Which they did. The small crowd of people who had been gathered disappeared through the doors.

A slightly musty smell invaded Gillian's nose when she entered the smallish room. Well, smallish compared to the cinemas she had been to with her children. Here, five rows of bright red chairs were arranged in a circle and, all in all, she guessed around a hundred people could be seated. Gillian's gaze was drawn to a huge round hole in the middle of the room. *What is this?*

"Come on. Let's sit down. It's going to start any minute now." Sam sounded as excited as a five year old on Christmas morning.

"I thought it would be more crowded."

Sam shook her head. "Not on a Friday evening. People go to cinemas on a Friday night or hang out in bars, meet with their friends for dinner. But they hardly ever find their way here."

After settling down next to each other, Gillian looked up. The ceiling was roundish. She scanned the room. Where was the projector?

Sam leaned slightly over and whispered in her ear, "Is it okay to hold hands in the dark?"

Gillian coughed. "Yes, it is. But only holding hands. No second or third base in here."

Sam leaned back again. "All right. I can live with that. But all bets are off later in the car."

"Nope. No way. I'm not turning into a teenage version of myself."

"Oh...so do tell me what happened in cars during your teenage days."

Gillian lifted an eyebrow. "That is going to be my secret."

The light dimmed slowly.

"It's about to start." Sam had barely uttered those words when, without further warning, the sound system nearly blew Gillian's ears away with Richard Strauss' "Also sprach Zarathustra".

She blinked. This volume could certainly wake the dead.

Something began to move out of the huge gap in the middle of the room but it was too dark to make out more than contours. Gillian leaned forward.

"That is the Zeiss Starmaster projector and the music is from "2001: A Space Odyssey", the opening of the movie," Sam whispered.

"Oh." There was the projector. Amazing.

"Ladies and gentlemen," a deep male voice said over the loudspeaker system. "Welcome tonight and thank you for joining us on a very special journey. 'Destination Solar System' will take us all through the small part of the universe that we believe we know and yet surprises us, again and again, with its beauty and majesty. Fasten your seatbelts and enjoy the ride."

Minutes into the show, Gillian had nearly forgotten where she was. A gigantic eruption exploded out of the sun. She pressed her back deeper into the seat and grabbed Sam's hand. "This is like sitting in a starship."

A deep laugh rumbled out of Sam. "Yeah, it's pretty cool, right?"

Gillian was lost. Positively, absolutely lost. And she loved every second of it. "It's unbelievable." Her breath caught in her throat as Sam's fingers skimmed the top of Gillian's thigh. "Stop that. Holding hands is where the line is drawn tonight."

Sam chuckled. "What a shame."

Instead of continuing the verbal play, Gillian wrapped her hand around Sam's arm and squeezed it slightly when they flew through Saturn's rings. "They are made out of small stones?"

"Well," Sam whispered, "the official description is 'small particles' and they're mostly made out of ice."

A comet brushed past them with a loud whoosh.

"Would it burst your bubble if I told you that there are no sounds in space because of the vacuum?"

Gillian turned her head and stared at Sam. "You're a geek."

"No, I'm not."

Gillian smiled and patted Sam's hand. "Shush now." She looked up again, just in time to see a blue planet coming closer. *Wow.*

Way too soon for Gillian, the male voice once again came over the sound system, "Thank you very much for travelling with us. We hope that you enjoyed the journey and that you will be joining us again in the future."

Seconds later the light came slowly up again.

Gillian took a deep breath. "That was awesome."

Sam got up from her chair and offered her hand to Gillian. "So, did you enjoy it?"

Gillian reached out, took the hand, and stood up. "More than that. This was mind blowing and beautiful and amazing and I can't believe I've never been here before." Her eyes locked onto Sam's. Those brown, gentle eyes. Breathing was becoming hard—as was forcing her hands to not reach out and touch Sam or not allowing herself to kiss those tempting lips. With all the discipline she could muster, she cleared her throat. "I have to take the children to one of these shows." She took a step away from Sam.

Sam opened her mouth and closed it again, thrusting her hands into her pockets.

Searching for a neutral thing to say, Gillian finally asked, "Have you seen the show before?"

"Yes. I have. But I don't think I'll ever get tired of it." Her smile didn't fully reach her eyes.

"Is everything okay?"

"Yes, sure." Sam looked at her watch. "Come on. I'll take you back to the apartment."

Gillian's stomach started to hurt. Where moments ago they had nearly been kissing, now the distance between them was a gaping chasm. And Gillian had a pretty good idea what had happened. "Hey." She reached out and took hold of Sam's hand.

Sam looked down at their linked fingers, confusion written all over her face.

"About the apartment." Gillian swallowed on a mouth gone dry, "I took a taxi. Would it be all right with you if you took me home?"

Sam's eyebrows nearly crept up her head. "To where you live?"

"Yes."

"All right. No, no problem at all. But...you're sure?"

Gillian shrugged. "No goodbye kisses in front of the house."

Sam grinned and this time her eyes twinkled. "We could provide them with a special kind of show."

"I'd rather not."

"That's a damn shame."

CHAPTER 12

LOUD MUSIC BLARED OUT OF a passing car. A tall woman with Doc Martens hurried across the street, a bright green backpack over her shoulder.

Gillian's gaze was drawn to the boots. *They look exactly like Sam's.* Her heart started to beat a bit faster. *Well, they would without the pink bootlaces.* And Sam would probably never wear a short skirt. Sam's ass was a lot hotter as well. And—

"Gillian, honey. Hello? Are you listening?"

Gillian tore her gaze away from the woman in the Doc Martens and looked at Rachel, who was dressed in a stylish white top, toffee trousers, and black heels—and still the Doc Martens stirred Gillian more. Much more. "Yes, sorry. I was daydreaming."

Rachel raised an eyebrow. "You certainly didn't hear one word I said."

Shit. "I'm really sorry. I'm a bit tired today." Gillian rubbed her eyes.

"You do look a little under the weather. You could have said no when I phoned and asked if you wanted to go shopping."

"I know." Gillian rubbed the back of her neck. "I know. But I had to go downtown anyway and pick up a dress for Angela at Murphy's."

"That sounds enthusiastic..." Rachel's eyes narrowed. "Is everything all right with you?"

Sure. I've been having amazing sex with women. Several times. One woman in particular and I can't stop thinking about her. I hate my life. I hate my dead husband. I'm a lesbian or bi or whatever...everything is perfectly all right. Peachy really. Gillian plastered a smile on her face. "Everything is fine. Thank you for asking. It's just that I woke up in the night and couldn't go to sleep again. It happens sometimes." One thing she had learned since Derrick's death was that playing on other people's pity was a good way of redirecting attention. And it wasn't a lie that she had trouble sleeping most nights.

"Oh, I know exactly what you mean. I have a hard time going back to sleep once I've woken up. Especially when Harry is not there." Rachel's voice was surprisingly gentle. She laid her hand on Gillian's shoulder. "You're still not used to not having Derrick around, right? I can't imagine how you cope without him."

Very well, thank you. "It's not easy at times." Gillian sighed to give her statement more emphasis. Guilt nagged at her conscience.

Playing the mourning widow wasn't a role she liked to play. Maybe meeting with Rachel had been a bad idea.

"You should really take up tennis again. Or come to the girls' nights." Rachel pursed her lips. "We could meet for breakfast again. We haven't done that for a few weeks."

Hell, no. There was no way she would be having breakfast or sipping cocktails with the wives' again any time soon—or ever. "Maybe. But...I think I need more time. And the kids need me."

Rachel stopped in front of a jeweler's display window. "Look, honey. This little beauty," she pointed at a Cartier watch, "is going to be part of my birthday present."

"Shouldn't birthday presents be a surprise?"

"No." Rachel shook her head. "I certainly don't like the kind of surprises Harry usually turns up with. He has no imagination and no empathy." A cold smile appeared on her face. "And since he has to make amends for doing something utterly stupid, this extra-flat Tank from Cartier is going to be one of my presents."

"It's a beauty." The watch practically screamed expensive understatement. Gillian stole a glance at Rachel, whose expression showed off the coldness of a diamond and not the fury of a ruby. *I wonder what he'd done this time to make her so angry.*

"We should go inside and find something nice to cheer you up. Look at those beautiful rings."

Oh dear Lord. A watch for over $30,000 was nothing that would cheer her up and a ring that was worth more than Sam's car wouldn't either. But this was a good time to drop the first bomb. Ignoring her plummeting stomach Gillian said, "No. I can't. Not at the moment. This will have to wait until we've settled into the new house."

"You're moving?" Rachel's eyes were wide as saucers. "Why is this the first time I'm hearing about this? Does your mother-in-law know?"

Bingo. "No, she doesn't." *But I'm sure she will at some point today.* Telling Rachel about the house was part of Gillian's scaredy-cat plan. If Rachel told Margret...well, then Gillian wouldn't have to. And then it would be Margret who would have to come to Gillian to talk about it—which was something the Dragon Lady despised. She wanted to hold court and have people come to her.

"Did you already sign?"

"No, but this weekend the kids and I will look at two houses on the short list." Gillian picked at a piece of lint on her jacket. "With a bit of luck it won't be too long before we can move."

"But where to? And why for God's sake. Your house is lovely."

Gillian shrugged. "There are just too many memories linked to the house. I feel that we need a new start. And as to where...that depends."

"But couldn't your father-in-law take care of this? I'm sure he has the best connections."

Not rolling her eyes was a major achievement. Hell would freeze over before she would ask him for help. "I'm sure he does. Absolutely."

Rachel stared at her, obviously waiting for an explanation.

It would have been so easy to give in, to admit that she would get a better offer if James took over. However, this was not what moving into a new house was about. This was about taking control of her life—even if it was scary as hell. Gillian squared her shoulders. "I need to do this on my own. And I need to know that I can do it on my own."

Rachel's sigh was overly dramatic. "Let's take a break." She pointed to the coffee shop on the other side of the street. "I could use an espresso or two."

"Sure. Yes." An espresso didn't sound like a bad idea.

A short while later they sat inside Marcello's, the loud whir of a frothing machine cutting through the room. Soft jazz music played in the background.

Gillian's gaze wandered around the room. She hadn't been to this place before. It was similar to all the other fancy coffee shops that had been popping up around town these past years. The full service wait staff set them aside from their competition and probably contributed to the large number of white-collar guests.

"I'll be back in a minute, dear." Rachel got up from their table. "Please order my usual, will you?"

Gillian nodded. This was going to be a long morning. She hated how difficult it was for her to stand up to others, and how easy it would be to give in and go back to her old kind of life. *Baby steps.* She needed to take baby steps. But for today, she would give it a rest. She had to prepare herself for the fight with Margret. That one would take all the energy she had. And more.

A waiter appeared at her table. "Welcome to Marcello's. What can I bring you?"

"Two double Espressos, please."

Sam inhaled deeply. The smell of freshly brewed coffee was something she could easily get addicted to. It was only rivaled by the smell of fresh bread. But fresh bread wasn't sold in this overpriced coffee shop, only sandwiches that cost more than a whole meal at her favorite hamburger joint. With a sigh she took the packet of coffee Linda had ordered her to pick up and handed two bills to the guy behind the counter.

"Here you go." He handed her the change back.

"Thanks." She threw a few coins into the tip jar.

Squaring her shoulders, Sam made her way to the exit, happy to be able to escape. This was so not her kind of place.

A guy in an expensive looking suit bumped into her. "Hey, pay attention to where you're going, will you?" His voice was rough, his suit expensive and his hair as oily as a can of sardines.

"You do realize that you bumped into me, yeah?" She hated those know-it-all, have-it-all guys. Guys like her father.

Suit guy looked down at her. "You better run along before I inform the manager that you," he looked her up and down, a sneer on his face, "are causing problems."

People from the nearby tables stared openly at her.

Sam clenched her teeth. She really, really wanted to burrow her fist into his stomach. That however, would no doubt lead to her being thrown out and utterly humiliated. If they didn't call the police and then things could get really ugly. That would not do. She knew that, with her dirty work clothes, she stuck out like a sore thumb. The payback for this shopping trip would be a bitch for Linda. No more buying coffee in fancy coffee shops just because a special kind of brew was on offer. Nothing was wrong with coffee from a supermarket. "I think that I'll now take a step to my right and walk around you. And then I'll leave and try my best to forget about whatever just happened. All right?"

"Just leave," he growled.

And she did just that, not remembering when she had last felt this shitty. She threw a glance over her shoulder.

His gaze was trying to burn holes into her body.

She slowly released her breath and was only a few steps away from the exit when a woman with blonde hair caught her attention. Strange how she always thought of Gillian when she saw someone with the same hair color or style. Sam stopped in her tracks. This woman did look amazingly similar to Gillian. Sam squinted. Was that...*Gillian. Wow.* It really was her. Sitting alone at a table. Sam bit her lip. For a moment she wasn't sure if leaving wouldn't be the better option. She had no doubt that the ape-man with a suit was still watching. However, the chance to see Gillian and talk to her...Sam couldn't resist. A smile spread over her face. Maybe killing Linda for this errand wasn't necessary after all. Sam pulled the free chair out at Gillian's table. The scrape of metal on the floor made her cringe.

Gillian looked up, an expression of surprise replaced by a short moment of joy. The moment of joy however was replaced by a frown—a frown that wasn't replaced by excitement or delight as Sam had hoped.

"Hi there, good looking." Sam sat down on the chair, her gaze glued on Gillian's face.

"Hi. What a surprise. What are you doing here?" Gillian cast a glance toward the other side of the coffee shop while biting her lip.

Sam stretched her legs out under the table. "Yeah, this is not my usual joint. But the coffee is supposed to be good and, unfortunately, Linda is a coffee snob. And as much as I'm not into this whole coffee scene...it's so nice seeing you here." Sam lowered her voice and leaned forward, her hands nearly touching Gillian's. "I thought a lot about you today."

Gillian drew her hand back and rubbed her neck. "Yes. Look, Sam. This is really not a good time."

"Oh. All right." Sam put slightly shaking hands on her knees. "You okay?"

A flicker of hesitation crossed over Gillian's face. "I am. But Sam could you please—"

"Everything all right, Gillian dear?"

Sam looked up into the blue eyes of a woman who was dressed like Sam's mother used to. Actually, a lot like Gillian was dressed today as well...all businessman's wife.

"Yes, thank you. I am fine. She," Gillian pointed at Sam, "was not feeling well. And sat down."

Confused Sam looked from Gillian to the other woman. What—

"Well, she looks pretty okay now."

Out of the corner of her eye, Sam saw the guy from earlier advance toward the table. She curled her fingers into fists until her knuckles stood out white against her dark blue trousers. She wet her lips. *Shit.* "I don't really think..."

"So," Gillian said, averting her eyes, "if you're feeling better...I believe my friend would like to sit down."

Sam stared at Gillian before she looked up at the friend. The memory of an early morning encounter hit her like a punch in the stomach. She had seen her before. This was the woman the annoying building manager had drooled over. And she had come out of the apartment with Gillian on the very morning Sam had seen her for the very first time. Together—as in early-morning-coming-out-of-the-same-apartment together. Sam tried to draw in a breath but couldn't. The walls of the coffee shop were pressing in on her. This couldn't be happening. It had to be some kind of joke or misunderstanding. She tore her gaze away from Gillian's "friend" and focused on her face. A face that was hard as stone. This was not the Gillian she had made love to. This was not the Gillian who laughed with her and made Sam feel whole. This was a Gillian she didn't know. And didn't want to know—because this Gillian made her feel sick and cheap.

A rough hand touched her shoulder. "Are you on drugs?" The guy from earlier had joined them.

"No." She shook her head.

"I'll get the manager. She's crazy." He walked toward the back of the coffee shop, determination in his steps.

Gillian's friend pointed at the chair Sam still sat on. "I hope the paint on your trousers was dry. I wouldn't enjoy having to send you an invoice from my drycleaner."

Sam blinked. It was as if all the air had been sucked out of her lungs. Everything in her screamed to get up and run, to leave this place. She looked into Gillian's pale face. Why was Gillian so quiet? Why didn't she say something? Anything? *Why doesn't she defend me?*

"This one." Suit guy was back, pointing a finger at her.

With him was the guy who had handed Sam her coffee. His earlier smile however had been replaced by a stern expression. He looked from Gillian to Gillian's friend and then to Sam, obviously trying to make sense of the situation. "I hear there's a problem?"

Gillian's friend was the first to react. "There is. This woman is in my chair."

"Ma'am," he looked at Sam, a frown on his face. "Maybe it would be better if you left."

"But I—"

"I have to agree." Gillian's voice sounded raw.

This had to be a nightmare, similar to those where Sam thought she could fly and then crashed down and died. Sam dared a glance at Gillian whose face was as pale as porcelain. There was no eye contact. There would be no help coming from Gillian. Sam was on her own. Forcing down her urge to turn and run, she stood up slowly. Her knees were shaky.

Gillian cleared her throat. "I—"

"I'm sorry." With as much dignity as she could muster—which was much more than she thought herself capable of at the moment—Sam turned around and left the coffee shop, head held up high.

Sam slowly closed the apartment door behind her when all she wanted to do was to slam it shut. However, she didn't have the energy to do that. She had barely found enough strength to make her way home and she seriously had no idea how she didn't cause an accident somewhere along the way.

Numb. She was numb. Which was good—numb didn't hurt as much as the pain caused by Gillian ripping her heart out. Sam stumbled into the kitchen and leaned heavily on the table. Why had she trusted Gillian so easily? Why hadn't she gone with her instincts and her experience instead of letting herself fall into those green eyes? Those damn green eyes.

Sam's cell rang.

She took it out and stared at Gillian's name on the display. *Shit.* Sam closed her eyes. She felt like vomiting. There was no way she was going to answer. With trembling fingers she laid the cell on the counter and waited until the only sound in the kitchen was the grumbling of her fridge.

I need to call Linda. Linda was waiting for the coffee. Waiting for Sam to come back. *I have to call Mr. Winter.* He was waiting for her to come over this afternoon and fix his toilet. *Shit. Shit. Shit.* Sam grabbed the half empty bottle of tequila that she hadn't touched for weeks.

Her cell rang again.

Sam stared at the device, torn between throwing the damn thing against a wall and letting the call once again go to voicemail. She took out one of her shot glasses. *I'll survive. This is not going to break me. I don't need her. I don't need anyone.*

The cell was quiet again.

Good. She took a deep breath before downing the tequila. *I have to call Linda.* She poured herself another shot and chugged it down.

The cell rang once more.

All right. That's it. With trembling fingers she picked up the cell. "What?"

"I'm sorry, Sam. I'm really sorry." Gillian's voice sounded frenzied.

"Stop calling." Sam looked at the bottle of tequila.

"I froze—"

"I don't care."

"Sam, I—?"

"Don't call me again."

Sam set the cell down on the kitchen counter before she slid down to the floor. Drawing her knees up to her chest, she wrapped her arms around her legs, crying for what she had hoped for and for what she had lost. Being numb had felt a whole lot better.

CHAPTER 13

HEAVY RAIN BEAT A STACCATO rhythm on the taxi's roof. The downpour hadn't stopped since early morning, and now, after dark, Springfield's streets had morphed into shallow lakes reflecting passing cars' headlights like glittering disco balls.

Gillian leaned her head against the cool window of the taxi that was taking her across town. She was so very tired. Sleep had eluded her for the past four nights—ever since the coffee incident. She watched the rundown houses and wavering forms outside without interest until they passed a woman with short hair and a powerful walk. *Sam.* Gillian's heart beat faster. She pressed her palms to the window, and then sunk back. *No.* A small child clung to the woman's hand. She couldn't be Sam.

Gillian closed her eyes against the painful reality of her life. She had failed the one person that had begun to really mean something to her. Even now she couldn't understand why she hadn't said or done anything to defend Sam back at Marcello's.

Frozen. Gillian had been totally, utterly frozen by panic. Completely unable to move or to speak—the only thing that had spiraled around in her head had been the fear of being outed there and then. The memory of that moment of cowardice was like an ever-thickening cover of frostbite around her heart. She had betrayed Sam's trust and probably destroyed whatever they could have had.

Stupid. Stupid. Stupid. She curled her hands into fists.

The taxi stopped, hurtling Gillian back to the present. She forced her eyes open.

"Here we are, ma'am." The driver turned in his seat to face her.

Gillian tried to get a look at the building outside. "This is 24 Hammond Street?" she asked, unable to see properly through the rain-smeared window.

"Yes, ma'am."

So, this was it then. With slightly shaking hands she took a few bills out of her wallet and handed them over. "I guess this isn't the most populated area of town, right?"

"No, ma'am. It sure isn't."

With her luck she would be mugged as soon as the taxi left. Gillian sighed. "Thanks. Keep the change, please."

The driver took the money and frowned at her. "Are you sure you don't want me to wait for you, ma'am?"

Gillian bit her lip and looked out the window. She didn't want to seem like a coward. On the other hand, it would be nice to have someone close-by if she needed to get away in a hurry.

She forced a smile. "You know, that isn't such a bad idea." She handed him some more bills. "How long will that keep you?"

"At least twenty minutes, ma'am." He took the money and turned off the engine. "Let's say I'll wait for half an hour 'cause I need a break anyhow and this place is as good as any."

Relief spread through her. "Are you sure?" Gillian put her wallet back into her purse.

"Yep." He settled more comfortably into his seat, clearly prepared to stay a while.

"Thank you." Gillian couldn't help smiling. *At least I've lucked out with the taxi driver.* Half an hour should be more than enough to find out if Sam was in her favorite club and, more importantly, if she wanted to talk to Gillian. *And if not? What do I do then?*

Hopelessness gnawed on her like a terrier on a bone. She was severely tempted to turn around and leave. Instead of walking into the lion's den, she could be home within the next forty minutes and enjoying a good book or watching something relaxing on television. There was always tomorrow. She could try to get a hold of

Sam on the phone. Maybe it would be easier to talk without seeing each other face to face.

Coward. Trying to find the easy way out again? It wouldn't work and she knew it. Sam hadn't answered any of her calls so far. Well, except the first one...when she had told her to not call again. Why should tomorrow be any different? *Get a grip. You came here to talk.* Gillian got out of the car and opened her umbrella with stubborn determination.

A waft of cold, wet air welcomed her outside. She shivered, cursing her decision to dress up. The black Vera Wang dress wasn't made for this kind of weather, but she wasn't above female tricks to help gain Sam's favor.

Clinging to her umbrella as if it was a lifeline, Gillian looked up at the neon sign on the building in front of her. The Labrys. *Couldn't the owner have been a bit more creative?* She had no idea what to expect inside. Her only knowledge of what a rundown lesbian bar looked like came from *The L-Word*. She very much doubted that Sam's favorite turf had much in common with the stylish clubs most TV shows featured or the clubs Gillian had visited downtown. She shook her head. Setting foot in a shabby lesbian bar was not something she had ever considered in the past.

Hesitating in front of the club's door, she felt almost sickened by her stomach's churning. She took a deep lungful of damp air to help clear her mind and calm her nerves.

"I'm not sure the door will open through sheer will power. At least it didn't yesterday," said a sultry voice behind her.

Gillian nearly jumped out of her skin. *Shit. Shit. Shit.* She gripped the keys in her pocket, prepared to fight any potential attacker. Clenching down on the icy panic in her belly, she turned around.

The pouring rain and shadowy darkness made it hard to see more than a bulky form. Her knees weakened with relief when she realized that the person standing before her was a tall, black woman with a friendly, lopsided grin on her face.

"Sorry if I scared you, honey, but you're blocking my way." The stranger took two steps to stand under the shelter of the eaves. "What lousy weather."

Gillian's heart still galloped. She took a second glance at the woman beside her. Even in the dim light Gillian could see that she was broad-shouldered. She wore a black leather jacket, blue jeans, and black steel-toed boots. Her soaking wet dreadlocks were plastered to her head.

A grunt of appreciation nearly escaped Gillian. She cleared her throat. "I'm sorry. I didn't mean to stand in the way." Her face grew warm when she realized that she had likely been observed staring at the door like a mouse hypnotized by a snake.

"No problem." The tall stranger opened the door before she said over her shoulder, "Do you want to come inside and have some fun downstairs, or would you prefer to continue seducing the unresponsive door?" She gave Gillian a wink.

Is she flirting with me? "I...I know that I must look stupid. It's only that...well, I've never been to this particular kind of club before." Gillian shuffled her feet, then immediately regretted her action when a wave of cold water seeped into her stilettos.

The other woman shrugged. "Everyone was a first timer once, honey. I learned there isn't much to be afraid of if you stick to a simple rule."

"And that would be?" Gillian tilted her head.

The stranger closed the door and leaned against the frame. She took her time to look Gillian slowly up and down. "The most important rule in life is to be very clear and upfront about what you want. And also about what you don't want. That is the best strategy."

Gillian snorted. "It sounds so easy. But it isn't."

"As a matter of fact, it is. It's just that women have a tough time with this 'cause we are taught to be friendly and understanding rather than open and honest." The woman shrugged a second time. "I personally find that this little rule makes my life a lot easier."

Open and honest? Surely it couldn't be so easy. On the other hand...it couldn't hurt to try something different for a change. Gillian gathered her courage and walked toward the door. "All right, I'm in."

"Good for you." The stranger opened the door. "By the way, I'm Skyler and I would very much love to buy you a drink."

Caught by surprise, Gillian didn't know how to respond. *So she was flirting with me.*

Skyler's dark eyes twinkled as she waited patiently for Gillian's reply.

Open and honest she said. Let's try it. Gillian graced Skyler with a gentle smile. "Sorry, but I'm here looking for my..." she swallowed, unsure what to call Sam. "For someone," she concluded with as much firmness as she could muster.

"See, that wasn't so bad, was it? Openness and honesty works just fine with me. Though I hope whatever or whoever you are looking for is worth it."

"She is." Gillian was surprised about the determination in her own voice.

"Then I hope you'll find her here tonight." Skyler ran a gentle finger over Gillian's cheek. "And if not...you know where to find me." Skyler's grin had a good-natured leer in it.

Gillian couldn't help chuckling. "Thank you. But if I can't find her here, I'll be going home." She stared at her damp feet. "But I hope you'll have some fun tonight."

Skyler snorted. "Oh, I have no doubt about that. I'm packed and ready to go."

Gillian tilted her head in question but got no response from Skyler except another wink.

Straightening her shoulders, Gillian made her way through the entrance, past Skyler, and down the stairs. The tang of cigarette smoke and beer welcomed her to the faintly lit room where a dirty-brown bar in desperate need of a fresh paint job dominated the left side of the room. One of Cher's older songs floated through the air.

This wasn't what she had expected. *This is what a lesbian bar looks like?* She took a deep breath, suddenly unsure if being here was really such a good idea.

The crowd at the bar was a mix of young and old women, most of them dressed in jeans, leather pants, and motorcycle jackets. A wolf whistle echoed from somewhere.

Gillian winced in response. *This is like walking into a group of horny teenage boys.*

"Don't let them get to you." Skyler appeared beside her. "Most are tough on the outside but marshmallows on the inside. And they treasure a good-looking, classy woman like you." Skyler slapped her shoulder lightly before she walked away.

Cher's song finished. For a moment, only the soft, unintelligible chatter of many voices could be heard, then a woman in the tightest leather pants Gillian had ever seen got up from her barstool and went over to the corner jukebox.

She fed the machine, and soon Cher started another song.

One of the women sitting at a table close by called loud enough for everyone to hear, "Hey, Sheryl, if I have to listen to Cher one more time, I'm going to perform plastic surgery on you."

Laughter and hollers came from the bar.

Gillian grinned and relaxed slightly. Maybe it wasn't so bad here. Torn between hope and anxiety, she started to look for Sam and turned to watch the couples swaying to Cher's *Love Can Build a Bridge* on the dance floor. Sam wasn't among them. Gillian clenched her fists against the sick feeling in her stomach.

There were some tables hidden in half-darkness behind the dance floor. Maybe...Gillian had walked halfway around the platform when she finally found the person she was looking for. All breath left Gillian's lungs. She felt as if someone had sucker-punched her right in the solar plexus.

Sam wasn't alone.

This was one of Gillian's nightmares in Technicolor, only that what happened between Sam and the blonde on her lap wasn't a movie or a dream. The slut in a cheap excuse for a dress couldn't possibly get any closer without crawling into Sam's body.

She has already replaced me. Gillian leaned heavily on the back of a chair. Tears blurred her vision. She had tormented herself with pictures of Sam suffering from the pain she had caused. And here Sam was, playing cozy with another woman. Obviously she hadn't wasted any time with shedding tears over what happened. All of Gillian's plans of asking Sam for forgiveness, her hopes of reconciling crumbled to dust.

"Did you think she would weep over you, Gillian?"

Gillian spun around and found herself faced with a woman with long, blonde hair.

"Excuse me?"

The stranger took Gillian's arm in a death grip and pulled her toward the bar. "Come over here before you make a fool of yourself or Sam. Sit down." The woman pointed at an empty barstool, then waved the bartender over. "Here, T, give us two Jack Daniels. Two fingers, straight."

"Got you covered, Linda." The bartender walked away to get their drinks.

"I don't drink whisky, especially not with women I don't know." Gillian glared at Linda. "And don't you dare touch me again!"

Linda glared back at her. "What? Jack Daniels too cheap for you?"

The bartender returned, setting glasses in front of them.

"Drink!" Linda said. She chugged down her own drink, and then slammed the empty shot glass down on the bar.

Fuming, Gillian didn't touch her glass. Seeing Sam might have crushed her hope but that didn't mean Gillian would allow a stranger to push her around. She stepped away from the barstool. "Who do you think you are?"

"My name's Linda. I'm Sam's best friend. So I'd say this is very much my business. Now drink up." Linda pointed at Gillian's glass.

Gillian opened her mouth and closed it again. *This is Linda, Sam's best friend? Shit.* Could this evening get any worse? Gillian sat down on the barstool. *Ah, what the hell.* She took the glass and gulped down the amber drink. The whisky burned a trail over her tongue and down her throat. She did her best not to grimace and failed miserably.

"Are you here to mock Sam?" Linda gave Gillian a warning look. "I saw you come in with Skyler. Looks like you already found someone new."

"No, I...I'm not here with Skyler. I just met her outside. I came in to talk to Sam." Gillian hated how defensive she felt and sounded. *I don't need to justify myself to Linda.* She sat straighter, toying with the empty glass. "But that is none of your business."

"Talk to her? Now? Maybe you should have talked to her in the coffee shop instead of pretending not to know her." Linda leaned closer, glowering at her. "And what about the bitch that was with you? Is she good in bed?"

What? Every single word hurt like a slap in the face. Gillian bit back the sharp words that burned on the tip of her tongue. What good would it do to infuriate Sam's best friend? Staring at the row of bottles on shelves behind the bar, she desperately wished for another whisky. But maybe it would be wiser to get drunk at home. She didn't have any reason to stay here any longer.

"What? Nothing to say to defend yourself?" Linda asked.

"If it was in my power to undo what happened, I would. But I can't. And the 'bitch' that was with me is only an old acquaintance. Nothing more." Gillian looked into Linda's hard eyes. "I made a mistake, a mistake that I deeply regret, but I came here tonight to talk to Sam, to apologize for what I did—or rather didn't do." She darted a glance at the table where the blonde slut was still plastered to Sam like mold on marmalade.

Linda slapped a hand on the bar. "Tell me something, Gillian. What was Sam to you? 'Cause I really don't get it."

"She is—not was." Gillian hesitated, unsure how to explain what she hadn't put in words before. Love wasn't the right label for hours of hot sex and some good conversation, but "casual fling" wasn't true either. She had come to care a lot more for Sam than she expected. "I feel a lot for her. And I...I don't want to lose her."

Once again, her gaze was drawn to the small table where Sam and the blonde slut played easy to get with each other. Gillian bit her lip hard enough to taste blood, but the minor pain didn't help dull the agony that burned inside her. "Seeing her with another woman...it hurts. A lot," Gillian said in a low voice, certain it was still loud enough for Linda to hear. She picked up the empty glass. "Can I have another one?" One more drink couldn't hurt.

Linda shook her head. "No, first you have to tell me how important Sam is to you."

"Very important." Gillian had no idea why she even answered Linda's question.

Linda snorted. "Is that why you pretended not to know her?"

Gillian cursed inwardly. Hearing those words hurt nearly as much as reliving the painful minutes again and again in her memories. "She told you?"

"Yep, though I nearly had to beat it out of her."

"I panicked." Gillian's neck muscles tensed.

"Excuse me?"

"I said I panicked." The urge to get up and leave grew. There was no way Linda or Sam would understand her background and the problems it caused.

"Why for God's sake? Did you believe Sam would hump you in front of your friend?"

Shame was replaced by a burning anger. "I'm not stupid," Gillian snapped.

Linda leaned an elbow on the bar. "So what, Gillian? Did you believe coming here dressed to the nines in that little black number would be enough to make Sam crawl back to you?"

"No, I..." Gillian inhaled around the knot in her throat. "I only wanted to talk to her." She didn't need to tell Linda that she had indeed hoped that Sam might forgive her, that she had dreamed about them becoming even closer than before.

Laughter echoed from a nearby table, distracting Gillian from her thoughts. A group of three women, each pierced in various parts of their faces, got up to leave. They oozed a raw sexuality that, even to Gillian, left no room for misunderstanding what they were up to. Gillian felt so out of her league. This wasn't her turf. *Why did I come? This will lead to nothing.* A heavy weight settled on her shoulders.

"I don't get you, Gillian. I really don't," Linda said, shaking her head. "But I have to give it to you...you have balls showing up here tonight."

"Yes, but that doesn't matter anymore, does it?" Gillian stared at her empty glass.

"You're serious about Sam?" Linda asked, arching an eyebrow. "I mean serious enough to grovel and beg, and not do the same shitty thing again?"

"I would, but what's the point?" Gillian nodded at Sam's table. "She's found a substitute. Maybe this is just as well."

"Oh, come on, Gillian. Sam is as drunk as a skunk. And little Barbie over there is just hoping to get laid." Linda snickered. "It seems she's not aware that Sam is in no shape to provide that kind of service tonight."

For a moment, hope blossomed in Gillian. She looked into Linda's brown eyes that had lost some of their coldness. "I'm not here to hurt her." She struggled for words, afraid to hope again. "Do you really think she's still interested in me?"

"Gillian, it doesn't matter what I think. The question is what you want."

There was no question about what she wanted. "I want her, I want 'us' back. And I want to..." Gillian swallowed hard. "I want to see if we can have more. Together."

A muscle in Linda's jaw twitched.

Gillian steeled herself against Linda's response.

"Are you ready to fight for her?" Linda held up a hand before Gillian could answer. "And I don't just mean tonight, Gillian. You have to treat her with respect no matter what comes your way."

Days ago she would have answered yes. Without any doubt. But life had taught her a painful lesson about herself. Truth was that she didn't have as much backbone as she thought. "I can only promise that I'll try my very best."

Linda's gaze became cold again. Her eyes drilled into Gillian and caused her to shiver. "I can't say that I like you very much or that I understand her infatuation with you. And let me tell you one more thing—you hurt Sam again in any way and I'll kick your pretty ass from here to your fancy place in the suburbs. But if she

means half as much to you as you do to her...
than go over there and teach Barbie a lesson.
Prove you're willing to fight for Sam."

Gillian stared at Linda, not sure if she
heard correctly. "I didn't think you meant
fighting literally."

"Oh, please. Gillian, get over there before little
Barbie hauls Sam home or before I rethink my
decision to encourage you." Linda pushed Gillian
off the barstool. "Now!"

Before Gillian had a chance to respond, Linda
turned her back and began chatting with the
bartender, simply ignoring her.

A bubble of anger heated Gillian's belly,
replacing the depression that had settled into
the pit of her stomach earlier in the evening. As
furious as Gillian felt about Linda's treatment,
the other woman was right. She had to do
something or risk losing Sam forever. If she left
now, all would be over. If she fought for Sam...
well, the worst that could happen was that she
would make a fool of herself. It was worth a try.
She didn't have anything to lose. Not anymore.

Gillian focused her attention as well as her
anger on the table where the blonde was sticking
her breasts—were those things even real?—in
Sam's clearly befuddled face.

Okay, that's it. No matter what happened
next, she refused to stand there and watch this...
this slut seduce Sam. She had to talk to Sam
and see if they could sort things out, but first

Gillian had to stake her claim before it was too late. She marched to the table and tapped the blonde's shoulder.

"What?" the woman muttered without turning her head.

"You're sitting on my lap." Vibrating with anger, Gillian loomed over the stranger, who finally deigned to look at her.

Surprise was clearly written on the blonde's face. She looked Gillian up and down. "Are you crazy or what? Go find yourself someone else to bother." She held out one hand and wiggled her fingers in a good-bye motion.

"No, you go bother someone else. I am sure you'll find a woman here who'll be more than happy to fuck you all night long. Only not this one." Gillian pointed at a confused Sam, who seemed to be having a hard time keeping her eyes focused. "This one is mine, and if you don't get up, I'm going to perforate your little ass with my Manolo stilettos."

Laughter and comments from women at nearby tables made it obvious that they had an attentive audience, but Gillian was past caring. She had to keep going if she wanted to take Sam home and scrub the stink of another woman's perfume off her.

The blonde climbed off Sam, who didn't look happy about losing her new plaything.

"No, shday...we'll...we'll have fun...lods of..." She tried to pull the blonde back onto her lap.

Jealousy and fury ate at Gillian until she trembled. She pushed the blonde out of her way and pointed a finger in Sam's face. "You listen to me. We are going home and we are going to talk. And if you want to have your slutty girlfriend back after our talk, I am sure, Ms.-I-Can-Go-All-Night over there will be happy to welcome you into her arms again. But tonight, I'm the one calling the shots, understood?"

For the first time, Sam's eyes met hers. Gillian's heart nearly broke from the pain reflected back at her, a pain that she had caused. "I am so sorry, love," she whispered.

"Does it look like Sam wants to go anywhere with you?" Apparently not ready to cave in, the blonde stepped between Gillian and Sam, her move effectively breaking their eye contact. "What you want here is of zero interest to anyone," she said snottily. "You'd better try your luck somewhere else and leave us the hell alone."

Gillian gritted her teeth, trying to rein in her temper. Never before had she come so close to hitting someone. She braced her hands on her hips, ready to use some of the obscene vocabulary she had learned from watching HBO, when suddenly a strong, coffee-colored hand reached around Gillian to grip the slut's shoulder.

"Roxanne," Skyler said. "Why don't you try your luck elsewhere? Preferably now!"

Giving them both murderous looks, Roxanne grabbed her purse and left.

Relief flooded Gillian's body. With a few pointed words Skyler had done what she could not. "Wow." Impressed, Gillian watched Roxanne walk over to the bar. "One day I would like to know what kind of history you two have."

Skyler grinned. "A gentlewoman never kisses and tells. Anything else I can assist you with?"

Now that the fight was won, Gillian wasn't sure what to do. She couldn't take Sam home with her but she certainly could take her to the city apartment. That way Sam couldn't throw Gillian out after waking up tomorrow. They needed to talk. The city apartment was Gillian's best bet. "Could you help me get Sam into the taxi outside?"

"Sure." Skyler bent down. "Come on, Sam. Don't let your lady wait."

"Shesch not my lady, no more." Sam shook her head.

The words cut razor sharp into Gillian.

Skyler chuckled. "Well, she seems determined to be your lady. And you know how these femmes are, right?" She whispered something in Sam's ear.

Gillian had never seen Sam giggle like a schoolgirl. But whatever Skyler said, worked. A moment later Sam struggled off her chair.

Good-natured whistles and shouts accompanied them as they left the bar, Skyler supporting Sam on one side, Gillian struggling to keep up on the other.

"Here we are, ma'am," the taxi driver said.

No! Gillian didn't want the ride to end and she surely didn't want to open her eyes. The length of Sam's body was pressed along hers, Sam's head cushioned on her shoulder. This moment felt so sweet, so wonderful. Reality was a bitch.

"Ma'am?"

Gillian sighed, opening her eyes. Through the fogged window on her right she saw they had stopped at the apartment building. With relief she also noticed that Thomas had stepped outside to see if his services were required. She knocked on the window, hoping to catch his attention.

His eyebrows drew up and he nodded.

Thank you. Gillian focused on the patiently waiting driver. "Sorry. I must have dozed off during the ride."

"Yeah, and you're not the only one. I guess you'll have to wake Sleeping Beauty there." He looked at Sam, who continued to snore in complete oblivion.

"Yes, I should."

The door on Gillian's side was opened. "Good evening, Mrs. Jennings. Is there anything I can do?"

"Good evening, Thomas. Indeed. Could you get over at Sam's side and help me get her into the apartment."

"Yes, ma'am."

Gillian took one of Sam's calloused hands into hers and squeezed it gently. "Hey, Sam. We're here. Time to wake up."

A smile played at the corners of Sam's mouth before she snuggled closer to Gillian.

At least she's not upset with me when she's asleep. That, however, made waking Sam even harder. "Hello, sleepyhead." Gently, Gillian brushed Sam's hair back and planted a soft kiss on her forehead. Right now she really didn't care what the taxi driver or Thomas thought of her behavior. A hint of bergamot and sandalwood teased her nose, a scent that reminded her of summer and the ocean. "This isn't your bed, honey. It's a taxi," she said. "You have to wake up."

Drowsy brown eyes opened a slit. Sam licked her lips and turned her head toward Gillian, obviously still caught in dreams.

Hot breath caressed the side of Gillian's neck, causing exquisite shivers to run through her body. She gasped when the warmth was suddenly replaced by wet heat as Sam began to nibble on her earlobe. Every nerve Gillian owned tingled with excitement.

The driver cleared his throat, shattering the moment.

"What?" Sam drew back and looked around, clearly disoriented. The tender trust which seconds ago had been present in Sam's beautiful eyes was now replaced by a pained suspicion. Reality had clawed its way back into the moment. Her dream was over. Sam flinched away from Gillian's touch, causing the leather upholstery to groan in protest.

"Do you think you can manage to get out of the car or do you need help?" Gillian's voice sounded rough to her own ears.

"I can." The tip of Sam's tongue appeared in the corner of her mouth, and her brows knit together in deep concentration.

Despite the pain that scratched inside her chest, Gillian smiled. Sam's expression was a perfect imitation of the one her son wore whenever he tried to solve a problem that was beyond his scope.

The door on Sam's side was opened and Thomas' head appeared inside the taxi. "Hello, Samantha."

Letting out a grunt, Sam leaned toward the open door, her momentum nearly causing her to fall out of the car.

Gillian grabbed the back of Sam's jacket. "Hang on there."

"I'll give her a hand." He took hold of Sam's arms and carefully maneuvered her out of the taxi.

Gillian handed the driver some more bills. "Thank you again for waiting for me, back at the bar. I really appreciate it."

"No problem. It was my pleasure." He winked at her.

With a tired smile Gillian got out of the car and into the drizzle that was falling lightly.

"Should we get her inside?"

Sam leaned heavily on Thomas' shoulder. Gillian knew she would have a hard time getting Sam inside without his help. "Yes, thank you."

After a minor struggle, the three of them finally stepped through the front door of the apartment building. Crossing the hall to the elevator wasn't as difficult as Gillian had feared. Sam was half asleep.

"She was still a teenager the last time I saw her this drunk." Thomas shook his head.

"You've known her that long?"

"Oh yes, I worked for her father."

Gillian pressed the elevator button. "We're nearly there, honey."

"Am not your honey. You...you shaid so." Sam swayed a little in place.

"Sam, you're still my honey if you want to be." Gillian silently counted to five. "But let's talk about this later. We have to get you into bed first."

"Am not going to shleep with you. No shex for you tonight! I don't wanna." Sam shook her finger in emphasis.

Gillian's face grew hot. She cast a glance at Thomas, who thankfully seemed more amused by the situation than anything else.

"All right, I got that," she told Sam.

"No shex."

"All right, no sex for me tonight." Gillian wanted to bury her flaming face in her hands.

The elevator rumbled alive, sparing Gillian from further embarrassment for the moment.

She looked at Sam, propped against Thomas' side, her head resting against the elevator wall. Even with dark shadows smeared like bruises under her eyes, she was gorgeous. *I wonder if she had problems sleeping?* Gillian had hardly been able to close her eyes, much less sleep since the café incident. Every time she tried, Sam's face appeared in her dreams. The pain and betrayal written over it haunted her. *Will she be able to forgive me? I don't know if I could if our roles were reversed.*

The elevator came to a halt and the doors opened.

Happy to escape, Gillian stepped out into the corridor before she turned around to help get Sam out of the elevator. Seconds later Gillian entered the apartment, locating the light switch without difficulty. She turned around just in time to watch Sam stagger into the bedroom, leaving her alone with a chuckling Thomas.

"I guess that's where my mission ends...right, ma'am?"

"Yes, I think I can manage from here. Though I can't thank you enough for your help tonight."

He beamed. "Ah, you don't have to thank me. I'm happy I was here. Give me a call if you need anything. I'm here until seven a.m. You know...I remember Sam when she was this tall," he gestured to his knees. "She was always a little daredevil. Her father hated that."

Stunned, Gillian didn't know what to say.

Thomas shrugged. "He wanted a daughter to show off and not a daughter who was as strong-willed as he was."

"She...she told me that she left home early..."

"I left the job before she left home. So, I can't tell you what happened to her. But knowing her father I'm guessing it wasn't nice."

"How—" Gillian broke off and cleared her throat as it threatened to close. "Did he hurt her?"

His smile vanished. "He did. Yes. Not physically. He beat her with words. She often came to hide in the garage where I worked for a while before I became the doorman in one of her father's buildings."

Gillian couldn't speak.

"I have to go downstairs. Call me if you need help. Have a nice evening."

She closed the door behind him. What a night, and it wasn't over yet. She had left her home in the suburbs in the hope of finding Sam, talking to her, and making up with her if possible. Afterwards, she had planned to go home, not spend the night in town. *So much for well-thought-out plans.*

So, what do I do now? One thing was sure: Right now Sam was in no condition for a chat. Gillian had to make sure that she was okay.

She rubbed her aching temples. Assaulted by confusion, guilt, and a host of other emotions, she went to the bedroom. Sam was lying fully dressed on the bed and soft snores floated through the air.

Gillian sat down on the edge of the mattress, taking in the slow rise and fall of Sam's chest, the flutter of her eyelids, her strong features, and full lips. Tempted, she reached out to lightly touch Sam's cheek before she carefully withdrew her hand again, tender feelings bringing a smile to her face. *What you do to me...*The power Sam already had over her life, over her heart made her dizzy. All she longed for was to lie down beside Sam, hold her, and be there when she woke up. Gillian sighed.

Sam mumbled something unintelligible, catching Gillian's attention. Half tangled in the sheets and still fully dressed, she surely couldn't be comfortable. Gillian could not leave her like that. It didn't take much effort to pry the black boots off Sam's feet. She put the boots down next to the wardrobe before she touched Sam's shoulder. "Come on, honey," she said. "You have to roll over on your side."

With a bit of effort Gillian finally succeeded in turning her over. It wouldn't do to let her lie on her back in case she threw up during the night. Gillian took the extra pillow and a rolled-up bedcover and put the items behind Sam's back to keep her in the same position. Glancing around the bedroom, she noticed the wastepaper basket behind a chair. She placed it on the floor beside the bed within easy reach. Just in case.

Carefully sitting on the edge of the bed, unable to stop herself from touching her sleeping lover, Gillian caressed Sam's soft cheek. *I don't want to live without you.* It was true. She couldn't imagine going back to the kind of life she had lived before Derrick died. His death had freed her. Or at least begun to free her...as bad as that sounded. However, she was a realist. As much as she wanted Sam in her life, Gillian had no idea how a life with her could work. In addition, she didn't know if Sam was even interested in taking their relationship to a more serious level. Or if she was even able to forgive Gillian.

A calloused hand wrapped around Gillian's fingers, nearly making her jump out of her skin.

"No shex," Sam murmured.

Gillian couldn't help grinning a bit. "No shex. Not tonight. I promise."

Obviously satisfied with the answer Sam began to snore again.

Gillian got up and walked back into the living room. She removed her stilettos and sank onto the leather sofa before she took her cell phone out of her purse and dialed her home number.

Tilde answered on the third ring.

"Hello, Tilde. This is Gillian. I have to ask a favor of you."

CHAPTER 14

LAUGHTER. SOMEWHERE PEOPLE WERE LAUGHING. Gillian pulled the blanket over her head. *Too early. Too loud. Don't wanna.*

A door banged shut. Keys jingled. Again laughter.

Damn. Groaning in frustration, Gillian opened her eyes. Sunlight filtered through the curtains. The city apartment... *Why...Oh. Sam.* Right, they were in the city apartment and Sam was in the bedroom. Gillian looked at her watch. Eight a.m. She rolled from the sofa and went to the half-open bedroom door, which she hadn't closed last night. Just in case Sam needed her at some point. But all Gillian had heard from Sam had been snoring and an occasional grunt. So, at least Gillian had gotten a few hours of sleep, although she had frequently woken up during the night, unable to stop worrying about the morning.

Sam was still snoring away on the bed, pretty much in the same position she had been in the last time Gillian had peeked into the bedroom.

For a moment, Gillian wondered if she should wake her. But then...what for? She was sure that Sam would feel like hell. Sleeping didn't hurt and Gillian didn't have to be anywhere until later in the evening. Tilde had agreed to care of the kids. *Coffee. I need coffee.*

The first sip of the dark brew was heaven on her tongue. Gillian closed her eyes and tried to find a Zen moment. So much had happened in the past twelve hours and yet nothing was clearer than it had been before she had found Sam at The Labrys. *Well, at least we're in the same apartment. She can't just run away. I won't let her.*

Gillian was just about to take another sip of coffee when the sound of retching cut through the apartment's silence. She flinched. *I guess that means Sam's up.* Suddenly the coffee had lost its appeal. She set her mug aside and followed the miserable sounds to the bathroom. The door was ajar. Gillian hesitated, torn between the longing to help and the fear of intruding on a very vulnerable moment. What if her presence made Sam feel worse? Guilt and insecurity held her frozen to the spot. *Quit dithering.* She reached for the doorknob and opened the door a bit more. Carefully peeking inside, she saw that Sam was hunched over the toilet.

Another round of retching started. Tremors shook Sam's body.

All Gillian wanted was to hurry into the room and help and soothe Sam. But would she accept the offer? Gillian ran a hand through her hair. This wasn't about their relationship. If Sam didn't want help, she would have to say so. Gillian pushed her doubts aside. She knocked at the door to announce her presence. When she got no response, she knocked again, this time louder and more insistent than before. She didn't want to enter before Sam acknowledged her presence.

"What?" Sam's voice was hoarse.

"Can I come in?"

A choked moan was the only answer.

All right. That's it. Gillian entered the bathroom, the sour stench of vomit almost making her gag. Trying not to inhale to deeply, she took a towel from a shelf. "Hey there." She wet the towel at the sink, and then knelt down next to Sam on the cool tile floor. "How are you doing?" She tenderly pushed the damp hair from Sam's forehead before she dabbed the cold sweat away.

For a moment Sam leaned into Gillian's touch. The connection—simple as it was—warmed Gillian inside. It was Sam who broke the contact and leaned back to the other side, her body resting on the tiles. "I hate this."

"I'll be back in a moment." Gillian got up and rushed into the kitchen. She remembered from her last pregnancy that one of the worst things about throwing up had been the graveyard taste left in her mouth. She picked up a glass, filled it with cold water, and hurried back to the bathroom, where she knelt down next to Sam again.

"I wanna die." Sam's voice was hoarse.

"No, you don't. And I wouldn't have a clue how to get rid of your corpse anyhow," Gillian said, softly enough to take any sting out of her comment.

Sam let out a dry chuckle. "Just leave my body in the hallway. Someone will pick it up." She clutched her stomach. "Oh, that hurt."

Gillian touched Sam's back. The T-shirt was clammy with sweat but there was nothing she could do about that. She didn't keep a spare set of clothes in the apartment. "Would you like to rinse your mouth? I have a glass of water."

"Yeah." Sam took the offered glass, her hand shaking. "Thanks."

Gillian rubbed soothing circles over Sam's damp T-shirt. "Do you feel like getting up?"

Bloodshot eyes turned toward her. "Why?"

"You'll feel better if you lie down," Gillian said. "Your stomach must be all cramped up by now. Sitting on the floor hugging the toilet won't do you any good. You need to relax."

Sam slowly shook her head. "No, I'll only have to throw up again."

"Sitting like this will not help. You should lie down." Gillian had enough experience with sick children to know that much. "I'm going to put a bucket next to the bed. You'll feel much more comfortable lying down. You need to drink a lot of water and take some aspirin as soon as you feel like you can keep them down. It will help. Trust me."

A bitter smile slashed a hard line across Sam's face.

Gillian flinched. "Sorry, I—"

"All right. I guess I can give it a try."

Surprise and relief washed through Gillian. "Good. Would you like to use some mouthwash first?"

A forced smile appeared on Sam's face. "What? You don't like the aroma of dead rat and wet dog?"

"No, and I'd guess you don't like it either."

"Yeah, that's true."

Gillian helped Sam up and stood guard beside her at the sink while she gargled and rinsed with the minty mouthwash. Thankfully, this didn't trigger another attack of throwing up.

"Would you like some help—"

"No, thanks." Sam struggled toward the door. "I can manage."

The dismissive tone hurt even if she deserved it. Gillian swallowed hard. "All right."

173

Watching Sam creep weakly into the bedroom was tough. *At least she hasn't asked me to leave...yet.*

"Shit." Sam breathed heavily and held her stomach. "Shit. Shit. Shit."

Gillian hurried over. "Come on."

She took Sam's elbow and led her to the bed before she carefully helped her to sit down. "Stretch out. It will help your stomach."

For once, a pale-faced Sam followed her instruction without questions or comments.

"Can I...?" Gillian bit her lip. "Are you feeling all right?"

"Yeah, this really feels better." She looked at Gillian through bloodshot eyes. "You wouldn't have a clean T-shirt laying around, would you?"

"No, I'm sorry. Maybe we could," she swallowed, "If you sleep some more now and when you're feeling better later...I could take you home?"

"Home? Yeah, that would be great."

Gillian watched Sam for a while until her breathing was even and her face relaxed. This was going to be an interesting day. Gillian leaned against the doorframe to the living room. Sam hadn't sent her away and she had even agreed that Gillian could take her home.

One step at a time. She had to take one little baby step at a time before she could dare hope that everything would be all right.

Gillian was beyond relieved when the taxi driver announced they had arrived at their destination. The late afternoon traffic had been a bitch. She cast a careful glance at Sam who was pale and looked utterly exhausted. "How are you doing?"

"Fine." Sam hesitated for a moment before she took hold of Gillian's hand and climbed out of the taxi. "Never better."

Gillian sighed. She wasn't sure how much of Sam's temper came down to her being here and how much was the hangover from hell. Still, she hadn't asked Gillian to leave her alone. Even though there was one moment, earlier, when Sam had looked long and hard at her. Gillian had expected to be sent home, but Sam had kept quiet. For Gillian, being here at Sam's apartment was more than just a baby step. A small blossom of hope had begun to grow inside her. She looked up at the house. It wasn't huge and probably held around ten apartments. "So, which floor are you on?"

"Ground level. Thankfully."

"All right." That really was a relief. Less walking was good. Very good. "Do you want me to help you inside?"

"No." Sam took a few steps before she murmured, "Thanks."

Gillian followed on Sam's heels, ready to jump as soon as Sam's knees buckled.

With shaking fingers, Sam took keys out of her pocket and opened the front door before she turned around. Sam wet her lips. "So...would you..."

Gillian held her breath.

"I mean...do you want to go home?" Sam's face was an unreadable mask.

Gillian's first impulse was to say yes, to turn around and leave. She knew that she was a coward. And leaving now would be her way out, the coward's way out. And she would hate herself later for running instead of fighting for a chance to win Sam's trust again. Maybe she would also hate herself if she said no, stayed and found no redemption. But then at least she wouldn't be a coward. She cleared her throat. "I'd rather stay a bit with you. If that's okay."

Sam turned around and stepped through the open door. "All right."

From the outside, the house was nice if a bit run down. Inside it was light and looked well-cared for.

Sam opened the door to her right and walked into the apartment.

Gillian followed and found herself in Sam's living room. Cream-colored walls, a flat panel LCD television on the wall opposite a brown leather sofa that looked unbelievably inviting, and shelves full of books. *So, she's a reader.* Gillian hadn't known that. There was so much about Sam she didn't have a clue about.

Dark rings had taken residence under Sam's eyes and her face looked ghostly pale. "I need to lie down." She walked into another room.

Unsure what to do, Gillian hesitated a moment before she followed. Her need to know that Sam was okay was stronger than the fear of rejection.

Sam was sitting down on her bed. "I'm still... could you bring me a T-shirt?" She pointed at the wardrobe.

"Sure. Wow." Gillian couldn't hide her surprise at the T-shirts, sweatshirts, and pants sorted into neat piles on the shelves. "That's quite impressive. You really like strict order at home, eh?"

"Saves a lot of time," came the grumbled reply.

Gillian's own closet looked more like a war zone. She picked a comfortable looking T-shirt, the cotton fabric soft and smelling of bergamot and sandalwood, scents she would always associate with Sam. Gillian handed the shirt over. "Do you...Can you manage changing on your own?"

"I'm not physically handicapped, you know," Sam snapped.

A palpable tension sizzled in the air.

"I didn't mean it that way," Gillian answered, a bit more sharply than she had planned.

"I'd like to change. Either you leave or you turn around. It's up to you." Sam slowly sat up, grabbing the hem of her T-shirt.

Gillian turned to face the wall. A naked Sam wasn't something she needed to see right now. Her senses, however, seemed to be of a different mind. The rustle of fabric triggered them and reminded her treacherous mind of the softness of Sam's skin, the way her eyes turned nearly black when she was aroused, pupils expanding to swallow the light brown. Heat rushed through Gillian's belly. *Don't. Think. About. This. About her.*

"I'm ready," Sam interrupted her thoughts. "You can turn around now."

Gillian looked at Sam, startled. Sweat gleamed on Sam's cheeks and forehead. She was as white as a freshly bleached sheet. "You really need to lie down," Gillian blurted.

Sam grimaced. "Yeah, I've been better but... Look, Gillian, I really appreciate you helping me and all that." She rubbed her forehead and looked down at the duvet. "I don't...I guess you need to be home or something, so...I think I can manage from here."

Cold fear gripped Gillian's heart. Was that it? Did Sam want her to leave? She had to be sure before she walked away. "Do you want me to go?"

Weary eyes met hers. "I don't know. Why would you want to stay?" Sam's voice cracked.

Maybe she doesn't want me to go but believes I don't want to stay, Gillian thought, a spark of hope flaring bright. Only honesty had a chance of repairing the gap between them, and she had nothing to lose anyway. "There's more than one reason why I want to stay, Sam," she said, pointing at the bed. "May I?"

The muscles in Sam's neck tensed. Her jaw clenched and unclenched in turn. Finally she nodded.

Gillian carefully sat down on the edge of the mattress, close enough to be able to reach out and touch Sam but with enough distance so she wouldn't feel crowded. *Please let me find the right words.* "I don't have to be home until later this evening. I..." She swallowed around the lump in her throat. This wasn't easy. "I want to talk about what happened in the coffee shop if you're willing to hear me out." She wanted to say so much more. The need to explain, to apologize burned inside her. "But for now I would like to take care of you and make sure you're doing okay. If you'll allow me to, that is."

Sam looked up, a quick brush of their eyes, before her glance fell back to the duvet. She smacked her lips. "I feel like I'm under a dehydration curse."

"Would you like some more water?" Amazed she had not been thrown out already, Gillian got up, ready to get whatever Sam asked for.

"Yeah. Thanks. The kitchen is the next door to the right. And Gillian?"

"Yes?"

"Thank you for being here. I can't make any promises, all right?" Sam rasped. "But we can talk."

"Thank you." Gillian hurried into the kitchen and came back with a glass of water.

Sam gulped half the glass down before she lay down on the bed and turned her back to Gillian.

Gillian was almost light-headed from relief. Just to make sure that Sam was really all right and didn't need anything Gillian stayed in the room, leaning against the door's wooden frame. Her gaze wandered through the room. A framed poster of Georgia O'Keeffe's *White Rose with Larkspur* hung over the bed. Gillian had spent a long time in front of the original during her last visit at the Museum of Fine Arts in Boston. The painting was an exquisite capture of the infinite beauty of flowers and one of Gillian's favorites. She would have never expected to see something so fragile in Sam's bedroom. *At the best I would have expected a black and white photo of a naked woman.* She shook her head at the assumptions she had made. *There's so much I don't know about her.*

She surveyed the rest of the bedroom. Three walls were painted in ivory, the fourth indigo blue, which contrasted nicely with the wardrobe whose front consisted of white glass and mirrors. If the living room was proof of Sam's more practical side, the bedroom seemed to reflect the softer side she hid so well most of the time.

Only when she heard Sam's soft snoring did Gillian leave the room. *Coffee. I need coffee and then something to eat.* She made her way back to the small kitchen.

The coffee machine was a simple apparatus that she hadn't seen in years. Most of Gillian's acquaintances had shiny, high-tech tools in their kitchens, impossible to operate without reading a tome-sized manual. Derrick had been adamant that they buy one of those digital, super-automatic espresso machines, not because it made good coffee—which it did—but because it was a status symbol, like his BMW roadster or the swimming pool or whatever could be used to show off. All of these things had been important to her as well—once. So much had changed over these past months. Sometimes she couldn't believe how snotty she had been, how limited her whole life and her worldview was.

Gillian opened the refrigerator in search of milk. She couldn't help chuckling. *Now, this is what I call a wasteland.* Three different brands of beer, a bottle of milk, and Chinese leftovers, which she didn't want to investigate too closely, as well as a jar of pickles, were the refrigerator's only contents. Preparing a meal was going to be a bit more challenging than she thought. In a cupboard to her right stood an opened box of Froot Loops. Her children would have had a field day if they ever learned about her eating something like this. Food with artificial flavor was banned from their home. They bought vegetables, fruit, and bread at the farmer's market. *Well, there is no need to tell the children that Mommy had chemicals for lunch. Maybe I should find a supermarket and stock up the fridge.*

What the fuck? Sam's mouth and lips were dry. Her eyes felt as if they were glued shut. She forced them open, only to notice a wet spot on the pillow below her. *Ugh.* She rubbed her cheek to get rid of any hints of drool.

The sounds of honking cars and howling police sirens invaded her bedroom. Through the fog in her brain, she pondered what had woken her up. The outside noises, as pesky as they were, she was used to. She moved her head a bit, then let it fall back on the pillow as her throbbing skull threatened to explode. *Ow!* Her body felt as if a steamroller had run her over. Twice. Every nerve ending hurt, including the few brain cells that had survived. And, if that wasn't enough, her tongue tasted as if something furry had curled up and died there.

Oh my God. She tried to focus on her breathing when an unfamiliar sound filtered into her dizzy brain. *Someone's moving around in my living room?* Sam strained her ears, her stomach lurching. *Oh, Gillian. Right.* Vague memories rushed back at Sam: Her flirting heavily with Roxanne, Gillian showing up and dragging her out of The Labrys and into the apartment, her vomiting, the promise that they would talk later.

Shit. The pounding in her head intensified. With a groan, Sam dragged her body toward the edge of the bed. She slowly sat up, relieved that she was dizzy but didn't feel the urge to throw up. She hated vomiting. The feeling of helplessness that came with losing the fight against her body, the taste in her mouth, the smell... If she remembered correctly she had not only puked like a teenager after having been served her first drink, if she remembered correctly, Gillian had witnessed all of it. Sam's face grew hot.

Gillian had said that she wanted to talk. What exactly did that mean? Did she want to ask for forgiveness? Her stomach fluttered at the thought that maybe Gillian felt bad about her fucked-up behavior at the coffee shop.

Sam snorted, angry for even allowing herself that kind of hope. Reaching over to the nightstand was like reaching through molasses, but she persisted until she found the aspirin bottle in her drawer. She took two pills, forcing herself to swallow them with the half-empty glass of water on her nightstand.

With careful movements, Sam propped her back against the headboard and closed her eyes. She needed time to let the aspirin do its job before she could face Gillian. *How did I get into this mess?* What had made her believe that Gillian cared for her? That she wouldn't cheat on her with a classier woman? Or did Gillian cheat on the classier woman with Sam? A bitter taste spread in Sam's mouth. *Who cares anyhow? I'm over her.* Sam let out a small bitter laugh. *Liar!* She wasn't really over Gillian. Not by a long shot. Sam's fists tightened on the duvet. Unable to lie still any longer, she ignored her body's protests and swung her legs out of bed. A wave of dizziness crashed into her. *Okay, take it easy is the goal for the rest of the day. On the other hand...*there was no way she could talk to Gillian while lying on her back, feeling sick. Lying down and feeling sorry for herself was an option as soon as Gillian left. And she would leave. Soon. There was no doubt about that.

Somehow Sam managed to make it into the shower. At first the water kind of hurt on her sensitive skin but she forced herself to stay put and after a while the sluice of water down her back had the same effect a skillful massage had on good days. Sam groaned. That was so good. She stepped out of the shower and toweled herself dry. For the first time after waking up she felt like a human being and almost ready to face Gillian again. Sam swiped the cold mist from the mirror and grimaced. *Well, that face has seen better days.* There were dark rings under her eyes and a pallor to her skin that was testament of too much alcohol and not enough sleep. She sighed. Alcohol really wasn't her friend.

After brushing her teeth Sam dressed herself in her most comfortable jeans and a sweater.

Determined to get it over with, she opened the door to the living room and stared.

Gillian sat on the sofa, an old *National Geographic* magazine in one hand, a cup of coffee in the other. Her bare feet were drawn up beneath her, her dress as short and form-fitting as could possible be.

A jumble of anger, longing, and hurt pulsed through Sam. Gillian's short, black dress accentuated her porcelain skin and blonde hair. *Damn. No one should be allowed to look so beautiful.*

Gillian's gaze met hers.

"Don't you look cozy?" The words came out as harshly as Sam had intended.

A flash of hurt whisked over Gillian's face. She slowly laid the magazine on the coffee table and sat up straight. "How are you feeling?"

"I'm fine." Sam needed to take control of the situation and put some distance between them. How could just seeing Gillian hurt so much and make everything that had been so clear, so black and white, so difficult and various shades of grey again? Sam straightened her shoulders and stepped into the kitchen. She gaped at the kitchen counter. A whole array of water bottles stood next to a packet of herb tea, two jars of jelly, and some white bread.

"I didn't know what you might like to eat or drink. Herbal tea is usually a good choice." Gillian's soft voice came from behind her.

A bubble of anger burst inside Sam. Gillian acting as if she cared was too much. She swung around. "What do you want, Gillian? Why are you here?"

Gillian paled and took a step back. "I... I wanted to talk. You said we could talk."

The pounding in Sam's skull increased, the pressure so great she wished she had stayed in bed. "What about?"

"I'm...I'm sorry about my behavior. I really am. I want to explain what happened. Back in the coffee shop."

Sam snorted. "Why should I even listen to you?"

"Because I wanted to ask your forgiveness for what I've done and for what I should have said and...I'm so sorry, Sam." Gillian rubbed a spot across her heart, her voice nothing more than a whisper.

To Sam, the ticking of the wall clock sounded like a bomb counting down. She opened one of the water bottles and drank straight from it. The cool liquid was balm to her scratchy throat.

"I'm so sorry for hurting you." Gillian took a shaky breath. "I would give anything to undo what I've done. I should have told Rachel who you are. I should have stood up for you. I should have behaved differently. But I can't go back and undo my shitty behavior."

Sam's fingers closed tighter around the bottle in her hand until the plastic made crinkly noises.

"You denied that we knew each other and then you let them humiliate me. You humiliated me. Hurt me."

"I know." Gillian didn't meet Sam's eyes.

"I trusted you. And you cut me."

"I know." Gillian's shoulders slumped.

"I...I..." Sam didn't know what to say. All she wanted to do was throw the plastic bottle against the kitchen wall.

"Can you forgive me?" The words were a mere whisper.

Sam's breath caught. She had expected to hear Gillian justify her actions, maybe beg her not to reveal their secret—not to ask her for forgiveness. That she hadn't anticipated. Sam blew out a frustrated breath and ran her hand through her hair. "Forgive you?"

"You have every right to be mad, Sam. I behaved like an absolute asshole." There were tears in Gillian's eyes.

Sam rubbed her temples. "It's not that easy, Gillian. You can't just come here, say you're sorry, and expect everything to be okay again."

"I know, Sam. I can't tell you how much I—"

"Stop." Sam held up her hand. "Why did you do it?" That question had kept her awake, night after night. Over and over the scene in the café had played before her eyes, a living nightmare that wouldn't go away. "Why did you pretend not to know me? And who was," she nearly choked on her next words, "the other woman?"

Gillian looked down at her feet. "I panicked. And the other woman was Rachel. She's an old acquaintance."

"Acquaintance? I saw you coming out of an apartment early one morning. Before we met in the club. Before you asked me to fuck you." Sam shook her head. "She's no acquaintance. She's a fuck buddy, right?"

Gillian shook her head. "No. She's not a friend. Not really. Her husband and mine worked together. They were lawyers in the same firm. That's how I know her. Well, and from playing tennis. And meeting for coffee and doing whatever wives do. The morning you saw us together... I picked her up for a breakfast meeting we've been invited to." Gillian took a step closer toward Sam. "I did not sleep with her." Gillian swallowed. "And I would never cheat on you. Never."

"I find that hard to believe."

The blood drained from Gillian's already pale face. "I know that my behavior is inexcusable. I panicked. I... I'm trying to turn my life around and I'm learning who I really am and that is good...but this is also hard. There are Derrick's parents, my old friends...though they are not really friends but..." Gillian's bottom lip quivered, "There are my children to consider. They have no idea." Gillian's voice was raw, her expression ghastly. "Sam, I made a mistake. A mistake that I regret more than I can express. The truth is...I'm scared." Gillian stared down at her hands. "Scared because I care about you. Very much. And I am so afraid that you won't give me a second chance and that I just blew what we could have had together."

Sam had a hard time absorbing Gillian's words. Anger and hope were fighting with each other inside her while she pondered how to respond. She had two options. She could cut Gillian out of her life. Right here and now. She could be cruel, hard, and unyielding to Gillian before she threw her out—a few well placed words were all that would be needed to make Gillian feel as shitty as Sam had felt in the coffee shop and for days afterward. The other option was to forgive her. *Forgive her. And then?* Sam's thoughts raced. "Gillian, I don't know what to say." She took another gulp of water from the bottle. "And I have a hard time believing that," she took a deep breath, "Rachel is just an acquaintance. But even if I do forgive you...I don't know if I'll ever be able to trust you again."

"Maybe it is better if I—" Gillian's voice cracked. "I can call a taxi, and then I'll get out of your hair."

A lump formed in Sam's throat. Was that what she wanted? She stared at the half-empty bottle in her hand. Did she really want Gillian to leave? She didn't know what to feel, what to think, but the idea of losing Gillian once and for all hurt more than the pain she had felt about the betrayal and was even stronger than her anger. What did that mean? Fact was that Gillian had gone to The Labrys to find her. She had apologized and asked for forgiveness. That had to count for something, right? Sam slammed the bottle down on the counter and followed a retreating Gillian to the living room. Just in time to see Gillian wiping tears from her face. *She's hurting.* They were both hurting.

"Wait."

Gillian turned around and looked at Sam, tears streaming down her face.

"You hurt me. A lot," Sam said, choosing her words with care while searching Gillian's face for something she didn't know how to ask for.

Tears glittered on Gillian's cheeks.

Sam cleared her throat. "But I don't want you to go."

They stared at each other.

Sam opened her arms. "Damn. Come here."

Gillian hesitated only a moment before flinging herself into Sam's arms.

A wave of Gillian's exclusive perfume drifted to Sam's nose, reminding her of a flowery meadow in the middle of summer. One of Sam's hands found its way to the base of Gillian's neck and began to gently knead the soft flesh. *This feels so damn good. Why does this have to feel so good?* She closed her eyes and let the closeness and warmth wash over her. A part of her knew that they needed to talk some more, but right now she was tired, felt like shit, and really needed more sleep.

"I'm so sorry." Gillian sobbed against Sam's chest. "So sorry."

Sam rested her chin on Gillian's head. "I'm sorry too."

Gillian looked up, her eyes wet. "Why? You have nothing to be sorry for."

"I should have answered your calls, should have talked to you instead of shutting down like this." She touched Gillian's lips with two fingers to stop her from replying. "I still believe that what you did was wrong. It was. We have to talk about it." She exhaled slowly. "But I missed you." Saying those words felt unbelievably good—as scary as they were.

Gillian let her head fall against Sam's chest again. They stayed like that way for a while, swaying slightly back and forth.

"Hey, Gillian?" Sam finally roused herself to ask.

"Yes," came the muffled reply.

"I don't know about you, but I'm really beat." Her back hurt, her head still hurt, and she was in desperate need of more aspirin.

"Me too."

"So what do you say about getting some sleep before we have our talk?"

Gillian glanced up. "Sure, let me just call a taxi. Could we maybe talk later today? On the phone?" Her voice quivered.

Sam swallowed. The offer didn't sound bad. Later she surely would feel more grounded than she did now. But the truth was, she wasn't ready to let Gillian leave, not when they had just begun to talk again. *Come on, you chicken. Just ask her.* "You look pretty much out of it yourself. Why don't you take a nap with me? My bed is big enough."

Surprise and delight replaced the shadows in Gillian's eyes. "Really? I mean, yes."

Encouraged, Sam bent to brush her mouth over Gillian's. It wasn't much of a kiss...too hasty, too tentative, too nervous but at the same time gentle and heartbreakingly familiar. There was so much between them that Sam really didn't want to lose. But she didn't know if they would be able to restore what had once been between them.

A short while later, Gillian traced her finger over the letters on the borrowed T-shirt.

Sam chuckled. Gillian's expression made it clear that she had problems with the slogan on the front. "You don't like it?"

"I'm not sure if a shirt with bright pink letters, stating 'Dip me in honey and feed me to the lesbians' is helpful for our first attempt at just sleeping next to each other." Gillian gave her a strained smile, looking pale and tired as she snuggled under the duvet.

"Well, it's either the one you're wearing, or 'She may wear the pants but I wear the strap-on,' or 'I eat from the bushy bowl.'"

Gillian grimaced. "That's gross."

"I thought that you'd like this one better."

For a short, awkward moment Sam hesitated in front of the bed. All of a sudden she felt shy around Gillian. Ignoring the unfamiliar feeling, she slowly crawled under the duvet. "I set the alarm for five o'clock. Is that okay for you?"

"Yes, thanks." Gillian tried to hide a yawn behind her hand. "I'm so tired. Sorry."

"Me too." The cool cotton felt good against Sam's sensitive skin. "Would you, um, like to—"

"Yes." Gillian scooted over, bridging the distance between them and laid her head on Sam's shoulder. "Can I?" Her hand hovered over Sam's stomach.

"Sure." The soft touch against her middle nearly melted her inside. A pleasant tingle followed, spreading up and down her spine. She was in no condition, mentally or physically to do more than revel in Gillian's presence, so she told her libido to back off. But she did allow herself to enjoy Gillian's warm presence in her bed, the soft and sweet-smelling body curled against her. *Hell, holding her feels so good*, was her last coherent thought before sleep claimed her.

CHAPTER 15

SAM PUT THE KEY IN the lock, turned it, and stepped inside the apartment. Darkness welcomed her. She held her breath. Only the low hum of the refrigerator could be heard coming from the kitchen. For a moment she wondered if she should leave again. It was nearly midnight. Chloe had school tomorrow and Victoria was obviously already in bed. A peek into the bedroom couldn't hurt. Maybe Victoria was still awake. Sam slipped out of her shoes and tiptoed to her sister's bedroom. The parquet was cold under her feet. The door was ajar. She opened it a bit further and took in the sight before her.

Victoria lay asleep in her bed. On her side. Even after all this time Martin's side remained untouched. A soft snore cut through the silence of the bedroom.

Sam grinned. *Nice.* She took a few steps toward the bed. Maybe there was some drool running down her sister's face. She squinted.

Nope. No luck. What a shame. Well, she could still tease Victoria about the snores that came out in regular intervals.

Torn between waking her peacefully slumbering sister and leaving, Sam stayed put where she was. A yawn overwhelmed her. She had only slept a few hours the last two nights since Gillian had left. Her thoughts started to run amok as soon as she closed her eyes. The long phone call with Gillian earlier tonight hadn't helped to calm her mind. Sam needed to sort out her feelings. Linda wasn't the best choice for this since her attitude toward Gillian was bordering on hostile. Which left only Victoria. Slowly making her way to the bed, she stepped on a creaky board. "Shit."

"What..." Victoria sat bolt upright in bed and pressed a hand to her heart. "Sam? What are you doing here?" She switched the light on before she looked at the clock on her nightstand. "Do you have any idea what time it is?"

Sam shrugged. "Sure I do. That's why I didn't call. I don't want Chloe to wake up."

"But you wanted to give me a heart attack?" She snatched the blanket over her head and fell back against her pillow with a grunt. "Go away."

"Sorry." Sam sat down on the other side of the bed. "But I really need to talk."

"Now?" Victoria's voice was muffled through the blanket.

"Yes, now."

"I'm too old for shit like this." She growled but put the blanket away. She curled up on her side, facing Sam. "What are we going to talk about?"

"Gillian."

Victoria made a gagging sound. "Young love. I hate it. And I don't want to listen to you talking dirty."

"Yeah, well. At the moment I hate young love too."

She cocked an eyebrow. "Did something happen?"

"No shit, Sherlock." Sam sighed and ran her hand over the duvet. The fabric was soft and cool under her fingers.

"Oh, all right. But you owe me. Big time." She climbed out of bed and slipped a pale blue bathrobe over her shoulders. Sighing, she pushed a hand through her hair. "We might as well have a glass of wine and some snacks to make this a real midnight party."

Sam followed her into the kitchen and closed the door behind them. Chloe wasn't a light sleeper but she wouldn't stay in bed if she heard her aunt. While Victoria opened a bottle of red wine, Sam poured herself a glass of water.

"Water? I do have cold beer."

Sam shook her head. Just the thought of alcohol made her stomach do not-so-funny things. "No thanks, water is fine."

"You really do look like shit." Victoria took a bag of pretzels out of the cupboard and opened it. "Want some?"

"Thanks." Sam sat down. "Yes."

"All right." Victoria plopped down opposite Sam and put the open bag between them. "Spill it."

Now, that Sam was sitting here talking suddenly didn't seem like such a good idea anymore. She picked up the glass of water and held it in her hands. How was she supposed to form coherent sentences about something that made her insides churn? She put the glass down again. "Gillian...she hurt me."

"How? What happened?"

Sam looked up. This was a safe place. This was Victoria. Sam took a deep breath and told her sister the whole sordid tale from the meeting in the coffee shop to what happened at The Labrys and the following day.

"Holy crap." Victoria leaned forward, elbows on the table, hands clasped. "Why didn't you call me after what happened at the coffee shop?"

"I didn't want to talk to anyone." Sam picked up a pretzel and crumbled it between her fingers. "I'm still not sure how I made it home that day without causing an accident. It was like sleep walking...or maybe more like nightmare walking." She blinked away the tears that threatened to fall. It didn't take much to make her cry these days.

"You're like a wounded animal."

Sam huffed.

"It's true. Every time you get hurt, you hide." Victoria reached over the table and grabbed Sam's hand. "But you don't need to hide, Sam.

I'm always here for you. Just like you've been here for us after Martin's death. We're sisters."

"Well, I'm here now."

"Yes. Though it doesn't necessarily have to be the dead of the night when you finally come out of your hiding place." Victoria squeezed Sam's hand. "So, you're talking again?"

"Yes. Over the phone."

"And that's a good thing, right?" A small crease appeared between Victoria's eyebrows.

"Yes, it is." And it was. Even though it was strange, talking about deep shit while not seeing the other person—it was also easier to do so at times. They had covered a lot of topics these past two nights.

"So, what is the problem?"

Sam stared down at the half-empty glass in front of her. "I'm not sure if love is enough."

"Enough for what?"

"For a future. Together."

Victoria let out a low whistle. "So, you're in love with her?"

"I don't know. I'm definitely close. But I'm not sure if I can trust her."

Victoria nodded and kept quiet.

"It's so strange. Because one always believes that once you're in love everything falls into place. But I...that's just not true." Sam fought to keep her voice steady. "I realized over the past few days since the coffee shop incident that love and trust both have to be earned. And freely given."

Saying those words out loud hurt as much as throwing them around in her head. "And it's not the love thing I have a problem with."

Victoria took a sip of her wine before she said, "It was a shitty thing she did."

"Yeah."

"So, I guess the question is if you're able to forgive her. And if you want to take another chance."

Sam sighed, drumming her fingers on the wooden table. "It's not that easy. I already told her that I forgive her and I really want to. But my heart still hurts and I'm still angry."

"I know. But, Sam...You'll never know how a relationship will develop or how it'll turn out. And even with the best relationship sometimes the universe throws you a curveball when you least expect it. But you can't let fear dictate your life."

Sam was tempted to destroy another pretzel between her fingers. Or to thump her head against the table. Anything that would help her get rid of the nervous energy coursing through her body. "I'm afraid."

"Yes. Life is terrifying. Love is terrifying. But love is also the one thing that makes getting up in the morning and facing life a lot easier." Victoria shrugged. "Love isn't the solution to everything. But it sure makes life a lot more interesting and colorful. And I really, really miss being in love."

Now it was Sam who reached over the table to take Victoria's hand in hers. "You'll find it again, Vic. You will."

"Maybe. Yes. But Martin set the bar pretty high." Her smile was sad. "Still, I'm open for something new. Well, I've started thinking about it. And that is definitely something new."

Sam shook her head and smiled. "And you have Chloe. That's something, right."

"That is everything. She reminds me so much of her father. Sometimes it takes my breath away."

Sam smiled. "She sure has some of his mannerisms."

"And his stubbornness."

"Though she could have inherited that one from you as well."

"Look, who's talking." Victoria stuck her tongue out.

Sam threw a pretzel at her and hit Victoria squarely in the head. "At least my aim has always been better than yours."

"I will not start a childish fight with you this late at night." Victoria leaned across the table. "But watch your back. I'll get you when you least expect it."

"In your dreams."

They stared at each other. Sam was fighting hard against the laughter that bubbled up somewhere deep inside her. Victoria always knew how to make her feel better.

Her sister's mouth twitched. "You're a goof. But seriously. What do you want to do? With Gillian?"

Sam huffed. "I want to turn back time. I want the relationship back that we had before."

"Well, if wishes were horses and so on."

"What if I trust her and she pulls another stunt like that?"

"Oh, Sam. I wish I could tell you that everything will be okay. But we're talking about real life here. From what you've told me she has some baggage herself. Being a single mother with two children...having this kind of background and above all not being out herself... This can't be easy for her." Victoria trailed her finger around the rim of her wine glass. "I admire her courage. To ignore whatever shadow was haunting her, to find you and to fight for you. That has to count for something, doesn't it?"

"I know." Sam sighed. "We've been talking about this a lot. And I do understand where she is coming from. I really do. But...I'm afraid. Really, really afraid. What if she breaks my fucking heart?"

"Sam, whatever you decide, I'll support you. And if she hurts you again I'll kick her ass, being the big sister that I am."

"You're the younger one."

"Yes, well. I'll behave like a big sister if it ever comes to that."

"All right." Sam grinned. She had no doubt that Victoria would follow through on the threat. "Gillian told me that she wants to go back to school."

"School?"

"Well, university. To pick up something she had started before she met her husband."

"I think that for you talking on the phone so much is really a good thing. Getting to know each other builds trust."

"She's sharing a lot of her daily life with me. And she's talking about the things she's afraid of."

"That's a good thing, right?"

"Yes, it is." Sam suppressed a yawn. Barely.

Victoria got up from her chair. "Come on, tiger. You can sleep here tonight, have breakfast with us, and decide how you want to play this in the morning."

"Will there be pancakes?"

"Yes, I'll even make pancakes."

"All right. But only if you promise not to snore."

Victoria stared at Sam, arms akimbo. "I. Do. Not. Snore."

"You absolutely do snore." Sam laughed out loud. "Funny. I feel so much better now."

They went into the bedroom. Victoria slipped out of her bathrobe and into bed.

Sam kicked her pants off, folded them, and plopped them on a chair. As she climbed into bed she realized that she did feel much better, much lighter than when she arrived. Even though no problems had been solved...just talking about it had helped lift the weight. A bit. With a sigh she put her head on the pillow. "Night, Vic."

"Night, Sam."

CHAPTER 16

"NIGHT, MOM." ANGELA GOT UNDER the duvet with a book in her hand.

Gillian sat down on the edge of her daughter's bed. "Good night, sweetheart. And don't forget about the fifteen minute rule, all right?"

"But, Mom—"

"Don't 'mom' me," Gillian interrupted with a smile. "It's already late. Fifteen minutes of reading time, and then it's lights out. Agreed?"

"But my friend Anne is allowed to stay up much later. I'm not a child anymore, Mom." Angela pouted.

Gillian bent down, pushed back a shock of dark brown hair, and kissed her daughter's forehead. *She has no idea how cute that grown-up act sometimes is.* "You will always be my child, and don't forget that the fifteen minutes of reading time is a generous gift. Michael's already asleep."

"But Mom, he *is* a child." Angela rolled her eyes. "He's only six."

"Daughter of mine, fifteen minutes. All right?" Gillian remained firm.

Angela took a deep breath, finally relenting. "Okay, but we have to talk about this. My birthday is coming up."

"We will, sweetheart. I promise. Good night." Tenderness for her oldest child filled Gillian's heart as Angela picked up her book and began to read. She was a bookworm—as Gillian had been and still was. Her childhood had been a constant battle with a mother who couldn't understand why her daughter carried a book around at all times. Gillian was happy that her daughter loved to read and didn't spend half of her life in front of the computer like some of her friends. Gillian stepped out of the room and walked down the stairs, grateful that another day was finally over and done with. Breathing a sigh of relief, she entered the kitchen.

"Hey, do you want some coffee?" Tilde sat at the kitchen table, a cup of coffee in her hand and an open newspaper in front of her.

Gillian shook her head. "No, thanks. I would like to sleep tonight. What is it with you Scandinavians and coffee at all times of the day or night anyhow?"

"We're a tough race, trapped in a freezing country where polar bears roam the streets twenty-four hours a day. Surely you understand the need for a hot drink to warm our icy bones?"

"Are you sure there's only coffee in your cup? Let me see." She took a step toward Tilde.

Tilde got up from her chair and sought refuge behind the table. "Go away, you crazy American, you. This is my coffee. Get your own."

Gillian laughed out loud. "Thank you very much. I prefer a glass of wine."

"Your loss." She sat back down again. "Nothing better than twenty-year old whisky mixed with a bit of coffee."

Eyes wide, Gillian couldn't believe what she had just heard. "You heathen. You didn't. Tell me you didn't."

Tilde shook her head. "No, just joking. But I found a whisky-flavored coffee today. It's really good."

Gillian went to the wine cabinet. "I really don't like that flavored stuff. A coffee has to taste like coffee." She picked a bottle of her favorite Shiraz and opened it. The slightly peppery aroma of the wine filled her nose. "And Tilde—I'll have to kill you if you tell my father-in-law that I didn't let the wine breathe."

Laughter followed Gillian when she left the kitchen to go into the winter garden. She carefully placed her glass on the little side table and sat down in her favorite chair, facing the garden. Dusk had settled. Only a few birds were still on the lawn, looking for a late meal. All was quiet. *The blessings of suburban life.*

This was the moment she had been looking forward to all day. Tilde wasn't the only adult in her life anymore with whom she could talk about the day's happenings, what needed to be done tomorrow, or whatever else was on her mind. Ever since she and Sam made up over a week ago, they had a standing date in the evenings.

Gillian tucked some hair behind her ear, retrieved the cordless phone and dialed a by now familiar number.

Sam slowly dragged her tired body into her apartment and straight into the kitchen. She longed for a hot shower, a cold beer, and a certain phone call. *I'm so pussy-whipped, and the weirdest thing is that it feels so good.* Talking to Gillian was the highlight of her day.

They hadn't been able to see each other after Gillian had left her apartment. Talking on the phone, however, was a set date every evening. Sometimes only for a few minutes but other nights they had talked until Sam had almost fallen asleep on the sofa. Tonight, however, would have to be a short call. Sam could feel every bone in her body and she needed to be bright-eyed and awake tomorrow for a job with a new customer.

A refreshing chill hit Sam's body as she opened the fridge. She decided against an ale, choosing a light lager instead. The smooth, refreshing taste of the brew washed over her tongue.

She was just about to undress and step into the shower when the shrill ringing of her phone cut through her apartment. Her heartbeat quickened. She hurried to the phone and picked it up. "Sam here. I live to serve," she said, suddenly embarrassed by the thought the caller might not be the person she expected.

"That's good to hear." Gillian's laughter bubbled through the phone like champagne. "Hi, honey, how was your day? And how is your back?"

Sam closed her eyes, letting Gillian's voice wrap around her, feeling better already. "Hi, Gillian. I'm so happy it's you. I was afraid I had another customer asking me to do more heavy lifting. Hang on a second, all right?" She walked over to the sofa and sat with a groan. Her back was going to kill her one of these days.

"That doesn't sound good."

"No, no, I'm fine. Today was okay, really. I only had to install a ceiling fan and some smoke detectors. Yesterday was tough. Moving furniture and boxes the whole day is no fun, but it's a good job. Today I even got warm pizza before I left."

"That's good. I was afraid you would have another night of Chinese left overs." Gillian chuckled. "Does that mean there's no more heavy lifting in your future?"

"Not in my immediate future, and that's just fine with me." Sam fiddled with the remote control. "So how was your day?"

"Oh, I met someone today. An old friend who is a dean at the college I told you about, and she said that I could sit in for some of the lectures."

Sam knew how nervous Gillian had been about the whole affair. To hear that she had taken another step was great. A feeling of pride washed through her. "That's cool. You're taking big steps."

"I am. Your encouragement and support means a lot to me. I'm not sure I'd be able to take these steps without you." The emotion in Gillian's voice came through clearly.

For a few seconds, Sam heard only breathing from the other end of the phone. She didn't know what to say. The only thing she had done was spend the last week listening to Gillian's dreams and encouraging her to do what she wanted to do. That was not really heroic. But the knowledge that Gillian thought so made her warm and fuzzy inside.

Just as she was about to break the silence, Gillian said, "I miss you."

"I miss you too." Sam swallowed hard. Talking about emotions, even saying mundane things like 'I miss you,' caused her stomach to clench up in knots. Past experiences had taught her that being vulnerable was like an intriguing invitation for some people to lash out and cause pain. Sam's first instinct was always to build walls to protect herself. But they had decided to be open and honest with each other. Gillian held up her end of the bargain and she would too. "I'm sorry my job takes up so much of my time right now."

"No, no, please. There's nothing to be sorry for. I just really, really miss you." Gillian cleared her throat. "And I wondered if you would maybe join us on Saturday? We're going to the zoo."

"The zoo?"

"Yes, Michael wants to and Angela, for once, didn't try to kill him for choosing something so childish."

"Right." Sam pressed the cold beer bottle against her forehead. "You want me to join you and the kids for the zoo? As in getting-to-know-your-kids at the zoo?"

"I don't plan to introduce you as my lesbian lover. I just want you to meet my children and thought that this was a good opportunity. But I guess it's stupid. I'm sorry."

"No. No." Sam sat up straighter, ignoring the pain in her back for the moment. "No, I just... You caught me by surprise. That's all. Gillian, this is big."

"I know."

Wow and double wow. Where was the woman who had nearly shit her pants when Sam had sat down at her table in the coffee shop? "All right. I have to admit that this makes me a bit nervous but I'm in."

"You don't have to if—"

"Hell. Yes. I have to and I want to." There was no way Sam was going to say no when Gillian had finally decided to move forward and do something so brave. "I'll wrap up the job on Friday. And then I'm all yours on Saturday."

"You sure?"

"Yes, absolutely." *I won't sleep the whole night. But that is another thing.* Sam yawned. "Sorry. The long days and short nights are taking their toll on my old body."

"Your body is far from old. But you should take a hot shower and go to bed early. I can hear how tired you are."

"Yes, Mom." Sam chuckled. "That's just what I'm going to do. Though I would rather shower with you."

Gillian let out an exasperated sigh. "You can't say things like that."

"Why?" A grin spread over Sam's face. Teasing Gillian was always a lot of fun.

"How am I supposed to go to sleep with the image of you and me together in the shower?"

"What do you think I'm doing with the same image when I'm in the shower? Ever heard of adjustable showerheads?" She could just imagine the blush flooding Gillian's face. She adored her innocence and at the same time it had been so great to see how Gillian slowly grew bolder.

"I'd rather have the real thing instead of a device." Somehow, Gillian managed to sound prim.

"Oh, Gillian. Me too, believe me." Another moment of silence lingered between them. Sam closed her eyes, imagining Gillian sitting next to her on the sofa and not so many miles away. "Is there any chance for some alone time, just you and me? Soon? I mean, I know that we said that we'll take it slow. And I want to. But...I miss you."

"Why, Ms. Freedman...are you asking me for a date?"

"Indeed, Mrs. Jennings. I am."

"Perfect, 'cause I'm free on Monday night. How does that sound?"

"Wonderful." They hadn't been able to see each other for what felt like an eternity. Phone calls were great. They had helped them to get to know each other better but still, nothing beat face-to-face interaction.

"And what would you say if I told you that I'm free the following Saturday. And not only free but without a curfew?"

Sam swallowed. "What do you mean?"

"The children will be staying with their grandparents from Saturday till Sunday evening."

A whole night together, not only seeing but maybe also touching Gillian. Touching, tasting, smelling. Sam's brain almost short circuited when she thought about the possibilities. She licked her suddenly dry lips. *Down girl. Down.*

Maybe she could take her to a romantic dinner. Sure, it was Gillian's turn to come up with a plan for a date...but having dinner together could be a great start for an evening. Some delicious but not too heavy food, some good wine, a lot of flirting, and then a whole night together. That sounded like a perfect plan. But would Gillian be ready to go out on an actual date? In public?

"Are you still there?" Gillian lost her earlier playfulness. "I understand if it's too short notice. We could just meet, and then I could drive home again. That's fine."

She grimaced at the insecurity she heard in the quiet voice. "Yes...no. I was just speechless for a moment. I would love to spend the night with you. Honestly. I was just wondering if you would like to go out or if you'd prefer to stay in for dinner." She braced herself for the answer. As much as she would love to have a romantic dinner somewhere, she would be all right if they stayed home and ordered takeout.

"Going out as in a date?"

"Yes." Sam held her breath.

"Our second one?"

"Well, actually our third one."

"That's true. So, our third date...I would love to."

Sam had a hard time containing her elation. "All right. That's great." She already had a place in mind. "Why don't we meet here around seven? I'll be dressed and showered by then."

"That's a shame, really." Gillian's voice dropped to a low, intimate tone. "But maybe we could shower together the next morning?"

Images of a naked and wet Gillian flashed through her mind. "You're evil."

Gillian chuckled.

A bright grin spread across Sam's face. "Great, I'll make reservations."

"Please, yes. Oh, and I hope you like hot dogs."

"Hot dogs." Sam scratched her head. "Yeah. But I planned on something more elaborate."

Gillian laughed. "No, sorry. My children insist on having hot dogs for lunch at the zoo."

"Ah, that's all right. As a matter of fact, I love hot dogs."

"Good for you, then. I don't, but the children are allowed to choose food on special occasions, so it's going to be hot dogs on Saturday."

Sam's jaw cracked as she yawned. "Sorry, it was a long day."

"You must be dead tired. Go on and have your shower. Alone," Gillian added.

Sam got up from the sofa "No can do. It's going to be me and my fantasies." She chuckled at the splutter of Gillian blowing a raspberry. "We'll meet on Saturday for the zoo, and then I'm going to see you on Monday evening and next Saturday and Sunday? I'm the luckiest girl in Springfield."

A whole night with Gillian. Sam really was on cloud nine. No time constraints, no hurry to fit as much sex as possible into the two or three hours they have had before. This time she could wine and dine her, take her time flirting, talk about everything and nothing, and then, well, and then she could also take her time seducing her. They had a whole night together. Wow. This was going to be beyond great.

CHAPTER 17

THE SMELL OF OILY FISH invaded Gillian's nose. Even with eyes closed, she would be able to identify the part of the Springfield Zoo they were in. That unique combination of odor and donkey-like braying was only found at the penguins' enclosure.

"Ugh. It stinks." Angela grimaced.

"Well, I wouldn't say it stinks. But yes, it's certainly a strong smell."

"No, it stinks." Angela sat down on a bench. "And penguins are boring."

Gillian resisted the urge to roll her eyes and sat down next to her daughter. "Michael likes them. He thinks they are cute."

"He's a baby."

"He's your brother."

"Baby brother." Angela had her arms crossed in front of her.

Oh dear Lord. Kill me before she hits puberty full on.

"Look, Mom." Angela pointed at the brochure she held. "The feeding starts soon."

"I know, Angela," Gillian replied. "Give Michael a moment, all right?"

Unlike Angela, her brother was fond of the penguins—so clumsy outside the water, but moving like a shot once they were in their element. They were his thing—the meerkats were Angela's.

Gillian cast a glance at her son, who stood beside Sam at the penguin enclosure. For a moment Gillian's breath caught. Being here with Sam and her children felt like a dream. A weird, but good dream. Still, some doubt still lingered inside Gillian. Was this really the right time for her children to meet Sam, even if it was only as one of her friends? Sam related easily to the children. Michael already had a small crush on her. Five years older than her brother, Angela had a harder time wrapping her mind around the fact that her mother suddenly had a friend who dressed and spoke so differently from her usual acquaintances.

"Mom, please." Angela's whining ripped Gillian out of her thoughts. "We're going to be late."

"All right. Let me talk to them." Her daughter was right. They had to hurry if they wanted to be in time for the feeding. Gillian got up and made her way over to where her son and her lover stood. She drank in the sight of Sam, who looked fantastic in blue jeans, light brown leather moccasins, and a boat neck sailor top that did nothing to hide her strong shoulders. A swell of desire coursed through Gillian's body. They hadn't seen, kissed, or touched each other for over a week. A very long week. She swallowed against a mouth gone dry. "Hey, you two. As wonderful as penguins are, there are some cute little meerkats waiting for us."

Michael's reaction to her words was a pout and a long drawn out, "Mom."

"We'll come back later," she ruffled his hair. "And then you can take your time watching them."

"But look." He pointed at a penguin that moved like a shot through the water. "They are so cool."

"Yes. I agree. But they'll be cool later as well. All right?"

"All right." The pout was back.

"Come on, Michael. Let's go and watch how the cute little carnivores make mincemeat out of the zookeeper." Sam winked at him. "Girls only see the lovely gray face and never wonder why they have eye patches like the Beagle Boys."

Michael frowned. "The what?"

"The Beagle Boys."

The frown remained on his face.

Sam sighed. "All right. I think that reference shows my age. The Beagle Boys were characters from the Scrooge McDuck cartoons, a gang of criminals just like these animals and look, they both have eye patches."

"Oh? What do the meerkats do? Do they bite? Are they dangerous?" His earlier disappointment was replaced by the kind of childlike joy Gillian didn't see often on her son's face, especially not since his father's death. He had always been a shy and quiet child, especially compared to Angela.

"What? You've never seen them eat?" Sam asked, her brows raised.

He shook his head.

"We haven't been to the zoo for nearly three years." Gillian smoothed down her jacket.

"Wow. Okay, pal, then it's about time. You'll be blown away."

As fast as he could, Michael ran over to his sister, most probably to tell her what Sam had said. Only in slightly different words.

"Please don't exaggerate stuff like that with him."

"Exaggerate?"

"I'm sure the meerkats just became monsters in his fantasy and that is what he's telling his sister right now."

Sam shrugged. "Honey, have you ever seen them eat?"

The way Sam's gaze slowly wandered up and down her body made Gillian's skin tingle, rekindling the barely extinguished desire that still lingered inside her. She held up a hand. "And you can't look at me like that."

"Is that so?"

Gillian groaned, taking a step back. "Stop it."

"I guess you're in for a surprise," a mischievous twinkle appeared in Sam's eyes.

"What?" Gillian held her breath.

Sam slowly bridged the distance between them. The cocky smile on her face made Gillian's inside go all mushy.

Sam stopped in front of her. "The meerkat feeding."

"What?"

"You're in for a surprise with the 'cute' little bastards. What did you think I meant?" With a wink, Sam stepped around her.

A hint of her perfume teased Gillian's nose, triggering memories not appropriate for a family visit to the zoo. At least it made her nearly forget about the fishy smell coming from the penguins.

Sam hurried toward Angela and Michael.

Gillian's pulse beat in time with the sway in Sam's steps. She was gripped by so many conflicting emotions and didn't know where and how to begin to sort them out. Guilt about the X-rated thoughts Sam unleashed in her was the most dominant right now. She guessed that this had to do with the children being around. However, no matter how often she told herself that what she had with Sam was special, there was always that nagging voice inside her saying otherwise—a voice that, on reflection, sounded very much like Derrick's mother. Gillian clenched her hands into fists. What she felt for Sam was so profound, going so much deeper than anything she'd had with Derrick. And she had known Sam only for a few weeks. She squared her shoulders and willed the nagging voice inside her to be quiet while she walked toward the three most important people in her life.

A short while later they stood in front of the meerkat enclosure, where a large crowd of visitors had already gathered. With a bit of luck and Sam's determination, they had found a spot in the first row.

Gillian leaned back into Sam's sturdy body, reveling in her closeness. She felt safe enough, with everyone around them standing close to each other, that nobody would notice the intimacy of the position she was in. With a grin on her face, she pushed back into Sam's body until she heard a slight gasp.

"You're playing with fire," Sam's voice was husky, almost a whisper.

She hummed in response. "No, I'm just testing your self control."

"Bitch."

Gillian chuckled. The knowledge that Sam wasn't immune to her actions warmed her inside. Every simple touch, every smile from Sam made her feel so much better, so much more alive. And it made her forget how complicated her life was... if only for a moment.

"Look, Mom." Michael pointed at the bustle of little tan bodies inside the enclosure. Some meerkats groomed one another, while only a few feet away, three wrestled with each other. Others lay under sun lamps, using their stomachs as solar panels.

Watching them interact was pure fun. Gillian had no idea what to expect when the feeding started, but she was sure Sam had exaggerated. These animals could be nothing other than cute.

"Look, this is the sentry," Sam said, pointing to a lonely meerkat standing on one of the bigger stones. His body tense, he kept a constant watch on the surroundings. "Hey, Michael, Angela?" she whispered.

The children looked up at her.

"See the group running around in front of the small door over there?" Sam pointed at a handful of the animals that were hovering at the other end of the enclosure. "The zookeeper will come through that door. They already know that it's about time. But the sentry is the one who sees her first and will signal her arrival to the group. Keep watching him."

Gillian frowned. "How do you know it's a she?"

"Eh?"

"The zookeeper. You said that the sentry will signal 'her' arrival."

Sam shrugged. "It could be a he, but it's been a woman every time I've been here with my niece."

Her niece. Right. So that is why she's so good with children.

Sam nudged her. "Look, it's about to start."

A woman in a dark green overall stepped out of a small building on the other side of the enclosure, carrying four stacked dishes in her hands.

"Now, watch the sentry," Sam said.

The sentry stood straighter, making a funny peeping sound. As if given a command, the other animals stopped whatever they were doing, moving together like a school of fish until they hovered in front of the small door Sam had pointed out earlier.

An excited murmur rose from the group of spectators around them. The whole scene reminded Gillian of the ancient Coliseum, the zoo visitors as spectators, and the meerkats like little gladiators.

Sam's breath was hot on her ear. "They aren't the only small mammals on high alert."

Gillian looked down at Angela, who gripped her digital camera tightly, ready to take pictures. Michael's hands were in constant motion on the railing.

"They are cute, but not as cute as their mother."

Heat rushed to Gillian's cheeks. Distracted, she turned her gaze back toward the meerkat spectacle.

The zookeeper closed the door to the enclosure behind her and was immediately surrounded by the whole group of small creatures.

Gillian couldn't believe her eyes. The formerly cute animals turned into a growling and squealing mass. Tails held in an upright position, the very same meerkats that had groomed each other seconds ago were now fighting and biting right, left, and center.

The zookeeper ignored the seething group at her feet, stepping over them. She took a few steps, turned to the left, and bent down to place the dishes on the ground. A wave of small animals followed her, swarming to the place where they expected the dishes to land.

Gillian held her breath and gripped the railing tightly. She was sure that the little beasts wouldn't discern between food and fingers when it came down to it.

At the last moment the zookeeper turned to her right and set one of the dishes down on meerkat-free ground while a murmur swept through the crowd. As soon as the dishes were on the ground, the zookeeper jerked her hands away not a second too late. The mob dug into the food as if there was no tomorrow.

Gillian didn't want to think about how flour worms tasted or how the feeling of a live worm must feel in a mouth. She concentrated on the zookeeper who, to Gillian's relief, didn't waste any time and placed two dishes a few feet away on the ground, and the last one several feet away from the others.

"It's a bit like watching the movie *Gremlins*," Sam said. "One moment they're so sweet you want to cuddle them; the next moment you think you need a weapon to defend yourself."

"Wow." Michael looked up at Gillian. "They are dangerous." Awe filled his voice.

"Mom, can we have some meerkats?" Angela asked, a dreamy look on her face. "They aren't big and we have enough space in the garden."

Sam chuckled but otherwise kept quiet.

"No, we cannot build a meerkat enclosure in the garden. We would have to move to..." she looked questioningly at Sam. "Africa?"

"Yes, Africa it is. That's where they live." Sam confirmed, smiling. "Anybody interested in watching raccoons eat? They're just around the corner."

Gillian groaned. "I don't even want to imagine what they're going to do to get their food."

"You'd be surprised."

Sam rapped her fingers on her legs. A swarm of crying, laughing, and screaming children was testing her eardrums and her patience. Keeping an eye on Michael while he went wild on the playground had sounded like a great idea. Back then. *Damn. Those kids are loud.*

Sam hugged the backpack closer to her and glanced around. The benches scattered on the playground were occupied by a majority of women and only a handful of men. She wondered how many of these women had husbands working on a Saturday? How many husbands didn't have to work today but had other things to do besides spend time with their families? And how many of the women were single parents like Gillian or part of a patchwork family. "Normal" families certainly were less and less the norm nowadays and she knew from experience that "normal" sometimes was just an ugly nightmare.

A bright red Frisbee whizzed over her head and smacked into something behind her. "Shit." She turned around. Thankfully, it had only hit a tree. Sitting there wasn't really for people with frail nerves.

She turned around again just in time to see Michael climb down the monkey bars while doing his best to get out of the way of three boys who were trying to break a speed record to the top. He was a great kid, lots of fun to be around and full of questions. Chloe would like him. Sam leaned back on the bench. Maybe they could include Chloe the next time they did something together. That could help her bond with Angela, who seemed more standoffish.

Michael made his way toward her. Heaving a sigh, he sat down on the bench. "I'm thirsty."

"No wonder. You conquered the monkey bars." She opened Gillian's backpack. "Let's see what I can find for you."

She found two bottles of water, one soda, and one sports drink. What now? Gillian hadn't left instructions as to what Michael was allowed to drink. *Better safe than sorry.* Painful experience with her sister had told her that mothers could be very peculiar. She picked a bottle of water and opened it for Michael. "Here, pal."

"Thanks." Michael took several gulps before he handed her the half-empty bottle back.

"Wanna have another go?" She pointed at the playground.

"No." He looked in the direction of the restroom. "Why do they always take so long?"

"Well, women are that way."

He looked up at her. "You didn't need that long when you had to go."

She was saved from answering by a woman passing their bench with a crying boy clinging to her hand. He was about Michael's age. The woman guided the boy toward the toilets. Only fragments of their conversation were audible, but it was obvious that the boy didn't want to go with his mother.

A tug on her arm made Sam look down into eyes that were the same color as Gillian's. "Yes, Michael?"

"Why is the lady so angry with the boy?"

"Well, I don't know for sure, but maybe she wanted him to go to the ladies' restroom and he didn't want to."

He nodded. "He's a boy. He needs to go to the men's restroom."

She bit her cheek to stop herself from laughing. She would have to make sure that she wasn't the one on toilet duty when he needed to go. "Yep, that's right, pal. And look who's on her way back," she said, pointing at his mother and sister, who had just emerged.

She glanced at her watch again. *Perfect timing.* She had an ace up her sleeve to help win the children over. Something that she hoped both would enjoy.

A few minutes later they had left the playground behind. Sam listened with only half an ear to Angela's story about last week's soccer practice, her mind occupied with other matters while they slowly walked toward their next destination.

"...and then Mrs. Sand told Patty off," Angela said, emphasizing her story with sweeping gestures.

Gillian nudged Sam's shoulder. "Are you okay? You're awfully quiet all of a sudden."

"Yeah, sorry. I guess last week's catching up on me. I'm a bit tired." She gave her a reassuring smile. It wasn't a lie; she *was* tired, although there was another reason for her absentmindedness. She wasn't sure anymore if the surprise she had planned for the kids would really knock their little socks off. *Maybe they'll think it's boring. Or stupid. But then, children love cute animals, right?* She wiped her clammy hands on her jeans. *No, they'll love it. Chloe would.*

229

Up ahead, she saw the Nocturnal House, an unremarkable gray on gray building that gave no hint about what it held inside. It was her favorite spot in the zoo, a place where day turned into night, and night-active animals from all over the world could be watched. She sighed. If the playground was any indication, the zoo was too crowded today to enjoy a quiet Nocturnal House. She would go crazy if she had to stand in a crowd of shoving and squealing visitors in front of the lemurs or the bush baby's enclosure. But then... they wouldn't have to today.

A blonde woman, dressed in the typical khaki trousers and sweater of a zoo employee, stepped out of the building. *Maisie. Right on time. Well, here we go.* Sam waved at her friend, who waved back. She ignored Gillian's questioning stare. With determined steps, she walked over to Maisie. "Hi, it's good to see you." They shared a hug. "Glad you could make it."

"Nice family you have there," Maisie whispered.

"Yeah." Releasing her, Sam rubbed the back of her neck. "Let me introduce you. This is Gillian, a good friend of mine, and these are her children, Angela and Michael."

"It's a pleasure to meet you." She shook Gillian's hand and smiled at the children. "Have you enjoyed your day at the zoo so far?"

The children nodded, one a bit more enthusiastic than the other.

"Good. I like hearing that. See, I'm one of the vets here," she said. "Sam told me you might be interested in taking a look behind the scenes?"

"Oh, can we, Mom?" Angela's eyes shone with an excitement that Sam hadn't witnessed often today.

Well, maybe my idea wasn't so bad after all. A weight lifted from her shoulders.

Michael chimed in. "Yes, Mom. Please."

Sam grinned. "Oh, please, Mom. We really want to."

"I wonder who's the biggest kid." She chuckled. "All right, as long as I don't have to touch a snake or kiss a crocodile."

Maisie shook her head. "No, you're safe. We have to release a slow loris back into his enclosure today. I thought it would be something you'd enjoy watching up close." She took a bunch of keys out of her pocket and opened a door to their right. "Please follow me."

Leaving the half-light of the Nocturnal House behind, Gillian stepped through the exit and squinted against the bright daylight. A light breeze ruffled her hair while the bamboo to her right whispered like the curtain in her bedroom sometimes did. As fascinating as the slow loris and Maisie's explanations had been, she was glad that this event was over. She couldn't shake the feeling that there was a connection between Maisie and Sam...that they had a past together. Once that thought had crossed her mind, Gillian had felt the green-eyed monster, otherwise known as jealousy, popping up.

Two kids ran past her. She recognized them from minutes ago when they had been told off for constantly pounding on one of the enclosure's glass front. Thankfully, her children behaved differently. *Well, at least when I'm around.* She couldn't delude herself into thinking that Angela and Michael weren't normal children who misbehaved once in a while. Still, the way they had acted around the slow loris, how they had listened to Maisie's instructions...it made her proud.

"Mom, that was so cool." Angela appeared next to her, beaming. "I think I want to become a veterinarian. The slow loris was sooo cute."

"That was great, Sam. Can we do that again?" Michael begged.

"Yes, Sam, please. Can we do that again?" Angela echoed her brother.

"I can't make any promises, but I'll ask Maisie and maybe there'll be another opportunity sometime soon. Why not?" She smiled at the kids before her questioning gaze met Gillian's. "Are there any particular animals you're interested in?"

"Well, I find female mammals quite fascinating." She held her breath, having no idea where that had come from.

Sam looked at her with wide eyes before she burst out laughing.

Gillian couldn't help joining in, very aware of the children's confusion.

"All right, all right. Sorry." She laid a hand on her stomach, trying to calm down. "I don't know about you, but I'm really hungry. Why don't we discuss this over some food?"

"There's a hot dog vendor just around the corner," Sam said with a wide grin on her face.

"Great. Michael, Angela, why don't you have a look and see if it's open?"

"Yeah!" They shouted simultaneously and ran off.

"Are you okay?" Sam asked, her smile faltering. "Is something bothering you?"

God, was she so transparent? She attempted to smile, but it was strained. Maybe it was better to get this out in the open before it festered inside her. She couldn't bring herself to look at Sam when she said, "I don't know if this is the right place to talk about it. But I..." Her stomach churned. "You and Maisie...was there ever anything between you?"

"No, never. Why...oh, sorry. I see." She took hold of Gillian's arm and nudged her over to a side entrance that was partly hidden behind the bamboo. "Look at me Gillian, please."

She grimaced. "Sorry, I know that was lame and—"

"No. Look at me."

233

She forced herself to meet Sam's gaze. "Yes?"

"There was never anything between me and Maisie." Sam took her hand, lacing their fingers together.

"She's good-looking," Gillian pointed out.

"You do have good taste in women." She grinned. "I won't say that we'll never run into someone I had sex with and yes, I've had a couple of short-term relationships with women who live in Springfield—but no, Maisie and I never happened. And honestly, there is only one woman I'm interested in. One woman that makes my heart beat faster. One woman who makes me smile. And that is you."

Gillian's face got hot. Jealousy really was a green-eyed monster. "I'm sorry. I just—"

"No." Her fingertips fluttered over the inside of Gillian's wrist. "Thanks for asking. We agreed to be open and honest with each other, right? And I'm being very open and honest now. You're the only woman I'm interested in. And I'm well aware that you come with baggage. As do I. Just different baggage. And I like your kids. I really do." Her smile was gentle and brilliant.

Gillian couldn't form words. Fighting down the fluttering in her chest, screaming at her that they were out in the open, she went with the need to show Sam how much she felt. Taking a step closer she pressed their lips together in a soft, tentative kiss.

Sam's arms slid around her waist.

Gillian released a contented sigh before she slowly pulled away. "Thank you for arranging the meeting with Maisie."

Sam rocked on her heels. "My pleasure."

Warmth flooded through her. "They like you too. The kids." Unable to resist the urge to touch her again, she brushed Sam's cheek with the back of her fingers. "Maybe it should scare me how easily you were able to win them over." She hesitated for a moment. "The truth is, it doesn't. You made today something very special...for the three of us."

What she said was true, but what she didn't say went even deeper. If she hadn't already known her feelings for Sam had turned from lust to something much bigger, better, and more frightening...today would have revealed the truth. She was falling in love with the woman who could make her blood boil, make her feel safe, and who treated her children with such respect. However, this was neither the time nor the place for such a declaration. *I'll tell her on our next date. We'll find a way to make it work between us.* She squeezed Sam's hand before letting go. "Come on. I'm sure the kids are already waiting for us."

Moments later, they nearly bumped into both children, who sped around the corner like a couple of cheetahs before skidding to a halt.

"Where were you?" Angela demanded, frowning.

"Sorry, child of mine," Gillian replied. "We are old women. Our feet don't move as fast as yours anymore."

"Mom, you're not that old." Michael rolled his eyes.

"Thank you." She turned to Sam. "These are the kind of compliments one simply hungers for at our age."

Sam chuckled. "She's right. You're really not that old."

Gillian playfully swatted at her. "Thank you... not."

A line had formed in front of the food pavilion. Chirping birds hopped around the garbage cans, picking at whatever tasty morsels had fallen on the ground.

Joking and laughing, the four of them stood in line until it was their turn to order. Four hot dogs were delivered quickly.

"Sam, could you help Angela and Michael carry their food over there?" She pointed at a table where a family of five was just leaving. "I'll pay and join you."

"Yep, can do." Sam took two hot dogs, which left the kids to deal with only one each. "But you better hurry or I'll eat yours." She winked at Gillian.

"Don't even think about it, Freedman." She shot Sam the most evil glare she was capable of. She handed the money over and grabbed some more napkins. Toppings were a sure road to disaster in her kids' hands—and on their clothes.

"Gillian. Gillian Jennings. Is that you?"

She froze. Even though she hadn't heard that voice for a very long time she recognized it. *Shit.*

What were the odds of meeting someone from Derrick's law firm on a Saturday in the zoo? *And Ben Shacker, of all people.* Turning around, she cleared her throat and plastered a fake smile on her face. "Ben. Hi. It's good to see you."

Ben pushed his shell-rimmed glasses higher on his nose. "Yes, what a surprise." He ran a hand through his thin, gray hair. "Hang on a second." He turned around. "Tamara, honey?"

A tall redhead who was at least half his age reacted. "Yes, honey?"

"I'll be right with you. Give me a minute."

The redhead's answer was a smile. At least she tried to smile as best as the Botox allowed.

Gillian's stomach churned. She knew Ben's wife, Winnie, from several summer parties and other events associated with the law firm. Winnie had been nothing but nice to her and had helped her settle into the group of 'significant others' as the wives were called in the firm. Political correctness was in high demand these days. Not too long ago, she had heard through the grapevine that Ben had replaced his wife with a younger woman. And, well, here they were.

"I haven't seen you in ages," he said while his gaze slowly travelled down her body, "but I must say...you look really good."

She wanted to throttle the sleazy guy or push her fingers into his eyeballs. Instead she mustered all the politeness she was capable of. "Thanks, Ben. How are you doing?"

"Oh, I'm doing great. I partially retired last month, which means more time for the grandkids and for Tamara." He waved over to Botox woman, who was glaring in their direction. "Are you here with your kids?"

Self-consciously Gillian looked over her shoulder to the small table where Sam sat with Angela and Michael. All three were laughing about something, looking so carefree that she had to fight the urge to simply leave Ben and join them.

Sam caught her gaze, frowning and tilting her head in Ben's direction.

Gillian straightened her shoulders and focused back on Ben. "Yes, I am here with my kids and a very good friend of mine."

Ben followed her gaze. "Nice."

"I'm sorry. I have to go. They're waiting for me."

"Sure, sure. It was nice to see you." He flashed her a smile. "Hey, we could meet up for drinks sometime. Talk about the good old times. Why don't you give me a call? I'd like to catch up. Maybe spend some time with each other. You must be lonely without Derrick."

She couldn't believe it. The little shithead was hitting on her while the woman he had betrayed his wife with was standing mere feet away. She wanted to throw up. "I really don't want to go out with you or meet you or whatever." She squared her shoulders. "Let me make it plain and clear. There is already someone else in my life, and I'm very thankful and happy about it. I am not lonely."

His gaze hardened. "Really. Good for you. Do I know him?"

"No, you don't." She turned around and made her way to her family's table, still fuming about Ben's insolence. When was the last time the guy had looked into a mirror? The redhead surely wasn't interested in his character, nor his body. And Winnie, good old Winnie had been left behind by this bastard. She plopped down on the wooden bench and stared at the hot dog before her.

"You okay?" Sam asked.

"Not really." She grabbed the plastic cup that stood next to the hot dog. She took a gulp and set the cup back.

Sam's expression became guarded. "All right."

"Sorry, let's talk about it later. Okay?" She hoped Sam understood that she wouldn't discuss what had happened in front of the children.

"Who was that, Mom?" Michael asked.

"He worked with your dad." She ruffled his hair. "And you know what? I just told him how happy I am to be here with you three."

A small smile played around Sam's lips. "Did you now?"

Gillian looked deep into her eyes. "Yes."

Sam's smile grew bigger. "That's good. 'Cause there's a snake exhibition today where visitors are allowed to touch the snakes, and we just decided that's where we *wanna* go next."

CHAPTER 18

THE SOUND OF CLASSICAL MUSIC drifted through the room, accompanied by the murmur of other guests. Only the occasional clatter of cutlery on porcelain broke the peaceful atmosphere. *L'Aubergine* was a restaurant for lovers with a fondness for each other as well as outstanding food. And even though—tonight was on its way up on the list of Sam's top ten most awkward dates ever.

A waiter hurried past, one plate in each hand. He set them down on a nearby table where a couple sat, easily chatting and enjoying each other's company.

Sam balled her hand into a fist on her knee and stared at the small piece of salmon that was left on her plate. How did they end up like this? Where was the easy camaraderie Gillian and she had during their phone calls or the wonderful companionship they had shared at the zoo? Tonight felt like a bad movie and not like the date Sam had been looking forward to.

She groaned inwardly, peeking at Gillian, who was concentrating on her Filet Mignon so hard that Sam was surprised the beef didn't combust beneath her stare. Gillian looked so beautiful in her dark green dress. She was breathtaking. And quiet. As quiet as Sam, who cursed her inability to form deep and meaningful sentences.

The critiques had raved about L'Aubergine. And it was great. The food was great. But it hadn't taken five steps into the restaurant for Sam to realize that she shouldn't have chosen this place. Being in an exclusive restaurant like that sure as hell put a knot in her stomach and in her brain. She had been so determined to find a place Gillian would enjoy that she had repressed her own distaste for everything rich and famous. The silence between them seemed louder to her than the background noise. *This is ridiculous.* Sam moved the salmon to the edge of her plate, not hungry anymore. She cleared her throat. "Good food, right?"

Gillian looked up with a smile that didn't reach her eyes. "Very good. Yes." She glanced at Sam's salmon before concentrating on her own food again.

The temptation to let her head fall face first onto the table rose by the second. She had to do something, be more eloquent or whatever. But how? She drummed her fingers on her pants. An idea popped into her head. This could backfire. Sure. But it could also save the evening. "Hey, Gillian?"

Tired green eyes stared back at her. "Yes?"

"How about a little game?"

Gillian tilted her head in the typical gesture that meant that she was confused. "A game?"

"Well, not really a game. How about we each get to ask two questions, nothing is off limits"

A frown appeared on Gillian's face. "That's not really a game. Unless there's a bottle involved. And if I remember correctly someone always ends up naked and drunk."

Sam grabbed her bottle of wine and held it up. "We do have a bottle. But there's no need to get drunk."

For a moment Gillian simply studied her, then set her fork down. "All right. Any question is allowed?"

Hesitating for a moment Sam finally said, "Yes." *Please don't let me regret this.* She wiped suddenly sweaty palms on her trousers.

"Can I go first?"

"Sure, go ahead." Sam held her breath.

Gillian pursed her lips and cocked an eyebrow. "Right. How about favorite writer and genre?"

Surprise and relief fluttered in Sam's chest. She hadn't expected this one. "Seriously? You can ask me anything you want and you go for reading material?"

"Yes. Consider it a warm-up for my next one." There was a twinkle in Gillian's eyes.

"Okay. Favorite writer...can I choose two?"

"Sure. Two are okay."

The first one was easy. The second one was a close race between two female writers. In the end she chose the one that would go with one of her favorite genres. "Neil Gaiman and Tracy Chevalier."

"I've heard of Neil Gaiman but who is Tracy Chevalier?"

"She writes wonderful historical fiction."

"So, I guess that historical fiction is one of your favorite genres?"

"Yes. Fantasy, in particular urban fantasy and historical fiction. Well researched historical fiction, I might add. Some of that stuff is just so badly researched that I get a rash reading it. But if it is well researched and well written..." Sam grinned, "then I'm sold."

Gillian took a sip of her wine before she said, "I was surprised that you own so many books. The shelves in your living room are better stocked than a small town library."

A sharp comment tingled on Sam's tongue but she swallowed it down. How often had she run into the prejudice that just because she worked with her hands people supposed that watching television, drinking beer, and belching was her favorite pastime? "Yes, I do like to read."

Gillian leaned back on her chair, the laugh lines around her eyes deepening. "Angela is the bookworm in our family. She goes through books like other children go through videogames. And I'm a sucker for autobiographies these days."

The waiter chose that moment to come over and pick up their plates. "Would you like dessert? We have a wonderful cheesecake tonight. Or maybe some homemade ice-cream?"

Sam looked at Gillian. "Would you like to share something?"

"I'm positively stuffed." She laid a hand on her stomach. "Maybe an espresso?"

Sam smiled at the waiter. "Make that two espressos, please."

With a nod he was gone.

"So, is it my turn for a question?" Sam ran her fingers over the tablecloth.

"Yes."

She didn't have to think hard about this one. "Okay, then tell me the most embarrassing moment in your life."

"That's not really a question."

Sam shrugged. "Okay, allow me to rephrase. What was the most embarrassing moment in your life?"

"Hard to choose. I've had a few. And the feeling of what was exactly the most embarrassing does change from time to time." Her brow furrowed so much that her eyebrows nearly touched. Then she smiled. "I think that one of the most embarrassing moments of my life was when Michael made Derrick's mother regret that she had grandchildren."

Sam muffled the sound of her laughter with the napkin. This sounded like a very promising story indeed. "What did he do?"

"Michael was three when we were invited to one of Margret's awful tea parties. She hosts them a few times each year and I have the suspicion that she keeps a list of the most boring people alive. The main reason for her parties is to show off her house and her family so we were invited—with children."

The waiter appeared with their espressos.

"Thank you." Sam inhaled the wonderful aroma that drifted from the cup. She dumped two spoons of sugar into it.

Gillian shook her head but didn't comment.

"What?"

"I think there's an equal portion of sugar and coffee in that cup now."

"That's just the way I like it. Hot and sweet." She winked at Gillian and wasn't surprised when the expected blush appeared. "So, what happened to make grandmother go bonkers?"

Gillian downed her espresso in one go, without adding sugar to it. "Nice. Well, Michael was terribly bored that afternoon and I was distracted by something. Anyhow, he suddenly showed up with his little feet stuck in high heels that he found somewhere, ran a few steps, bumped into and smashed a very expensive Chinese vase."

"Oh. Bad." Sam chuckled.

"Yes. But that's not the best part of the story."

Sam leaned forward. "Yes?"

"He was sitting on the floor, crying. I couldn't lift him up since I had a broken arm, thanks to a stupid accident. So I asked my mother-in-law, who stood next to me, to check if he was okay."

"Yeah?"

"Well, I only had to ask twice before she finally complied." Gillian's smile could positively be described as devilish.

"Go on."

"Michael threw up all over her."

"Oh God." Sam laughed so hard, she had tears in her eyes.

"Twice."

"Unbelievable." That must have been a sight. "Did she make child-kebab out of him?"

Now it was Gillian's turn to laugh. "No. She didn't lay a hand on him. But she was not amused. And all I wanted was to disappear—in a cloud of smoke or something equally desirable. I can laugh about it today but at that moment I was so devastated and embarrassed."

A few guests stared over at their table. Sam didn't care. She was having fun and they were finally talking. It was great.

Gillian tipped her espresso cup at Sam. "So, my turn again?"

Sam steeled herself against the next question; pretty sure that whatever would come wouldn't be as easy to answer as the first one. "Yes. Go on."

"Since we're talking about family..." Gillian's voice was gentle. "Tell me a bit more about yours?"

Sam's stomach tightened. She crossed her arms over her chest. "There's not much to tell."

"I don't want to overstep. Sorry."

Shit. Sam really didn't want to talk about her childhood, her teenage years, or her family at all. What she wanted even less, however, was to go back to how the evening was before they started their little game. She wanted to move forward—with Gillian. "It's all right. It's just a topic I don't like to talk about. Anything specific you'd like to know?"

"I heard from Thomas that you have a... strained relationship with them?"

Sam snorted. "I'm sure that's not how he described it."

"No, it wasn't."

"So, what did he say?"

"Not much. He mentioned that you never had a good relationship with your father. That you spent time hiding in the garage. With Thomas. And that...that your father hurt you."

Sam nodded and began to peel the label off the wine bottle. "He did. Yes." She really, really didn't want to talk about it. But she couldn't condemn Gillian for wanting to know. Sam took a deep breath to center herself. "My father and I haven't spoken to each other since I left home."

Gillian reached across the table and put her hand over Sam's. "At seventeen?"

Sam narrowed her eyes and stared at the warm, soft hand that covered hers before looking up again.

A flash of hurt crossed Gillian's face. She started to pull her hand away.

You idiot. "No." Sam grabbed her hand. "No. Sorry, I love to touch you and be touched. I just..." She looked around and tried to gauge if the other guests paid any attention to them. Lowering her head, Sam finally said, "I wasn't sure if you had forgotten that we are in a public place."

"No, I didn't forget. I just decided that I don't want to care about things like that anymore."

Sam blinked. Twice. Gillian was really moving out of her comfort zone—date in a restaurant, touching Sam in public. Maybe it was time to do the same. She wouldn't go into details. Not here. Not tonight. "Did Thomas tell you about me leaving at seventeen?" She ran a thumb over the soft skin of Gillian's hand.

"No, you did."

"Oh, right." Sam nodded slowly. *How did I forget about that?* Rolling her shoulders to get rid of the tension, she said, "I don't exist for my father anymore. Which is just fine with me. I'll be happy if I never have to see him again. He left my mother around ten years ago. I have no contact with her either. She's a very religious person. And there's a brother who is a successful investment banker and a total moron. No contact there either." Sam hated the bitterness in her voice. "And then there's my younger sister. Victoria. And her daughter, Chloe."

"You are in contact with them, right?"

Sam grinned. "Yes. And it eats my father alive that I'm Chloe's godmother."

"Did you stay in contact with your sister after you left home?"

Sam shook her head. "No. Victoria is five years younger than me. But she reached out to me before Chloe was born. I promise to tell you the whole sordid story one day. Victoria can be very determined. And we do have a close relationship. She's not only my sister but also my friend. And Chloe...she's great. I think that Michael and Angela would like her."

"We should get them together someday."

Sam smiled. "Yes, we should. Maybe another visit to the zoo?"

"That is a great idea."

They smiled at each other, their hands still linked on the table.

"So, is it my turn to ask another embarrassing question?" Sam teased.

"Yes, but that this is your last one for tonight."

"Let's see." Sam hesitated for a moment. But she needed to know, even if it was totally stupid. "How did you meet Derrick?"

Gillian was silent for a moment before she said, "He was my boss. At the law firm." A small smile tugged at her lips. "I was his secretary. Which is pretty clichéd, right? And let me assure you that my former job didn't really make me the most attractive daughter-in-law for his parents."

"You were a secretary?"

"Yes. I'm one of those secretaries who married her boss."

"Oh." Gillian had been a secretary. *She married her boss.*

"You look as if I just told you that I'm pregnant."

Sam's mouth fell open. "What?"

"I'm joking. I'm not pregnant." Gillian chuckled. "You should see your face."

A myriad of emotions and thoughts tumbled through Sam. A secretary. Not a lawyer herself or a...whatever rich girls studied. *I'm really, really an ass.* She realized that she had fallen into the same kind of thinking that she hated from other people, to assume things about someone else without having any idea about his or her background. *That's what assholes do.* She gathered the remains of her dignity. "Good, I prefer you being a secretary to you being pregnant."

"That's a sentiment that I share. Two children are great but absolutely enough." Gillian got up from her chair and winked at Sam. "I'll be back in a minute."

What a night. Sam ran a hand through her hair. She was still processing the fact that Gillian had been her husband's employee. Weird. In Sam's experience rich people married rich people—especially those coming from old money. So what had possessed Derrick to marry Gillian? What kind of guy had he been? *I guess that's a question for another time.*

"All right." Gillian stood next to Sam's chair. "Let's go."

"Ugh...shouldn't we pay first?"

"That's already been taken care off." Gillian leaned down and whispered, "I have to be home in thirty minutes and I need some hot kisses before I drive away. Hot, hot kisses."

"Oh." Like a teenager, Sam's cheeks warmed. "Sure, yes. Let's go." She got up from her chair and followed Gillian outside.

Moments later they stood in front of Gillian's car. Just like they had on their first date.

"You're so amazing." Sam sighed.

Gillian's smile was gentle as she stepped close, pressing her body against Sam's. "Maybe. But in my eyes...you're the beautiful one. Inside and out."

Sam slid both arms around her waist. "Hi there."

"Howdy." Green eyes twinkled.

Sam buried her face in the crook of her neck, deeply inhaling the scent that was so typically Gillian. Sam pressed her lips against the soft skin and lingered there for a moment before she drew back again, tracing her left hand along Gillian's jaw, fingertips tingling at the sensation. "I enjoyed this evening. A lot."

"I'm glad you liked the food."

Sam chuckled. "Yeah. The food wasn't bad."

"And the wine."

"Wasn't too bad either."

"The music," Gillian teased with a playful smile.

"You're a goof."

"Maybe. But I'm your goof."

"That you are." Sam pressed her lips to Gillian's in a soft, tentative kiss, eyes drifting close. She could get lost in this kiss and stay here forever.

Gillian complied with slow, tentative strokes of her lips and tongue, pressing even closer to Sam than seemed possible.

Sam released a contented sigh. Licking her lips, she rested her forehead against Gillian's. "Go. Now. Or I will not be responsible for my actions."

Gillian whimpered. "But I wanted more hot kisses."

"You're killing me." She took a deep breath. "This really isn't the place for making out."

A pout appeared on Gillian's face.

"Oh, look at that. A pout." Sam planted another kiss on those tempting lips. "And now... drive away before I lose my self-discipline."

With a sigh Gillian got into her car. "I hate you."

"No, you don't." She leaned down until she could look into those green eyes. "And I promise you that you will be the one begging me to stop kissing you on Saturday."

"Think so?" Gillian batted her eyelashes.

"No. I know so."

CHAPTER 19

"WHICH ONE OF YOU IS it going to be tonight?" Gillian's fingers trailed over the dark green cotton nightie that accentuated her eyes and fit her like a second skin before she touched the cool dark blue fabric of the short cut silk pajamas that could almost be described as lingerie. She loved the way the smooth silk caressed her skin at night. A touch, soft like the hand of an experienced lover. *Sam.* Her eyes fluttered closed at the image of a naked Sam, of her firm, hot body, of the way she looked when she came. Beautiful. Desirable. Unbelievably hot. Gillian's knees went weak. She sat down on the bed. The longing for Sam, for her touch, was so powerful and scorching that at times it threatened to overwhelm her. There was lust, a lot of lust actually. She loved Sam's touch, her take charge attitude during sex, and her thoughtfulness. She had freed Gillian to voice her needs—needs she hadn't even known she'd possessed. But it wasn't just about sex anymore.

And hadn't been for a while. She wanted to be there for Sam and offer a massage when her back hurt. She wanted to make sure that she ate properly—no one could live on cold pizza several days a week. And she wanted to go to bed and to wake up beside her.

Gillian touched her lips, remembering the kisses they had exchanged after their last date. There was no denying Sam's raw sexual power. She trembled inside. Little had she known that sexual desire could mix so well with...love.

The sound of running feet jerked her back to reality.

Seconds later her daughter rushed into the bedroom. "Grandma is here."

Gillian groaned. Margret was the last person on earth she wanted to talk to right now—actually ever. Why hadn't Charles, the chauffeur, come to pick up the children as usual? Talking to Margret when all she had on her mind was Sam and how many times and ways she wanted to come tonight...*Crap.* She took a deep breath to steady her nerves. "All right, thank you," she said, composing herself. "I'll be down in a minute, sweetie." She put the silk pajamas into her overnight bag. Both children knew that she was going to Sam's for a sleepover. Talking about her close friendship with Sam was a first step. The children didn't need to know that her kind of sleepover would be a lot different from the ones they went to.

Gillian turned to her daughter and noticed for the first time that she held one book in each hand. "You're staying for one night at your grandparents. You don't need to take a whole library with you."

Angela rolled her eyes. "I wouldn't need to choose which book to take if you bought me an e-reader. And if you don't have a cup of coffee with Grandma before we leave, we'll be the ones who'll be grilled like in a bad police series. Grandma always wants to know everything...like what's going on in our lives..." She lowered her voice, "...and in yours. And you never know what children say in their parents' absence."

Gillian's pulse quickened. "Excuse me?"

"Sheesh, Mom. I was only joking." Her brow furrowed. "There's not a lot to tell anyhow. Your life is pretty boring."

"Boring? Thank you very much." She couldn't help laughing. *You have no idea.*

"Yeah." Angela held her hands up in the air. "I mean with you staying home and being...you know, a mom and all. So are you having coffee with her before we leave or not?"

She didn't want to spend time with the dragon lady, but Angela was right. If she didn't have a cup of coffee with her, she would interrogate the kids. *Which she's probably going to do anyhow.* Still, not talking to her wouldn't be fair to the children. And—as awful as the timing was—she had wanted Margret to come and meet her on her own turf. "As I said, Angela, I'll be down in a minute, and yes, I'll have a cup of coffee with your grandmother," she said, praying to God to give her strength.

Gillian's stomach flip-flopped like an old tumble dryer as she looked down the wooden staircase that would take her to the living room, to Margret and an argument Gillian didn't want to have today. She put a hand on her treacherous stomach. Arguments with her mother-in-law were like a showdown in one of those bad westerns Derrick had liked to watch. The outcome in those movies was nearly always the same—the hero won...wounded, maybe close to death but he won. That was the big difference to arguing with Margret. The hero never won. Margret did, leaving behind wounded enemies and Gillian had been wounded too many times to count until she had given in and played the game—don't disagree, don't force your opinion or even better...don't have an opinion. Changing this habit was not only difficult but painful.

Breathe in. Breathe out. You're a grown woman. It's your life. Gillian bit her lip. *All right.* Straightening her shoulders she took another deep breath before she closed her eyes. *I am strong. I won against the blonde bimbo in the bar. I won Sam back. Sam.* The flip-flops in Gillian's stomach area slowed down a bit. *I can do this. I will meet Sam later tonight. And I will move out of this house and start a new life. Sam is back in my life.* Gillian put a hand on the banister, the wood under her hands cool to her touch. *I am strong. I am not alone.* She opened her eyes. *I am not alone.* Warmth spread through her. That was what she had to cling to—she wasn't alone. She had Sam at her side. *I can do this. I will do this. Margret has no power over my life. Not anymore.* Slowly Gillian walked down the staircase.

As she was about to set foot on the last step Tilde came out of the living room, rolling her eyes. "I brought her a cup of coffee," she hissed. "Unfortunately we are out of cyanide."

Gillian couldn't help but grin. At least there was a united front against Margret between the grown-ups in this household. "Wish me luck."

Tilde only lifted her eyebrows. "I'll make sure the kids are ready to leave."

"Thank you." Gillian ran a hand through her hair and went over to the door that led into the living room.

Margret stood at the window, looking out into the garden and onto the freshly mowed lawn.

Gillian flexed her fingers. The first pain had already set in after spending two hours with an activity she wasn't used to. Mowing the lawn was hard work. She entered the living room and cleared her throat. "Margret. Good afternoon."

"Indeed." Margret turned around, her eyes hard and blue like a frosty mountain stream. She crossed the distance between them and lightly grasped Gillian's elbows before dropping a single kiss to her right cheek. "How wonderful of you to join me."

The scent of *L'Aimant* and old money tickled Gillian's nose. "Unfortunately I don't have a lot of time before I have to leave."

Margret scoffed. "I'm sure you can spare a few minutes for your mother-in-law." She sat down in a chair, and crossed her legs, her eyes never leaving Gillian's. A cup of coffee stood on the side table next to the chair she had chosen.

"I see that Tilde already brought you some coffee. Do you care for anything else?"

"No, thanks dear. But maybe you would like to enlighten me as to who did mow your lawn? Do you have a new gardener?"

Here it comes. Gillian's heart beat a little faster but she plastered a smile on her face. "No, there's no new gardener. I did it."

Margret scrunched up her forehead. "You did what?"

"Mowed the lawn."

Margret opened her mouth and shut it again before finally saying, "Why? We could have sent Ricardo over. There are people who get paid for this kind of work. There was no reason for you to do this on your own."

Gillian shrugged. "The weather was nice. I had time. And it is a good work out."

Margret stared at Gillian as if she had just confessed murder. "I really don't know..." the sigh that followed was dramatic. Margret broke the eye contact and took up the cup of coffee. "Is this a new brand?"

Unsure why they were now talking about coffee instead of Margret drilling into her some more regarding the garden Gillian shook her head. "I don't think so."

"Well, it sure has a strange aftertaste." She set the cup down again.

Gillian bit the inside of her cheek, remembering Tilde's words about the lack of cyanide in the household. "Oh, maybe that's Tilde's new coffee. She went for something whisky flavored."

"Does she want to kill me or only my taste buds?"

Gillian rubbed her temples. "I need some coffee. Would you like me to bring you a new cup? This time without flavor?"

"No, thanks." Margret leaned back in her chair.

"I'll be back in a minute." Gillian fled to the kitchen. Caffeine was the last thing she needed. Her heart was beating fast enough as it was. But getting a cup of coffee was a good excuse for a short break. She took a look at her watch. A quarter past five. She had to leave in fifteen minutes. With a sigh she opened the cupboard and stared at the cups, her gaze wandering to the few mugs that had found their way into their household since Tilde lived here. Gillian grinned and picked up a pink mug that was so ugly that she had considered throwing it away on several occasions. Margret would hate it.

After filling it up with steaming coffee Gillian went back to the living room, as ready for round two as she would ever be.

Margret was sitting in her chair as if holding court, every inch of her looking as formidable and unbending as a queen.

Gillian sat down across from her mother-in-law and placed the pink mug close to Margret's cup—a cup that belonged to a set of the finest porcelain money could buy.

Margret's eyebrows nearly crawled off her forehead, her gaze fixed on the pink ugliness that was sitting on the table.

For a moment Gillian expected Margret to pick up the mug and throw it to the floor or do something equally dramatic.

"Did you accidentally pick up charity waste somewhere, dear?" Margret scoffed.

Biting her cheek Gillian leaned back in her chair. Antagonizing her mother-in-law was as clever as waving a red rag in front of a bull. "Why?" She looked at the mug. "Oh...you mean the mug?"

"Yes."

"Oh no. It was a present."

Margret's lip curled. "From a blind beggar?"

"No, from Tilde." Gillian picked the mug up and enjoyed the taste of the smooth, hot beverage. "So, how is James doing?"

Margret's jaw worked and Gillian expected another biting remark, fully prepared to counter it with an equally snarky remark.

"He's...he's well. Thank you." Margret crossed her legs. "Michael Sherman, the new managing partner, asked him to mentor two new associates. James enjoys working with the young lawyers. He says it makes him feel young again."

Gillian wasn't sure if she was more surprised that Margret let the mug issue go or that James was still working what sounded pretty much like a fulltime job. "I thought he wanted to reduce his workload?"

"He did cut down, but he's not made for staying home." Margret avoided Gillian's gaze.

"But what about your plans to travel to Europe?"

"It's a pleasure deferred. There's always next year." Margret picked at something on her blouse before focusing her eyes again on Gillian. "But enough about us. Tell me what you've been up to. We haven't spoken for such a long time."

Gillian fiddled with a corner of the table runner. "There's not much to tell. The children keep me busy."

"I met Ben Shacker in church," Margret said in the same tone she would use if talking about the weather. "He mentioned that he saw you at the zoo."

And there it was...so far, everything had been foreplay but now the first real gauntlet had been thrown. Gillian's flattened the cloth with slightly trembling fingers. What had Ben seen and more importantly, what had he told Margret? Gillian swallowed hard. *Don't defend yourself. Play it cool.* "Yes, the children and I had a lot of fun."

"He mentioned that you weren't alone." Margret's smile didn't reach her eyes.

"That's right. A friend was with us."

"Oh, do I know him?"

This was like a game of chess. Gillian shook her head. "It was a her, and no, you don't."

"Ben didn't mention it was a woman. He only said that he had no idea who your friend was."

"Ben doesn't know my friends. Why should he? He certainly isn't one of them."

"And I don't know her either?"

"No, you don't. And honestly, meeting Ben was rather unpleasant. I still can't believe that he left Winnie for that red-haired bimbo. Have you seen her lately? Winnie, I mean."

Margret frowned and sat up straighter. "We met for dinner last week. She's a strong woman."

"I guess she's stronger than I would have been in her position." Gillian had often wondered if Derrick would have left her at some point. If he would have decided that he wanted to be free of her and the children. *Guess I'll never find out.*

She leaned forward, her elbows on the table. "How many of your friends have been left by their husbands or been cheated on?"

Margret stiffened. "I don't know. Why?"

"That many?" Gillian chuckled dryly. "We wives stay at home and take care of the kids; we try to look good if we have to attend an event with our husbands, and we're supportive of their careers in every way. In return we get nice houses, nice dresses, and nice presents. I sincerely doubt that we get the better part of the deal. There is no space, no encouragement for us to evolve, to grow as people. Being attractive, quiet, and accepting isn't something I find fulfilling anymore."

The silence between them hung heavily in the air. Gillian's heart raced. She didn't even dare to look at Margret, sure that all she would receive was a sneer. If there was one rule that stood above all in that society she despised so much it was that one never talked openly about the dishonesty and hypocrisy that controlled their lives. Affairs weren't mentioned. One just ignored them. Gillian ran a finger over the table runner. If she remembered correctly this one had been a present—from Margret. As had been the chairs they were sitting on and some of the furniture in the house. Gillian put her hands in her lap. She would sell everything. Not only the house but the furniture. She would allow the children to take what they want. But the rest—

Margret cleared her throat. "I also met Rachel who told me that you're about to move into a new house."

All right. This changing of topics was a bit like driving slalom—one stayed on the same slope but had to be careful not to crash into anything. Time to change the game. No more tiptoeing around. Gillian looked up. "Yes. I actually signed yesterday. We're going to move in around three months."

Margret put her hand on her chest, her eyes wide. "So, it wasn't a bad joke of hers."

"No. I found a house that matches exactly what we need. I checked the background, I have the finances and the children like it as well."

"Gillian." Margret's voice got louder. "You can't just pack up and leave. You have to think of the children. This is your home."

"The children are what I am thinking about. I want them to enjoy life and find their own way. I want them to be happy and responsible. And no, this isn't my home, our home anymore. And it hasn't been for a very long time."

Margret's face had reddened slightly. "Happy? Why can't they be happy here?" She got up from her chair and stood, arms akimbo. "They have everything they could wish for. They go to a good school, they have their friends here, they have everything. Well, except their father."

"Their father." Gillian's jaw tightened. She had enough and got up from her chair as well. No way would she be forced to look up at Margret. "Their father was never here for them because he spent every minute of his free time with one of his 'lady friends'."

Margret's nostrils flared while she took a step forward. "There is no need to talk about this unpleasant subject. I would rather talk about what is going on in your life at the moment."

"Well, what would you like to know?"

"I don't understand—"

"Mom, Angela says I can't take my boomerang with me."

Gillian turned around.

Michael had entered the room, his brightly colored boomerang in his hand.

Angela stomped in behind him. "He's already taking his stupid remote control truck."

"The truck is not stupid. You are." He shot back, taking a step closer to his sister.

"Stop, you two. Now." Gillian waited until the bickering calmed down. This was her chance to get Margret out of the house. "Each of you can take one thing. You already have lots of books and toys at your grandparents' house. Now go and get your bags. You'll be leaving in two minutes."

"But—"

"No, Michael." Gillian forced herself to be calm, despite her still churning stomach and Margret's eagle eyes that drilled holes into her back. "There's no discussion. Go and get your things. Grandma is ready."

With slumped shoulders both of her kids left the room. Amazing. It was a shame that this didn't always work.

"Are you trying to get rid of me?"

Gillian turned around and faced Margret. "What?"

"We were in the middle of a conversation as I recall."

"Margret, the longer we let the children wait, the more restless they will get. And I'm sure you wouldn't want to have them run around your house and those antiques of yours like little energizer bunnies."

"You could join us. We could continue our talk while the children are in bed."

Over my dead body. "I'm sorry, but I'm meeting a friend in town."

"What about breakfast tomorrow morning, then? James could join us."

Gillian bit down on the bark that was trying to escape her mouth. Sure, Margret and James ganging up on her. That sounded just like the kind of breakfast she would love to join. "I can't. I'm staying in town overnight."

"Oh." For a moment Margret seemed lost for words. "This talk isn't over."

"Well, it is for today." And with that Gillian turned around and left Margret behind in the living room.

CHAPTER 20

GILLIAN CLOSED HER EYES, ENJOYING the wonderful pressure of strong fingers on her scalp. Her head was cushioned on a soft lap, she was lying on a comfortable couch, music playing quietly in the background, the taste of the pizza they had enjoyed earlier still lingering on her tongue. She couldn't possibly be any more comfortable...or content.

The anger about the conversation she had earlier with Margret still gnawed at her, but she had promised herself to stay in the moment and to enjoy whatever the evening might bring. With Sam. Tomorrow...well, tomorrow would be here soon enough, and then she could fret again. Tonight, she simply wanted to revel in the unexpected love and happiness she had found. With a moan, Gillian snuggled deeper into Sam.

"Sounds like you're enjoying yourself." Sam whispered.

"If you continue like this, I'll soon be asleep." She shifted until she was able to look into Sam's eyes.

"Oh, then I'd better stop."

"No. Don't even think about stopping. I would have to hurt you."

"Are we talking about good hurt or bad hurt?" Sam purred.

Gillian ran her hand along Sam's leg. "Want to find out?"

"Maybe." Sam's fingers wandered lower and began to lightly caress Gillian's earlobe.

The touch sent shivers down her spine.

"Want to show me?"

Desire mixed with a sense of calm determination washed over Gillian. She scooted up until she faced Sam. The cocky smile she saw made her stomach flutter. "Hey, you. Fancy meeting you here."

Sam chuckled. "Yeah, haven't been here for a long time, but I thought that maybe I'd get lucky tonight."

"What? Did you hope to find a hot date?" The playful banter between them dispersed the few dark clouds that had remained in Gillian's soul. All complications, problems, and misgivings vanished when she looked into Sam's eyes. Eyes that were filled with love and understanding—and mischief.

"Yes, I did. And so much more." She took Gillian's hands and planted butterfly kisses on each palm. "Here I am with the most beautiful, wonderful, intriguing, and sexy woman I've ever met. Lucky, lucky me." The smile on Sam's face was making Gillian all tingly inside. "To know that this isn't one-sided makes me deliriously happy."

"Oh, Sam." Something very warm and pleasant spread inside Gillian. She knew that Sam wasn't a sweet talker which made the words so much more meaningful. Gillian softly brushed her lips over Sam's before drawing back.

"Mm...that was nice." Sam licked her lips.

"You liked that?"

"I loved it. And I think I need more of where that came from."

"Do you now?" Her lips again sought out Sam's. But this time she didn't draw away. She deepened the kiss, explored without haste the hot sweetness, encouraged by the sensual moans coming from her lover. Their tongues were stroking, reaching, playing with each other. Skillful fingers found the sensitive skin behind her ears. Liquid heat scorched her from the inside. Breathing heavily, she broke the kiss. "Wow."

A soft smile played around Sam's lips. "Wow indeed. Anybody ever told you what a great kisser you are?"

Gillian laughed. "No. Never." Her mood grew sober. "The things I remember went more along the line of me being a 'cold fish'."

Anger blazed in Sam's eyes. "Who said that?"

"Derrick." She took a deep breath, not sure how much she should share. "He said that he... well, he said that a blow-up doll had more fire."

Those words had hurt. Deeply. She swallowed hard. "And one of the women I had a one-night stand with before we met said that it was no wonder that she wasn't able to have an orgasm with someone who was such a bad lover." Unable to look into Sam's eyes, Gillian picked at a piece of lint on the couch.

"Stupid assholes. Both of them." Gentle fingers cupped her jaw and turned her face upwards. "Gillian, I've had many lovers. It's not something I'm proud of. Not anymore. I'm proud that you're the one loving me. And there is no one that has ever made my blood boil the way you do. I could explode from a simple touch. You're a fantastic lover."

Tears sprang into Gillian's eyes. "Oh God." She let her head fall against Sam's shoulder and burrowed into the contact.

Soon a hand traced warm circles on her back. As much as she had enjoyed the sex with Sam right from the start, a part of her had still believed herself to be an inadequate lover. Sam had always been the one to take the initiative, to suggest things, or to inquire about Gillian's desires. Maybe it was time to let go of another part of her past. Looking up from her safe spot, she asked, "One touch from me and you explode?"

Sam chuckled. "Yes. Sometimes simply watching you walk in front of me makes me itchy as hell. You have a gorgeous ass."

Gillian felt heat rise on her cheeks. "Show me."

"What?" Sam looked confused down at her.

"Show me that one touch from me makes you explode." She rushed the words out so that she couldn't take them back.

Sam regarded her with a combination of amusement and gentleness. "Does that mean you would like to see my etchings?"

"What?"

"The drawings in my bedroom." A teasing grin played around Sam's mouth.

Gillian couldn't help giggling. "Give me a break. Did that line ever work for you?"

"As a matter of fact, yes. But I like this one even better." She pressed her hands to her heart. "Baby, your outfit would look great in a crumpled heap next to my bed."

Gillian took Sam's hands, unable to resist the urge to touch them, and rubbed her thumbs up and down calluses that were proof of her profession. "Ugh, that is so bad."

"No, it's true." Sam kissed her nose before she slightly brushed their lips together. "And I really, really want to make love to and with you tonight. I need you, Gillian. All of you. Your heart, your mind, and your body."

A shiver of excitement spread through Gillian's body like a fire-breather's plume of flame. She lifted her head until she found Sam's lips. This time her kiss was far from gentle and soon repaid in kind. Delicious heat bloomed between her legs. Maybe being daring wasn't a bad thing.

Sam broke the kiss. "Come." She held her hand out. "The etchings are in my bedroom. And I'm too old to have sex on the sofa. Not good for my back."

Gillian's mouth curved into a smile. Willingly she took the offered hand and followed.

When they entered the bedroom, her gaze wandered to the framed poster of Georgia O'Keeffe's *White Rose with Larkspur*. Not too long ago she had thought the poster unfitting for someone like Sam—someone so tough, so butch. Now she knew that the fragile and delicate flower simply mirrored a part of her lover's personality that was rarely shown to anyone. *But I'm allowed to see it.* And that made her proud and humble at the same time. "Some years ago I saw the original in Boston." Gillian pointed at the poster. "I think I stood in front of the painting for nearly half an hour and marveled at Georgia O'Keeffe's ability to capture the essence of the rose. She was a marvelous artist."

Sam nodded. "I had no idea who the artist was when I bought the poster, but the vibrant colors got to me. It's a beautiful thing. I like looking at it when I lie in bed. It touches something inside me." She brought her hands to Gillian's hips and drew her nearer. A smile spread over her face; her eyes were filled with a tender glow. "As do you, Gillian."

Sam covered her mouth with her own.

Gillian wrapped her arms around Sam and was soon lost in the feel of soft lips. An enthusiastic whimper escaped when her bottom lip was nipped. Parting her lips, she allowed Sam's tongue inside. Blood pulsed in her ears, her excitement surging with every stroke of their tongues. She didn't think she'd ever get enough of kissing Sam. This was what she wanted, whom she needed.

Gillian's body began to thrum like a high-tension wire when Sam cupped her breasts and began to softly knead them, sending a light, hot shock through her body. "Don't...don't stop."

"Never."

Gillian's hand wandered to the inside of Sam's thigh and slowly higher to the crotch of the jeans. She began to massage the soft flesh under the stiff fabric, producing irresistible sounds from Sam. Sounds that affirmed the earlier spoken words about the power Gillian held over Sam.

An idea formed in her head. Deciding to go with a spontaneous impulse for once in her life, she broke the kiss and took a step away from Sam.

"What...everything okay?"

Gillian's chest quivered when she took a breath. She could do it, could take the initiative. "I'll never forget the first time I saw you in that club," she said, "all tough-looking and so very, very sexy." She slowly opened her dress, slid out of it, and let the garment fall to the floor.

Sam's eyes widened. Her breathing hitched.

Knowing full well how much watching her strip turned Sam on, she couldn't hide a smile. "I also remember you telling me to take my bra off." She undid her bra and let it drop next to her dress.

Sam's hungry gaze fixed on her breasts.

Gillian's nipples hardened. Intoxicated by Sam's response, she felt herself getting wetter.

"And my panties." She added her underwear to the pile on the floor and brushed her fingers over her belly, enjoying the little jolts that the touch created. "Then you asked me how I wanted to come." Gillian chuckled. "No one had ever asked me that before. I was so perplexed and had no idea what to say." She brought her hands to her breasts and, with slow movements, pinched her own nipples. Heat built all over her skin, inside her. Her voice sounded rough to her own ears. "Tonight I know what I want." And it was true. She did.

"Then tell me." Sam licked her lips.

She stepped closer and opened the two top buttons of Sam's shirt with trembling fingers. She planted a gentle kiss on the soft flesh in front of her before she looked up into chocolate brown eyes. "I want you to tell me what you want, what you like. You always put my needs first. Tonight I want you to tell me what you want."

Sam stiffened.

Gillian's stomach tightened to a knot. Had she overstepped? She opened her mouth to take her words back.

But Sam beat her to it. "I..." She cleared her throat. "Wow, this is a first." A warm hand cupped Gillian's cheek. "No one ever asked me that before."

"Really?"

Sam nodded. "Really."

Gillian gathered her courage. "Why wouldn't...?"

Sam frowned. "Most people have a certain image about butch women and how to act around them."

"Oh." Gillian frowned. "But I really want to know. Please tell me."

Hesitantly Sam bent her head and whispered into Gillian's ear. "Actually, there is something I have wanted to do since the first time we met."

Gillian's knees nearly buckled when Sam began to tease her earlobe with her tongue.

Strong hands held her. The teasing stopped. "I would love to be inside you...as close to you as possible. So, if you'd really like to know what I want..." She hesitated for a moment, and then dropped her voice even more. "I'd like to use a toy, a dildo. I want to be inside of you, want to look into your eyes. I love seeing you when you come...but it's okay if you don't want to."

Surprised by the insecurity in those last words, Gillian didn't need to think twice. "I'd like to try it." Truth was that she had thought about the possibilities of toys before. And the idea of Sam with a dildo...Gillian's stomach dropped. She'd love to try it.

"Yes?"

The insecurity Gillian saw in Sam's eyes tugged at her heart. She nodded. "Yes. I love making love with you. And this...well, it sounds like it could be fun."

"It can be. Absolutely. Wow." Sam didn't waste any time and stripped out of her shirt. She was naked underneath, without a bra.

Gillian drank in the sight of the broad shoulders, the strong arms, and the proud breasts. A tribal tattoo covered most of Sam's right upper arm. The need to touch the tattoo, to feel those pert breasts burned inside her, but she forced herself to stay still.

With lightning speed Sam stripped out of her jeans and out of her panties. She stood looking like a proud warrior of olden times.

Unable to hold back any longer, Gillian reached out and covered Sam's breasts. Hot, soft flesh filled her hands. "I love your breasts."

Sam sucked in a breath when Gillian began to trace circles around the tips of her lover's breasts. Seeing how the buds tightened under her fingers, how affected Sam was by her touch... this was heaven and it filled her with fire.

"Oh, Gillian." Sam's face was flushed, eyes half-closed. Unable to be still for long, one of her hands began to play through soft curls before tickling a sensitive spot beside Gillian's clit.

Gillian gasped.

"Lie down, honey."

Fighting against the dizziness that cursed through her Gillian made it to the bed and lay down on the duvet. The cloth underneath was rough on her sensitive skin.

Sam walked to a small wooden trunk that stood half-hidden beside the wardrobe and opened the lid. She took a harness, a bottle of lube, and a light blue dildo out of the trunk and put them on the nightstand, before turning to Gillian. A soft smile played around Sam's lips. "You take my breath away. You know that, right?" Her gaze intensified when she crawled onto the bed with slow, graceful movements. "Hi there." She bent down and planted a kiss on Gillian's knee.

Goosebumps spread out all over Gillian's body. Her breathing hitched when a lick on the inside of the knee followed the kiss.

Soon Sam was caressing her way up Gillian's body again, not stopping too long at any point but kissing and licking every available inch of skin.

Gillian was about to explode. Never before had she felt so loved, so lusted after. A moan that soon turned into a growl escaped.

Chuckling, Sam settled between Gillian thighs, supporting herself on her elbows. A beaming smile spread over her face. "You're adorable." A kiss on Gillian's nose followed. "I'm so thankful to have you in my life." A slow, soft kiss on her lips followed that statement.

Gillian needed this. Needed Sam. She swallowed against the knot in her throat. "I love you." Her hand trembled when she reached out to caress Sam's cheek. The skin under her fingers was smooth and warm. She gently guided Sam's face closer. "Totally."

The kiss that followed was welcoming and hot. The body above hers trembled mirroring her own overflowing emotions.

Soon Gillian's whole body burned from soft touches and hot kisses. Full, naked breasts pressed against hers. Running her hands over Sam's back, the muscles flexed and twitched beneath her fingers. She loved the taste of earth and salt that was so typical of Sam. Soft flesh over muscles, hard as iron.

Hungry for Sam, for everything she had to offer, Gillian couldn't get enough of touching her. But soon, too soon, Sam dropped feather light kisses down Gillian's breasts, her belly, her hips, the top of her thighs. Then fingers dipped into her wetness, swirling around her folds, the nub of her clitoris.

Gillian moaned, raising her hips to enhance the contact, but the fingers drew away.

"You're so wet. For me?" She asked.

"Only for you," Gillian replied, her mouth almost too dry for speech.

"Good answer." Sam's fingers returned to the needy spot, playing around her clit, driving her crazy. Good crazy, but crazy nevertheless.

Her hands clenched the sheet when Sam's finger slid inside her vagina. This felt so damn good. Soon Sam followed with a second finger, hitting sensitive spots in deliberate teasing. Just when Gillian got used to the sensation and wanted to get lost in the wild feelings, Sam withdrew both fingers.

A whimper of disappointment escaped Gillian. "No."

"Oh, baby, we're just getting started." Sam planted a soft kiss on her clit, followed by a gentle lick that made Gillian jump. "I want to take my time tonight. I'm just not sure if I can." Sam took the harness and attached the blue dildo. With experienced movements, she strapped it on.

The sight was...weird. Gillian swallowed, suddenly not so sure if using an artificial blue penis was something she would enjoy.

"Hey, are you okay?"

"I...Yes." But she couldn't draw her eyes away from the blue "thing" dangling from Sam. "Well, maybe..."

"We don't need to do this. Honestly." Sam put her hand on the dildo.

"No. Wait." Gillian bit her lip. As much as this was starting to freak her out—the knowledge that this was what Sam wanted stopped her from shying away from a new experience. "It's just...I need time to get used to it." She stared at the dildo. "This."

"All right." She frowned. "You sure? I don't mind if we don't go through with it."

"Yes. Just give me a few minutes. Please."

Sam's hand stroked lightly over Gillian's cheek. "Take all the time you need, honey." Her tone was as soft as the smile on her face. She took a step back and opened the drawer on the nightstand. "Maybe you would like to help me?" She took a condom out of the drawer and held it in her hand.

Gillian nodded and took the condom with shaking hands. This she had done before. "I've never touched one."

"A dildo?"

"Yes."

A small smile tugged on Sam's lips. "So, you're a virgin?"

"Only a dildo virgin." Gillian took the condom out and slowly rolled it over the dildo. She put some pressure on the toy.

Sam's hissed.

Gillian let go of the dildo. "I'm sorry. Did I hurt you?"

"No. That was...wow. Nice."

"Oh." Encouraged by those words Gillian took the dildo in her hand again and pushed the base a bit more firmly before releasing the pressure again.

A gentle hand cupped hers. "You want to be careful here." Sam gasped. "I *wanna* make you come first. Lie back."

And with those words all fears vanished into thin air. She lay down.

Soon tender fingers ran through her pubic hair and reached her clit. Fingertips were teasing hot, slick warmth. For a second, Gillian tensed, holding her breath.

"Relax. Trust me." Sam slowly began a rubbing motion on the side of Gillian's clitoral shaft.

Gillian moaned. She closed her eyes. This was a stimulation she deeply enjoyed. Waves of pleasure began to build inside her.

"You're so wet."

"Yes." The touch...Sam's touch...was driving her mad.

"Open your eyes, baby."

She did, instantly captured by eyes that were almost black with arousal. The connection between them was something Gillian had never experienced before. This here, between them, was so much more than sex. It was a connection that made her feel loved, cherished, and...wet.

"Could you?" Sam took hold of the bottle of lube.

With trembling fingers Gillian took the bottle. Where moments ago she had been nervous and unsure...now her head and heart were filled with only one thing—anticipation. With a pleasant shiver, she applied plenty of lube around the dildo's head. She swallowed around a lump in her throat. "I'm not afraid anymore."

"No?"

"No!"

"Good." Sam's fingers went back to what they were doing before, driving all coherent thoughts out of Gillian's head.

She let the bottle fall next to the bed.

The smooth head of the dildo slid through her wetness, making her gasp. Through heavy-lidded eyes, she watched Sam use her hand to guide the dildo slowly inside.

This was so good. A moan escaped her throat.

Sam took her time and drew it out again.

Gillian nearly cried out from the sensation of loss. "Please."

"I'm right here. I'm right here with you," Sam promised in a whisper, this time pushing steadily forward until the dildo was buried inside Gillian. It filled her, stretched her, then Sam slowly began to thrust. With each stroke, a new wave of pleasure sizzled through Gillian.

"You feel so damned hot." Sam's voice, almost a growl, penetrated Gillian's fog of bliss.

She hissed when Sam hit an especially sensitive spot, a pleasure that only increased when Sam slowly rotated her hips during her thrusts. Gillian trembled. This wouldn't take long. She was already tumbling toward the edge.

Throughout it all, Sam's gaze never left hers. At each new stroke, Gillian had to fight against the urge to close her eyes. The muscles of Sam's back and shoulders quivered under her hands. Soon she found a rhythm, anticipating each stroke, longing for it, grinding against the dildo as Sam thrust into her. Soon the familiar fluttering in her belly began. An ocean of sensation emerged within her, overwhelmed her.

Clinging to Sam's shoulders, she couldn't delay it any longer. Fire surged, shooting like lightning through her body, wave after wave after wave until her bones and muscles seemed totally liquefied. At last, vaguely aware of Sam stopping her thrusts and withdrawing the toy, she let out her breath in a deep sigh. "Oh, dear Lord."

Sam's laugh was gentle. "Nope, not exactly."

Her vision hazy, Gillian watched Sam get rid of the toy and the harness before joining her on the bed again.

"You're so beautiful, so vulnerable when you come. I love watching you." Sam pushed some hair away from Gillian's face and kissed her slowly. "You okay?"

"Yes. More than okay." Gillian ran her thumb over Sam's lips, her whole body sluggish and relaxed. A grin spread across her face when Sam took the thumb into her mouth and started to suck on it. "Come here." She didn't have to ask twice and soon was snuggled against Sam, who was stretched out full-length beside her. "I need a moment. That was...phenomenal. Thank you."

"Mm...phenomenal indeed. That was unbelievable. I felt so close to you."

For a moment, no more words were spoken. Gillian lightly caressed Sam's skin, tracing the tendons in her arm, the small scars around her wrist, and the calluses on her hand. "I love touching you." She took the hand and kissed every finger. "I love being with you." She turned and looked into Sam's eyes, a thought forming in her brain. "Tell me, is this harness a 'one size fits all' thing?"

Gillian slowly drifted awake. Reveling in the warmth and comfort of Sam's body tucked next to hers was like floating in warmth. Last night had been perfect. And, boy, had she rocked Sam's world with their little role reversal. Gillian felt her face get hot thinking about all the different ways they had each other, kissed each other, loved each other until the early hours of the morning.

"You awake?" Sam asked, her voice rough from sleep.

Gillian chuckled. "No. I think I'm still dreaming. Reality can't be this good."

"Then don't wake me. I'm still floating in some kind of unbelievable bliss." Sam closed her eyes again.

Gillian ran her fingers up and down Sam's back until goosebumps followed her path. As much as she wanted to stay like this for the rest of the day or even better, the rest of her life, she couldn't. A glance at the alarm clock showed that it was already late morning. No wonder she was tired; sleep hadn't come for either of them until just a few hours ago. "Sam?"

"Mm? Just keep going."

"I'm sorry, honey, but I have to leave in two hours, and I thought...well, maybe you'd like to have breakfast together." She held her breath, still unsure how much reality Sam was willing to accept. Instead of having another marathon sex session or at least spending the day together, they would have to work around Gillian's schedule and her kids' demands.

Sam gazed at her, a grin on her face. "Well, we could risk a look into my fridge."

"Yes, we could." Gillian grimaced. "But I'm not really that fond of pickled eggs."

"O ye of little faith. That was before I did some major shopping for my favorite girl." Sam yawned heartily. "Good sex always leaves me starving the next morning. And I had some mind-blowing sex last night, let me tell ya."

Gillian kissed her gently. "Yeah, me too. And the funny thing is...you were there, too." She rolled away from Sam's pinching fingers until she nearly fell out of bed. Laughter filled the room. "Stop it. I need to use the bathroom."

Sam slowly stretched her glorious body. "All right, I'll make coffee in the meantime."

"Thank you." Gillian got up from the bed, feeling slightly sore, but every little pain she felt was worth the love she had found. For the first time she was really, truly positive that being with Sam would work out, and the thought was a damn good one.

CHAPTER 21

WHITE FLAKES FLOATED DOWN TO the frozen ground. Sam leaned her forehead against the cool glass and gazed out into the garden. Everything was covered in a light blanket of white, untouched and pristine. Only a cat's footprints were disturbing the frost and snow that covered the grass. Sam sighed. Living in the suburbs really had its advantages. Downtown Springfield sure wouldn't look like something out of a winter dream and more like the marriage between a mud hole and some abused snow.

"Hey, Sam. Do you want your eggs scrambled or fried?" Tilde's voice intruded on her thoughts.

"Fried," she shouted back, causing the glass in front of her to fog up.

"Sunny side up or down?"

"Down."

"All right."

If the white fluffy stuff continued to come down like this...maybe she could build a snowman with the children later on. Well, with Michael. Angela was probably too old for that kind of stuff.

She saw Gillian's reflection in the glass before arms found their way around Sam's waist. A soft kiss landed on her neck.

"Good morning." Gillian's breath tickled her skin. "What an amazing sight to wake up to."

Sam laid her hands over Gillian's. "Yeah. It's going to be a bitch driving home later today. But it sure looks nice."

"Yes, the winter wonderland outside is a nice view as well...but I meant you, being in my home in the morning." Another kiss found its way to Sam's sensitive skin. "Only seeing you in my bed waking up could have topped this."

Sam pressed her body into Gillian's, enjoying the warmth, comfort, and thrill that coursed through her every single time she touched her girlfriend. "I like being here. With you."

"I like having you here."

Sam turned around. "The view from here is even better."

"You sweet talker you." Gillian's eyes sparkled like sapphires.

Sam put a kiss on Gillian's nose. "Just telling the truth as I see it."

"Is that it?" she frowned.

"I bet that the children will run into this room at the exact moment my lips touch yours."

Gillian grimaced. "All right. You have a point."

They had agreed to take it slow. After Thanksgiving, Gillian had told her children that Sam was not only a girlfriend but her 'girlfriend.' They had spent more time together and last night had been the first sleepover—with Sam staying in the guestroom and waking up alone in a huge bed and a strange room.

"Breakfast is ready."

"Having a maid is not half bad."

Gillian pinched Sam's waist. "She's no maid. She's an au pair."

"Yeah, well. Same difference. But she sure comes in handy."

"That she does." Gillian took Sam's hand. "Come on. Let's sit down."

They crossed the hall, holding hands. When Sam wanted to withdraw hers before stepping into the kitchen Gillian didn't let go but gave her a squeeze.

Three pairs of eyes welcomed them—one with kindness, one with childlike joy, and one with caution. Sam sighed. Angela had a harder time accepting what was happening than Michael. She restrained herself around Sam, not trusting her. At least she wasn't openly hostile. She tried to imagine what would melt Chloe if Victoria showed up with a new prospective partner. Patience and kind perseverance with a healthy dose of humor would probably be the key. *It's worth it. She's worth it.* "Good morning."

Gillian gave her hand one last squeeze before letting go and sitting down at the table.

Sam took a deep breath before seeking Angela's gaze. "Hey, is it okay if I sit here?" She pointed at the empty chair next to the girl.

A polite smile appeared on Angela's face. "Sure, if you want to."

"Thanks." Sam sat down, smiling at the wink she received from Gillian.

Tilde put a plate with two fried eggs in front of Sam before sitting down as well. *"Smaklig måltid!"*

"That is Swedish and means 'enjoy your meal'", Angela explained.

"Thanks." Sam's gaze wandered over the table. She whistled through her teeth. Amazing. She couldn't remember the last time she'd seen a breakfast table that held such a variety of food. She usually had a cup of coffee more or less on the go and maybe a sandwich that she picked up somewhere. But this...wow. There was everything from scrambled eggs to bacon to cheese and fresh fruits as well as cereal...it was more like having brunch in a hotel. "Do you always feast like this in the mornings?"

Angela shook her head. "Nope. Only on Sundays." She dumped some cereal in a bowl and filled it up with milk.

"Sam?" Michael's smile was sweet. Very sweet.

"Yes."

"Do you like snow?"

Oh, he's good. "I do."

A grin appeared on Gillian's face but she kept her eyes glued to her plate.

"I do too."

"Well, then you're one lucky boy. I don't think it will stop snowing anytime soon."

Michael bit his lip. "Would you like to go outside after breakfast?"

"Outside?" Sam tried her best to act innocent even though she was pretty sure she knew what he was up to.

He nodded "Yes."

"I bet he wants to build a snowman. All kids do." Angela spit out, her distaste for childish activities obvious.

"I didn't."

"Sure, you do."

"Actually, I'd love to build a snowman." Sam turned to Angela. "And maybe you could help us?"

There was no spark of interest in her eyes. "I'm not a child anymore."

I hate puberty. Maybe a different approach..."I saw your drawings yesterday. You're really creative. And I think it would be cool if our snowman was different from the rest of the neighborhood. They'll all be jealous because ours will be so much cooler."

Angela tilted her head a bit. "How different?"

"Well, I don't know. I'm not the creative genius here." Sam put her fork down. "What do you think?"

The ringing of the phone stopped whatever Angela wanted to say.

"I'll get it." Gillian got up.

"Good morning, Margret." Her voice definitely sounded more businesslike than usually.

"Grandma." Angela groaned.

Tilde grimaced.

There was no way in hell that Sam would comment. Her dislike for the woman she hadn't even met was huge but she'd keep her opinion to herself.

"No, we can't." Gillian shook her head. "I told you that we'll be spending Christmas Eve and the following day at home."

Oh. That isn't going to go over well with the dragon lady. She kept her eyes on Gillian.

"No, Margret. We spent Thanksgiving with you. And I told you then that we're not going to celebrate Christmas with you."

Gillian rolled her eyes. "We're not alone. Tilde will stay over Christmas and Sam is here."

The voice on the other side of the phone was so loud that even Michael looked up.

Sam winced.

Angela poked her with the elbow. "Maybe we could build a snowwoman instead of a snowman."

"That's an interesting idea." Maybe they could build two snowwomen who were kissing each other. Then Gillian wouldn't need to worry about how to come out to the neighborhood. "But what about building something that—"

Gillian's voice was louder and held a cutting edge. "Well, Margret. I'm sorry for destroying your Christmas but I won't change our plans. The children will spend two days with you if you still want that but we'll spend the rest of the time here as a family."

Oh shit. That was not going well. Sam held her breath. As much as she had been looking forward to spending Christmas here...

Gillian's face reddened. "The children and Sam are my family and Tilde is a part of it as well."

Sam wondered if it would help or make things worse if she got up and—

"You will have to get used to me being in a relationship with a woman. That is not going to change." She slammed the receiver down, her breathing heavy.

Sam got up and went over to where she stood with a trembling chin. "Hey, come here." She opened her arms and Gillian took the offer, nearly burying herself into Sam.

For a moment no one said anything. Not a sound came from the table and Sam had no idea what to say with the children in the same room.

"Hey," Michael broke the silence. "You're under the mistletoe. You have to kiss each other."

Sam looked up. He was right. Well, not exactly. They stood around half a foot away from one of the sprigs Tilde has distributed throughout the house.

Gillian's chuckle sounded a bit strained. "I don't even want to know how my six-year old son knows about mistletoes and kissing."

"I bet you don't want to know what else he knows." Sam planted a kiss on her head. "And I'm not kissing you with Angela's eyes drilling holes in my back."

Gillian looked up into her eyes. "I..."

Even though it hurt to form the words, she had to say it, "If it's easier for you then I'm fine if you spend Christmas—"

"No," Gillian tightened her jaw. "It's not easier. I want to spend Christmas with you."

"All right." She smiled. "I'd love to spend Christmas here."

Gillian took a deep breath and stepped out of the embrace. "Good. That's settled then." She took Sam's hand. "Let's finish breakfast and enjoy the day."

"Fine with me. Let's talk later." Sam turned around.

Angela beamed at her. "So, about the snowwomen. What about building a movie scene? Like something out of Harry Potter?"

Michael jumped up from his chair. "Yes!"

"Cold, cold, cold." Gillian rubbed her hands together against the chill that was invading her clothes. They had really pulled it off. A Harry

Potter snowman stood next to Hermione and Dumbledore, three sticks protruding from where their arms where and pointing at a creature that could be interpreted as a cat, a dog, or a shrunken Death Eater. They had been running out of snow toward the end.

"Look at that." Sam's nose was as red as Michael's and her grin matched his as well.

Tilde and Angela were putting the finishing touches on the Death Eater.

Gillian couldn't remember the last time they had had so much fun together. "All right." She clapped her hands. "Tilde, you take the pictures while I go and prepare the hot cocoa for us."

"I'll help you." Sam followed her inside.

A few minutes later, the milk was simmering on the stove while Sam prepared coffee for Tilde and herself.

"Oh, nice and warm." Gillian put her hands over the pot that held the milk. "I thought my hands were going to fall off."

Sam chuckled. "Yeah, that is absolutely the most ambitious thing I've ever built out of snow." She closed the distance between them, took Gillian's hands in hers, and rubbed them gently. "How are you doing?"

There was caution in her brown eyes. Caution linked with a fear that Gillian hoped would disappear with time. "I'm doing good." She leaned forward and put a gentle kiss on Sam's lips, lingering for a moment. "And if I have to choose

between you and someone else, something else...
I'll always choose the children and you. Always."

"But it hurts you—the way you have to fight?"

Gillian sighed. "I'm not a fighter but I'll never back down when it comes to you. I'll always fight for my family."

"I'm family?" Tears were forming in Sam's eyes.

Gillian reached out and cupped Sam's cheek. "Yes, you are part of the family. My family. Our family. Got it?"

"Got it."

A touch of caution remained in Sam's eyes. Gillian knew it would take time to build trust and prove to her that those words were not empty promises but, luckily for them, they had all the time in the world.

EPILOGUE

SIX MONTHS LATER

The flesh beneath Sam's fingers was hot. Her heart raced, her muscles trembled. This was heaven. Or at least as close to heaven as she would ever get. Minutes ago she had finally managed to pin Gillian up against the kitchen door and now she had one hand on a soft breast while the fingers of her other one were rubbing small circles over Gillian's clit. "I. Love. You."

Gillian moaned. "Yes. Yes."

"I want you to come. And I want to see you explode."

A groan was her answer.

Sam slid two fingers inside Gillian. So slick, so wonderful.

A door banged.

"Shit." Gillian's eyes were wide.

"No. No." Sam whimpered and pressed closer against Gillian. "They aren't supposed to be back before five. This is not fair." She had wanted to cross sex in the kitchen off her bucket list. *Damn. Damn. Damn.*

Gillian exhaled audibly. "I'm sorry, sweetheart."

"Me too."

"Mom? Where are you?"

"It could have been worse." Gillian smiled. "Two minutes later and I would have considered giving them up for adoption." With that she planted a soft kiss on Sam's lips and stepped away. "We're in the kitchen."

Sam rubbed her face, trying to calm down. Gillian's smell was all over her fingers. *Shit.*

She confined the traitorous hands into the pockets of her jeans. A trip to the bathroom was in order. As soon as possible. Dating a mother of two really had its downsides. They had agreed to not be too explicit around the children. Occasional kissing was okay, holding hands was fine, and hugs and cuddles were mandatory. Anything PG or above, however, was not.

The smile on Angela's face couldn't have been brighter. "I got the new book. Look." She held out a cover that showed a dragon and a girl with a sword on it. "Grandma bought it."

"I'm happy that you're happy, dear." Margret's fake smile was darkening the kitchen. Her eyes found Sam's. "Hello. What a nice surprise."

Sam sucked in a breath and stiffened. *What's she doing here?* The dragon lady was a total bitch whenever their paths crossed. Tonight was supposed to be the first barbecue of the season and they had planned to have fun and family time. And now she was here. Sam lowered her eyes to the floor, slowly counting to ten. She would stay calm whatever was thrown her way.

A hand around her waist drew her closer, until her side was pressed against Gillian's. Sam looked up.

The smile on Gillian's face sent several messages—the most important one being 'I'm here at your side.'

Sam couldn't help but mirror the smile.

"Mom, look. Look." Michael stormed into the kitchen, a tablet in his hands. "Grandma gave me an iPad."

The hand around Sam's waist tightened. "That is great, Michael. Why don't you put it down in your room? And Angela?" Gillian addressed her daughter. "Please take your book to your room. We're going to start the barbecue a bit earlier than planned. Michael still has to put the finishing touches on the deck. With Sam."

"Yeah." Michael turned around and hurried to his room.

"And Angela, you wanted to paint the new chair. If you do it now there's a chance that you can use it tomorrow."

"Oh, yeah. That would be great." She left without another glance at her grandmother.

The laser beams coming out of Margret's eyes were meant to pulverize but the smile on Gillian's face didn't falter for one second. "Thank you for bringing the children back." She looked at Sam. "I'll start with the salad. I thought maybe a light green one and I prepared the potato salad this morning. Is that all right? Or would you like anything else?"

God. She wanted to kiss Gillian senseless. But that would have to wait until tonight. "No, thanks. Steak, potato salad, and a cold beer sound perfectly fine to me."

A muscle in Margret's left cheek ticked. "Gillian." Her voice had the quality of fingernails on a chalkboard. "Do you have a minute?"

"I'm so sorry Margret. But no. We really need to get on with the preparations if we don't want to eat late. Maybe you could give us a call the next time you'd like to come over?"

Sam had to bite the inside of her cheek to keep from laughing. This was priceless.

"I don't—"

"That's right, Margret. You don't get it. But that is your problem." She planted a kiss on Sam's cheek before facing her former mother-in-law again. "Sam is part of this family. She shares our lives. The children love her. And I love her. So, if you want to stay in the children's lives you better try harder."

"Excuse me?" Margret's facial expression reminded Sam a lot of the moment several weeks ago when Michael had sucked on a lemon.

Gillian didn't respond. She just stared at Margret as if daring her to say more, to finally cross the line.

Margret opened her mouth but no words followed. Her lips clamped together before she turned around and left the kitchen. Shortly afterward, the slamming of the front door echoed through the house like a gunshot.

"Wow." Sam faced Gillian. "Wow and double wow."

"What?" Gillian frowned. "I'm fed up with her obnoxious behavior. We've tried to be nice. We've invited them to dinner. Several times. First they didn't show up, and then they started fight after fight." The dark look on Gillian's face was the one reserved for whenever they talked about her parents-in-law. "Enough is enough. Either they come around or not. But I won't try anymore. I think she realized today that no matter how expensive the presents she can't win against us."

"Us?" Happiness filled Sam.

"Yes. Us. We are their family." Gillian said "I won't ban their grandparents from their lives. But I won't make excuses for them anymore."

Sam tingled all over. Gillian had said 'us' and meant it. "Thank you."

"No." Gillian shook her head. "No. Thank you for coming into my life."

"I think we found each other."

"Yes, I think we did."

The smell of grilled meat and charcoal hit Gillian's nose as she stepped through the double glass doors, balancing two salad bowls and a plate of cheese on a tray. Sunlight slid through the trees' canopy, bathing the newly installed wooden deck and the new teak furniture in a warm light. It was a wonderful May day with just a slight breeze. Perfect for a family barbecue.

She walked over to where Sam and Michael stood at the glowing grill, talking about the perfect wooden deck they had built over the past couple of weeks. Michael sported two Band-Aids on his fingers but had otherwise escaped unharmed.

"Hello, beautiful."

Michael made a gagging noise.

Sam shot a grin his way. "I'm so looking forward to you having your first girlfriend."

Michael gagged. "Never. I hate girls."

Sam ruffled his hair. "Yeah, well. Believe me… that is going to change."

The look on his face reminded Gillian of Margret's earlier today. "How much longer do those need? I'm starving." She pointed at the steaks that were slowly searing on the grill.

Sam took a gulp of her beer. "The burgers are just about ready."

"Great. Michael, go and get Angela, please."

"Okay." Michael sat his glass down and hurried inside.

"Teasing him when he shows up with a girl will be great." With a twinkle in her eyes, Sam tipped the bottle and emptied half of it in one swallow.

"And I'm looking forward to you teaching him all he needs to know about contraception."

"Me? Why me?"

"Why not?" Gillian couldn't help but laugh at the panicked expression on Sam's face. "Want a kiss?"

Sam's mouth curved into a slow, satisfied smile. "Always."

Gillian's mouth moved gently over Sam's, not deepening the contact. "I'm looking forward to continuing what we started earlier."

"Behind closed doors."

"Absolutely."

Sam chuckled.

With lots of laughter Angela and Michael stepped out on the deck.

Sam planted another kiss on Gillian's lips before grabbing a plate. "All right. Who's hungry?"

Gillian sighed. Maybe her life wasn't all happily ever after—but it was damn near perfect.

ABOUT EMMA WEIMANN

Emma Weimann knew at an early age that she wanted to make a living as a writer. She knew exactly how and where she wanted to write the books that would pay for her house at the beach and the desk with a view of the ocean.

Even though she has had those dreams for over thirty years now, neither the house nor the desk exist. Not yet. But she's making a living producing books, not just as a writer but also as a publisher, establishing Ylva Verlag and its international pendant, Ylva Publishing, in 2011 and 2012.

Connect with Emma Weimann online

Blog: http://emmaweimann.wordpress.com/
E-mail: emma.weimann@gmx.net

OTHER BOOKS FROM YLVA PUBLISHING

http://www.ylva-publishing.com

WHEN THE CLOCK STRIKES THIRTEEN

LOIS CLOAREC HART, L.T. SMITH, EMMA WEIMANN, JOAN ARLING, DIANE MARINA, ERZABET BISHOP, R.G. EMANUELLE

ISBN: 978-3-95533-155-9
Length: 175 pages

Midnight Messages by Lois Cloarec Hart

Luce Sheppard can't ignore it any longer. She has to make a decision and time grows short. But refusing to make a decision is a decision, and she retires to bed, prepared to accept the results of her non-decision. That night an unexpected midnight visitor lands on her doorstep. Keira Keller, a distraught teenager, has lost her way home after a disastrous party. Luce steps in to help and in doing so receives answers to questions she didn't know she'd asked.

Batteries Not Included by L.T. Smith

Alex Stevens is a workaholic and a loner. Nothing and nobody can get past the cool exterior and solitary walls she has painstakingly created.

Until one night in October. One night that makes her step back and reassess what it means to be alive.

Lost and Found by Emma Weimann

Laura Sullivan flees to her grandparents' old cottage to escape the haunting memories of finding her brother in bed with her girlfriend. But even in rural Ireland, tranquility is easier to find than peace—especially when she meets an otherworldly being that leaves her a reminder she didn't count on.

Chrysalis by Joan Arling

Tara is a nice little girl. Her friends, on the other hand, are... peculiar... A breeze of a story. Or the other way 'round.

Sisters of the Moon by Diane Marina

The week before Halloween, Nicole joins her friends on a local ghost tour. In addition to visiting spooky sights and haunted grounds, she meets an enticing woman who makes her spine tingle. Who is the mysterious stranger? And how will the encounter end?

Wolf Moon by Erzabet Bishop

Seeking diversion from her job as a bookstore manager, Lindsay goes to a Halloween party at a convention center—and finds much more than she bargained for.

Werewolf Detective Taggert responds to a bomb threat at the convention center. An explosive situation, especially when raw chemistry hits them full force.

Can Lindsay open her heart and accept the fierce love of a red-hot shifter, or will they go their separate ways?

Love Bites by R.G. Emanuelle

New Orleans. Vampires. Jodi goes to the former and finds the latter. She feels a mysterious pull that leads her to The Big Easy and to freedom, passion, and the startling revelation of what having too many daiquiris can make her do.

HEARTS AND FLOWERS BORDER

(revised edition)

L.T. SMITH

ISBN: 978-3-95533-179-5
Length: 291 pages

A visitor from her past jolts Laura Stewart into memories—some funny, some heart-wrenching. Thirteen years ago, Laura buried those memories so deeply she never believed they would resurface. Still, the pain of first love mars Laura's present life and might even destroy her chance of happiness with the beautiful, yet seemingly unobtainable Emma Jenkins.

Can Laura let go of the past, or will she make the same mistakes all over again?

Hearts and Flowers Border is a simple tale of the uncertainty of youth and the first flush of love—love that may have a chance after all.

COMING HOME
(revised edition)

LOIS CLOAREC HART

ISBN: 978-3-95533-064-4
Length: 371 pages

A triangle with a twist, *Coming Home* is the story of three good people caught up in an impossible situation.

Rob, a charismatic ex-fighter pilot severely disabled with MS, has been steadfastly cared for by his wife, Jan, for many years. Quite by accident one day, Terry, a young writer/postal carrier, enters their lives and turns it upside down.

Injecting joy and turbulence into their quiet existence, Terry draws Rob and Jan into her lively circle of family and friends until the growing attachment between the two women begins to strain the bonds of love and loyalty, to Rob and each other.

IN A HEARTBEAT

RJ NOLAN

ISBN: 978-3-95533-159-7
Length: 370 pages

Veteran police officer Sam McKenna has no trouble facing down criminals on a daily basis but breaks out in a sweat at the mere mention of commitment. A recent failed relationship strengthens her resolve to stick with her trademark no-strings-attached affairs.

Dr. Riley Connolly, a successful trauma surgeon, has spent her whole life trying to measure up to her family's expectations. And that includes hiding her sexuality from them.

When a routine call sends Sam to the hospital where Riley works, the two women are hurtled into a life-and-death situation. The incident binds them together. But can there be any future for a commitment-phobic cop and a closeted, workaholic doctor?

Mac vs. PC

Fletcher DeLancey

ISBN: 978-3-95533-187-0
Length: 148 pages

As a computer technician at the university, Anna Petrowski knows she has one thing in common with doctors and lawyers, and it's not the salary. It's that everyone thinks her advice comes free, even on weekends. That's why she keeps a strict observance of her Saturday routine: a scone, a caramel mocha, and nobody bothering her. So when she meets a new campus hire at the Bean Grinder who needs computer help yet doesn't ask for it, she's intrigued enough to offer. It's the beginning of a beautiful friendship and possibly something more.

But Elizabeth Markel is a little higher up the university food chain than she's let on, and the truth brings out buried prejudices that Anna didn't know she had.

People and computers have one thing in common: they're both capable of self-sabotage. The difference is that computers are easier to fix.

SIGIL FIRE

ERZABET BISHOP

ISBN: 978-3-95533-206-8
Length: 131 pages

Sonia is a succubus with one goal: stay off Hell's radar. But when succubi start to die, including her sometimes lover, Jeannie, she's drawn into the battle between good and evil.

Fae is a blood witch turned vampire, running a tattoo parlor and trading her craft for blood. She notices that something isn't right on the streets of her city. The denizens of Hell are restless. With the aid of her nest mate Perry and his partner Charley, she races against time before the next victim falls. The killer has a target in his sights, and Sonia might not live to see the dawn.

COMING FROM YLVA
PUBLISHING IN FALL 2014

STILL LIFE

L.T. SMITH

After breaking off her relationship with a female lothario, Jess Taylor decides she doesn't want to expose herself to another cheating partner. Staying at home, alone, suits her just fine. Her idea of a good night is an early one—preferably with a good book. Well, until her best friend, Sophie Harrison, decides it's time Jess rejoined the human race.

Trying to pull Jess from her self-imposed prison, Sophie signs them both up for a Still Life art class at the local college. Sophie knows the beautiful art teacher, Diana Sullivan, could be the woman her best friend needs to move on with her life.

But, in reality, could art bring these two women together? Could it be strong enough to make a masterpiece in just twelve sessions? And, more importantly, can Jess overcome her fear of being used once again?

Only time will tell.

BARRING COMPLICATIONS

BLYTHE RIPPON

It's an open secret that the newest justice on the Supreme Court is a lesbian. So when the Court decides to hear a case about gay marriage, Justice Victoria Willoughby must navigate the press, sway at least one of her conservative colleagues, and confront her own fraught feelings about coming out.

Just when she decides she's up to the challenge, she learns that the very brilliant, very out Genevieve Fornier will be lead counsel on the case.

Genevieve isn't sure which is causing her more sleepless nights: the prospect of losing the case, or the thought of who will be sitting on the bench when she argues it.

The Return

Ana Matics

Near Haven is like any other small, dying fishing village dotting the Maine coastline—a crusty remnant of an industry long gone, a place that is mired in sadness and longing for what was and can never be again. People move away, yet they always seem to come back. It's a vicious cycle of small-town America.

Liza Hawke thought that she'd gotten out, escaped across the country on a basketball scholarship. A series of bad decisions, however, has her returning home after nearly a decade. She struggles to accept her place in the fabric of this small coastal town, making amends to the people she's wronged and trying to rebuild her life in the process.

Her return marks the beginning of a shift within the town as the residents that she's hurt so badly start to heal once more.

Heart's Surrender
© by Emma Weimann

ISBN: 978-3-95533-183-2

Also available as e-book.

Published by Ylva Publishing, legal entity of Ylva Verlag, e.Kfr.

Ylva Verlag, e.Kfr.
Owner: Astrid Ohletz
Am Kirschgarten 2
65830 Kriftel
Germany

http://www.ylva-publishing.com

First edition: June 2014

Credits
Edited by Anne Smith
Cover Design by Streetlight Graphics

CPSIA information can be obtained
at www.ICGtesting.com
Printed in the USA
FFOW01n1628101114
8691FF